HEADFIRST INTO HELL

The Complete

Cases of Jerry Frost

1930–34

HORACE McCOY

illustrations by Arthur Rodman Bowker

cover by Jes Schlaikjer

BLACK MASK

2025

Table of Contents

The Mailed Fist

Jerry Frost, of the Flying Rangers,
goes after the Big Shot

THE MOMENT CAPTAIN Frost's eyes became adjusted to the owl-light of the Adjutant-General's office he realized the Great Man was gravely concerned. He stood in a corner by an open window, gazing fixedly at the wide-terraced slopes of the Capitol lawn, his broad bulk framed against a massive bookcase; yet Frost observed, and not without admiration, that even in this moment of duress his commander suffered not one whit in comparison with the dignity and sturdiness of the surroundings.

The Adjutant-General was not aware of the presence of his flying Ranger until the door clicked behind, but even that noise only partially roused him. He barely looked up. His eyes caught the slender form of the crack airman and he quietly said, "Sit down." Then he looked through the window again as if somewhere on those green contours lay the solution of his immediate problem.

Frost knew his chief, knew his temperaments and so, understanding, he sat down and said nothing. He sank into the soft cushion of a luxurious chair and the first contact he had had with comfort in some time caused him to close his eyes wearily. The lean warrior of the Border skies was tired. He was more than that: he was frayed and haggard. For twenty-six hours now he had been under high pressure; twenty-six rousing hours in which he had fought two battles—one on the ground and one above the ground—and four trucks loaded with rifles and originally destined for a revolutionary army in Mexico.

"I suppose," said the Adjutant-General, his voice low, "you wonder why I ordered you up here so suddenly."

Frost smiled. "Yes and no," he said. "But it gives me a chance to report that in the St. Alto cañon ten miles north of the Rio we took the gun runners and approximately two thousand rifles."

The Adjutant-General nodded and walked with measured tread from the window to the chair behind his desk, and dropped into it with a carelessness he could not have felt.

"Also," Frost went on, "we recaptured Knight, one of the four men who escaped from the Eastern Express."

The head of the Texas Rangers acknowledged and dismissed the statements in a single sentence. "I know," he said. He went on in the same tone, "I've been looking over those books you got from the Black Ship gang in Mexico. They're damned interesting." He humphed derisively. "We're in them."

Frost laid his helmet in his lap and hitched his heavy chair closer. There was a faint trace of wonder in his bronzed face.

"I don't understand, sir," he said.

The Adjutant-General pushed an open ledger across the top of the desk and said, "Have a look." He pointed with an incredibly long forefinger to an entry made in clerical fashion:

Captain Jerry Frost, $2500 (cash)

The Ranger captain looked up, puzzled, and then returned his eyes to the book as if he had not seen aright the first time. The entry though had neither changed nor vanished. The full import of the thing dawned on him and into his tired eyes there flashed a spark of anger and perplexity so closely intermingled as to be almost indistinguishable. He set his jaw grimly and looked up.

"Why," he managed. "I don't know anything—"

"Of course you don't," the Adjutant-General said. "No more than I understand this one—" he pointed again to the page, lower, where another entry was inscribed in the same handwriting:

The Adjutant-General (Texas), $10,000 (cash).

Frost sat back in a state of complete bewilderment. His fingers drummed nervously on the arm of the chair.

"That's a damned lie!" he exploded. "I never took a dime off them!"

The Adjutant-General nodded. "Yes, it's a damned lie. You know it and I know it—but suppose this ledger had got into the wrong hands. Get the idea?"

"I guess," Frost mused, "it would have been just too bad."

"Exactly. And they didn't write those things in there for

their own private amusement. They had a purpose—but they evidently didn't figure on losing the books—before they were ready to lose them. Now"—he picked up another ledger— "there are some names in this one"—he thumbed idly through the pages—"intended for their eyes alone and written by a different hand." He paused briefly and fired an abrupt question. "Got any idea who is the real leader of that outfit?"

"Weisberg?"

"Not even close."

"One of the men who got away in the escape?"

"Still not even close." The Adjutant-General interlaced his fingers to form an inverted V and with it he rubbed his lower lip.

"Then I give up," Frost said.

"Well, if I told you you'd think I'd gone crazy. Look!" He pushed the second ledger across the desk and laid his finger above a name.

Frost saw and sat back as if he had been slapped in the face. He said, "Umph!" and looked out the window. Then he looked back at his chief and said, "Maybe—"

"No," the chief cut in. "I know what you're trying to say— and you're all wrong. I wish to God you were right!" His voice trailed off. "No doubt about it. He's our man."

"But a man like that!" Frost said.

"Yes—a man like that! Rather complicates things, doesn't it?" He went on a little bitterly: "They weren't gummed up enough before. No-o-o-o! So this had to happen."

Frost was quiet for a moment and the sharp roar of traffic and students' trick automobile horns rolled through the window. "Well," he said finally, "what are we going to do about it?"

The question was a perfectly natural one. The name the men had looked upon—the name of the head of the Black Ship gang, a highly organized syndicate which dealt in all manner of contrabands and lawlessness, and lately had undertaken a revolution in Mexico—that name belonged to a very important man in the Southwest. His reputed wealth had made him a legendary figure, and although he had in recent years retired from political life, there had been a day when he had pulled the wires that make the marionettes of a political system hop.

The Adjutant-General got to his feet heavily. "What are we going to do about it?" he repeated. "Well, I'll tell you," he went on, staring into the eyes of his squadron commander. "I'm going to throw him in the penitentiary if it's the last thing I ever do—and it probably will be. That, by God, is exactly what I'm going to do!"

All the ruggedness of that deep-toned office, all the strength contained in its cumbersome furnishings, seemed to flow, of an instant, into his frame. The Adjutant-General faced, and he knew it, political oblivion; but he was a descendant of those stalwarts who had perished on Mexican steel in the Alamo: the personification of the code of his famed constabulary—Get Him! No matter what the cost—Get Him!

"It's a rotten business," he went on slowly, still standing. "Good and rotten. The only way to straighten it out is to start blasting." He exhaled his breath deeply. "I'm figuring on you and your men to the last ditch."

Frost nodded. "We're with you, sir," he said. "To the last ditch." He lifted his eyes and the two men stared silently across that space for an instant. An instant was enough. "I'm ready, Commander."

A smile hovered on the Adjutant-General's lips. "You're a damned fine soldier, Jerry," he said solemnly. "Damned fine! And you're one of the few who can go after this fellow and keep your guts. His name'd scare the others to death. Now here's what's happened in twenty-four hours:

"That Catherine woman you got on the boat in the Gulf has been released on bond. That's the Government's business. Three of the higher-ups in the gang are at liberty—one is our prisoner. Confidentially, I'm not worried about anything now but that big fellow. What we've got to do—what you've got to do—is get him good. Maybe this ledger would be enough to indict him, but I'm not taking chances. He used to have a lot of influence—maybe he has now. I'm not taking any chances. We've got to nail him so there isn't a chance in the world for money and high-powered lawyers to get him out. I'm gambling you can get him like that, and I'll tell you frankly I'm glad I'm not after him. I wouldn't know how to start.

"Now beat it back to your hotel and get some sleep before you fall over from exhaustion. Then go—and *get him!*"

Captain Frost offered no observations. The long speech finished, the Adjutant-General sat down and rolled a brown cigarette and twisted the end. A match flamed and he inhaled.

"Good luck, Jerry!" he said.

"Thanks, Commander!"

Frost got up and walked noiselessly from the room.

HE WENT STRAIGHTWAY to the hotel where the clerk beamed upon him as if he were a potentate and said, "The Adjutant-General phoned about you." He handed a key to a bellboy, changed tones as facilely as a ventriloquist, and went on: "Show Captain Frost up." Frost turned away and said, "Thanks."

On the tenth floor the boy briskly preceded him to a room, inserted the key and flung open the door. "That all, sir?"

"No—mind drawing my tub. Just warm," he said flatly.

Frost was preoccupied. The name he had seen in the ledger stuck in his brain. It made the present assume an aspect of unreality. It shook one's faith in things. It seemed almost incredible that a man with such a reputation could actually be leader of a powerful crime organization. For the hundredth time since he had left the Adjutant-General's office Frost told himself a mistake had been made—and for the hundredth time he got precious little consolation. There was no mistake: this was his man. And he had to get him.

But getting him, Frost told himself, would not be child's play. Wealth, prominence, position—those were the redoubts he had to assail and overcome. The Adjutant-General had been right, of course. The ledger would not have been enough. Had they gone into court with only that they would have been in a fair way to get hooted out of their own temple.

Here was another Herculean assignment, here was another opportunity to catch and hold the Arcadian stag. Here was need—dire need—of the mailed fist.

"That all, sir?"

The bellboy's query caught Frost in the act of slipping off his athletic shirt and brought his speculations to an abrupt end.

"Water warm?"

"Yes, sir!"

"Towels—loads of 'em?"

"Yes, sir!"

"Okey. There's half a dollar on the desk for you."

"Thank you, sir."

The boy pocketed the half dollar and went out the door. Frost stepped over and locked it. He threw his athletic shirt across a chair, kicked off his shorts at the bathroom door and jumped into the tub without the loss of a step.

There was a soft *ploomp!* and Frost slid comfortably down the tub. He reclined, crossed his legs and tried to forget that name. But he couldn't, so he sat up and rubbed himself vigorously. That failed, so he tried whistling. That, also, was no good.

"Hell," he said, and got out.

He used three towels to dry himself, stepped into the room, pulled down the shade and jerked back the counterpane on the bed. He got into bed determined to go to sleep and rest.

But for once he had not accurately reckoned with his powers of endurance. He did go to sleep, but it was not dreamless. He rolled and tossed. He tried to relax, but the harder he tried the worse his condition became. The name haunted him. He saw it in countless forms. Once it was a branding iron—the handle the man's body and the name was his head. It blazed and drew close. Frost swore and lashed out....

Again he had the strange feeling that he was awake. He lay on the bed staring at the ceiling. Suddenly things began to revolve. The bed went one way, the ceiling another. He felt that he was about to be thrown off and he clutched the sides tightly. The ceiling was spinning like a propeller... faster... faster.... He remembered thinking nothing could go that fast and stay together. Something had to give way. Something did. It was his brain. *Crash!* The ceiling splintered and from every direction came the names... millions of 'em... things alive... darting...

swooping… closer. Frost ducked his head.

And sat bolt upright in the semidarkness, sweat in every pore of his body. He lay down again and was aware that his fingers hurt. He looked at his hands. The nails on each index finger were broken from gripping the sides of the bed.

"Hell!" he said, and got up.

He pulled the shade and recoiled as the sun burst into his eyes. Then he assembled his clothes and dumped them in a heap on the bed. He put them on.

He walked out of the room like a prisoner pardoned, and left the door open.

At the desk he paused briefly and said, "Check me out."

The clerk was panic-stricken.

"Anything wrong, sir?"

"Everything. Call me a cab."

He walked across the lobby to the door and lighted a cigarette. He puffed for a few minutes, until a gaily-colored automobile drew up in front. He went out and got in it.

The driver looked around, a question on his lips.

"The flying field," Frost snapped.

Taxi drivers in college towns are notoriously independent, and this one was irritated by the brusque tone. He got away with a jerk and went two blocks where he was stopped by the traffic warning. He smiled in vicarious amusement.

"Hey!" said Frost.

The driver turned his head but said nothing.

"Keep going!"

"The light's against us," he grumbled. He looked back to the front.

"Hey!"

The driver turned again, and this time he stared in undisguised anger. He was beginning to get hard. Which was no long process.

Frost flipped back his chamois windbreak and revealed a gold badge.

"Have a look—and then step on it!"

The driver grunted, but by this time the bell had sounded and released the pent-up line. They rolled away swiftly.

In ten minutes they were at the flying field. Frost got out and handed the driver a dollar bill. "Keep it," he said.

For the first time then the driver warmed. He smiled and nodded his head several times.

Frost walked to the Number Two hangar and spoke to a group of men who were idling inside.

"My bus serviced?"

"Yes, sir!"

"Thanks. Get it on the line."

Four men snapped to do his bidding and trundled the little black ship out of the hangar. Frost pulled on his helmet, took a look at the sky and the wind cone, and went out to it. He crawled in and kicked the starter. There was a long whirr, and then he contacted and the motor barked into life.

Captain Frost got away in a rush of wind and a screaming of wires. He cleared the hangars, pointed his course, and then adjusted his long legs to the cockpit.

He smiled at the old friends on his instrument board, and the roar of the wind gave him new confidence and strength. The task that had, thirty minutes before, seemed hopeless now diminished in size. Captain Frost was in his element. Old friends. No hallucinations. No aberrations. No fears. The clouds… his ship… his guns… he glowed all over.

Get him, eh?

Okey!

He named the sun as a personal adversary for the time being and raced it to Gentry. He thundered over the alkali strips, past the purple flatlands that are the South Plains, and over the barren square that was the flying field of the Texas Air Rangers on the muddy Rio Grande. He dived down at close to eighty miles ground speed, and as he came across the field the dying sun was glinting off the four silver ships that were Hell's Stepsons'.

And then he saw a fifth one—a strange one. It was light blue and was one of the new Curtiss models. He wondered whose that could be as he came to the starting line and was met by Bob Lunsford, the mechanic.

Lunsford scotched a wing, Frost kicked the rudder around and stopped his tiny ship in its slot as neatly as a mosaic. He cut his switch, the propeller gasped for air, and then died for want of it.

Frost got out and faced his chief mechanic.

"Hello, Bob. Who's here?"

"I don't know, sir. But those two men you got in the smuggling have gone. Captain Stuart took 'em."

"Oh, yeh. Whose blue wagon is that?"

"I don't know, sir. He's inside." Lunsford beamed in retrospect. "But I'll say he can sure handle 'er. He barreled over the hangar at fifty feet and dropped her within twenty yards of where she is as pretty as you please. He—"

His voice was beating on empty air. Frost was moving across the field.

He stepped upon the porch and through the open door into the room where Hell's Stepsons were sitting. There were unheard greetings, and Frost became aware that an unknown form was between him and the fading sun that came through the window. He paused curiously.

"Hello, Jerry," boomed a deep voice.

Frost took a step closer, but still could not see. The other man, however, was unaware of that. He said again, "Jerry," and this time he came forward with his hand outstretched.

Frost saw they were about the same size, and the man now had shifted until he was able to see he wore a heavy mustache. He knew he didn't know the mustache, but he was dimly conscious of knowing the face behind it.

He took the hand and said, "Hello," rather indifferently.

The other man was slightly taken aback. Hell's Stepsons were grinning amusedly.

"Forgotten me? Is it possible? You don't remember eight years ago when you and I and Maranga—"

Frost's mouth popped open. "No—no! Not Tommy Tucker?" Simultaneously he reached for the hand again and shook it warmly.

The man nodded. "Li'l Tommy Tucker," he said. "In person."

They fell into each other's arms and Frost banged him on the back with both hands.

"Tommy Tucker! By gad, this *is* great! But for a moment I didn't know you."

Tucker grinned dryly. "I noticed that."

"Well, have a chair and get the weight off your feet, Tommy. I suppose you know all the gang?"

"Yep—I was master of ceremonies myself. God, Jerry—it's

good to see you again. And what the hell kind of business are you in now?"

"Oh—law enforcement. I'm a copper."

"Well, you're a sweet copper. I heard about you down in Mexico City."

"What were you doing in Mexico City? Where have you been, Tommy? What have you been doing? Gad, you'll never know what a relief it is to see you!"

Tucker grinned and lighted a cigarette. "It's a relief to be here. You've got a great layout—and your flyers—say, I'm for them. They've gone over big with me."

Hell's Stepsons smiled, and Frost could tell in a single look they approved the newcomer.

"Yes, but where'd you come from?"

"Well, I've been negotiating—"

"Still hiring out to fight?" Frost asked.

Tommy Tucker inhaled and admitted it. "I was on the inside of the biggest graft I ever saw in my life when blooey! you spoil the picture!"

"I?" Frost unbuttoned his jacket. "Whaddya mean, I spoiled it?"

Tucker looked at Hans Traub. "Shall I tell him?"

"Sure," said Traub.

"All right—" He turned back to Frost. "Well, after six years trying to teach a lot of lousy punks down in Brazil how to stay up in the air, I resign and drift back. In Mexico City I stop, and the first pop out of the box I get an offer to join a 'good cause.' The pay is a thousand gold U.S. dollars a month and a good job when we win—but I'd heard that job gag before and paid no attention. They meant business. They produced two thousand berries for the first two month's pay and there was nothing to do but loaf around Valbuena and let the federalists take care of my ship. That was rich! I waited three weeks for orders and then I learned these guys not only wanted to start a revolution but that they wanted a guy to occasionally duck across the Border with some stuff—"

"Wait a minute," Frost said, sitting up. "Who hired you? Remember his name?"

"Sure—his name was Knight."

"All right, Tommy. Go on with the story."

"Well, I told the guy that smuggling was way out of my line, but that I'd do a lot of fighting for a thousand bucks a month. He argued and argued, but I said no and that finally was that. Then he happened to say that maybe I was afraid because I'd run across Jerry Frost, and I asked a few guarded questions. That's how I learned where you were. Knight finally said I wouldn't be mixed up in the smuggling, and this morning I got written orders delivered by a messenger to proceed to the Los Hermicillos ranch of a man named Palmer."

Frost was staring, wide-eyed. "How long since you've seen Knight?"

"Oh—a week or so."

"Ever seen anybody else in the outfit?"

"Not that I know of. When I started to Palmer's ranch, I saw your hangar and thought I'd look in and get the low-down. I don't want to get in bad with my government."

Captain Frost grinned. He looked at Skipper Hinsdell. "How much of this have you all heard?"

"All of it," Hinsdell replied. "I was telling Tucker that this Palmer used to be a pretty big egg in these parts."

"Used to be?" said Frost. "He still is." He laughed. "Here I nurse a secret all day—and all the time you fellows knew it. Well, I don't mind telling you the Old Man is higher'n a kite about Palmer. And he's the one we've got to get."

Eddie Giles pursed his lips. They all were more or less familiar with the reputation of Paul Palmer. "You mean this is on the level? Palmer is—"

Frost nodded. "Not a doubt about it. Palmer is."

Tommy Tucker interposed himself into the conversation again. "Now, look here, Jerry. I don't mind helping along with a revolution, but how about all this mystery business?"

Frost spread his arms out on the table. Rowdy Perry got up and switched on the light. Hell's Stepsons had not before noticed that the countenance of their leader was wan and tired.

"It's like this, Tommy," he said. "For a long time we've been having trouble with a gang. They've done everything imaginable. Even to counterfeiting. There's no telling what'll happen if we let them keep on. But so far we've got the little fellows. That gang is the one you're mixed up with. They've been hot for a revolution—but there is a lot of stuff you'll have to do if you stay with them. My advice is to forget all about it."

For a moment Tucker was silent. "I guess maybe you're right, Jerry. It looked pretty damned funny to me, too."

He reached his hand inside his pocket and laid a letter on the table before Frost. "Here's what they gave me."

Frost picked it up and read it:

"Mr. Paul Palmer:
    This will introduce Mr. Tucker, one of the new airmen, who has accepted a commission.

                                    K."

He held it in his hand and said, "This looks like a queer way to do business. Haven't you ever seen Palmer?"

Tucker said he hadn't. "They sent me the letter and directions how to reach his ranch. I wasn't to hurry. I understand he was back in Texas for the first time in a couple of years."

"And Palmer has never seen you?"

"Not as far as I know," Tucker laughed.

Frost's eyes suddenly lighted and he banged the table loudly and got to his feet. "By all that's holy, I think I've got it!"

Hans Traub stared at him interestedly, almost enviously. A plan had been forming in the ex-Bavarian's mind, but it had been completed first by Frost. "Got what?" he said.

"A plan. Listen!" The wan expression was gone from his face now and he was vitally alive. His eyes were wide and his lips spread. "There's no secret about it—I've got to get Palmer. Orders. Tommy, stand up."

Tucker shrugged his shoulders and got up. Frost walked around and stood back-to-back with him. "How much difference?" he asked.

"Not more than an inch," volunteered Rowdy Perry. The plan was beginning to dawn on Hell's Stepsons.

Frost turned around. "Do we look alike?"

They agreed. "Only Tucker's got a mustache," said Traub.

"Yes, but if I had a mustache—"

Skipper Hinsdell roared, "Great! Positively great! You'd be dead ringers!"

Frost faced Tucker. "See, Tommy? I want to take the letter and your plane and impersonate you. And I want you to hang around here until I get back. If I get him—"

But Eddie Giles dissented. "Aw, Jerry—that's suicide. You

can't get away with that!"

Frost, however, was in the grip of an inspiration. "Why not?" he demanded, justifying himself. "Why not? Palmer's been in Mexico for two years and here's a flyer he never saw. The only man of the gang who saw Tucker was Floyd Knight—and *Knight's in jail!* This is the break I've been waiting for—and if you think I'm going to boot it, you're just plain off your nut!"

"I say it's a crazy idea," Giles argued.

"Lissen, Eddie. All my life I've traveled on hunches. Tommy Tucker knows that. I worked with him for two years and many's the time my hunches came in handy. Eh, Tommy?" He got the necessary corroboration and went on: "This is a hunch—and I'm riding it. And if it goes through I promise you Tommy'll be a Texas Ranger."

And there the thing ended. There were loud discussions, but in the end Frost won as he always did. He had a hunch, and he was, as he said, riding it.

SIX DAYS LATER a blue airplane winged its way out of Mexico and crossed the Rio Grande at thirty-five hundred feet. Ten miles northeast of the tip-end of the Tierra Viega range it was flying at five thousand feet and as it emerged from a cloud-bank and came out over the vast Los Hermicillos rancho it was at seventy-five hundred.

Below lay one of the greatest estates in the Southwest. From where Frost sat it resembled a veritable fairyland. Even in a country of big ranches Los Hermicillos was big. Thousands and thousands of head of cattle roamed its ranges. Its buildings were modern and luxurious. It boasted one feature few ranches yet had—a large hangar. To the south a range of mountains marched across the sky, flushing pinkly against a blue background; other peaks alternately changed from lavender to purple, deepening in the cañons and passes. The first view of Los Hermicillos was as breath-taking as was the glimpse of the negro Christophe's amazing fortress in the Haitian wilds.

Frost blipped his motor and sailed down. He stroked his young mustache and smiled complacently.

Not once had he permitted himself to consider what would be his fate if his plan failed, if he were discovered. Such thoughts were alien to his nature. He was now, as ever, supremely confident in his enterprise, relying wholly on his intuition. Some day, of course, that intuition might play him false. But until that day....

His blue ship bounced into the field and came to a stop at the ditch near the hangar, and two men ran out. Both were dressed in the regalia of flyers who do their own mechanical work. Frost sized them up as a couple of tough clucks. He got out and stretched his legs.

"This Los Hermicillos?"

"Right," said one. "Where're you from?"

"Mexico City. Mr. Palmer here?"

"Well—" began the second man.

"He ought to be," Frost went on evenly. "He left for here a week ago."

"What do you want?"

"I've got a letter. I've been working for him down in Mexico City," he answered casually.

"Oh," said the first man.

"Oh," echoed the second man.

"Yeh," said Frost. "I guess I better go see him."

"I guess so," said the first man. "Tarver's my name." He extended his hand, which Frost took.

"Tucker's mine."

"This is Shorty Merrick."

Frost shook hands with him. "Hello, Shorty."

The man named Tarver started across the field with Frost.

"Big place," Frost observed.

"Biggest in these parts," Tarver said.

"Keep many planes?"

"Three or four. Voughts. Know 'em?"

"I'll say! Good buses, too."

"Not a bad wagon you got."

"No, it isn't. New Curtiss pursuit."

They went through the patio on to the porch. The house was a long rambling structure done in Spanish and early Texas architecture. Tarver knocked on a door and presently the bland face of a Chinese appeared.

"Tell Mr. Palmer we wanna see him," Tarver said. He led Frost into the room. It was an enormous room, evidently used for a sun parlor. It was equipped with innumerable wicker chairs of odd shapes and sizes and they were covered with multi-colored cloths. Frost reflected if this motif was preserved throughout the entire house, its owner had a palace.

"This is the first time in more'n a year he's been home," Tarver confided when they were inside. "He's been living in Mexico and Jim Shelburne's been running the place."

"Yes?" said Frost. The statement added to his courage. He was glad to have the fact verified that Palmer had been living in Mexico. It lessened the chances that he had seen any of the publicity which had attended the forays of Hell's Stepsons. Or any of the pictures—

And then, almost noiselessly, Paul Palmer came in.

He was big and rawboned and seemed about forty years old. He wore riding pants and soft boots that were badly oil-stained, and his flannel shirt was open at the throat. He came forward slowly.

"What is it, Tarver?" he asked.

"This fellow just landed, Mr. Palmer. Said he had a letter—"

"All right. You may go."

Tarver said, "Yes, sir," and walked out of the room. Frost took a step forward and extended his hand. "My name's Tucker," he said, with the same familiarity as if it had been. "I've got a letter." He looked into Palmer's face. The features were even, his eyes clear and deep, his chin firm and his mouth determined. And Frost, knowing men, knew that here was big game. This fellow was no piker.

"Oh, yes," said Palmer. He shook hands perfunctorily. "Sit down, Tucker." He reached for the letter, tore it open and read it silently. Then he sat down and crossed his legs.

"They told me about you," he said. "Old-time flyer, eh? And not so anxious to do anything but fight." He emphasized anything.

Frost smiled. "Fighting's my business, Mr. Palmer," he said. "The other isn't. I've always tried to stick to my business."

"Not a bad idea," Palmer said, appraising him sharply. "Still, when you work for the other fellow—"

"You ought to follow orders," Frost finished.

"Exactly!" Palmer said heartily. "I hope you will remember that."

"I will. I've been knocking around long enough to know when I've got a good thing. I hope to hold it."

"That depends," said Palmer. He lighted a cigarette and offered Frost one. Frost took it. "But I hardly know what to do with you here. I'm something of a stranger around these parts myself—"

"Great country!" Frost put in enthusiastically.

Paul Palmer fastened his keen eyes on Frost's face and abruptly asked: "What did they tell you about this business?"

Frost shook his head. "I don't understand what you mean."

"I mean," Palmer went on, without lifting his tone, "that they told you certain things when they hired you. What were they?"

"Oh," ejaculated Frost innocently. "You mean how much do I know about what's going on?"

Palmer bobbed his leonine head sharply. "Yes—that's what I want to know."

"Well, sir," Frost replied, inhaling, "I was hired to help with a revolution. Revolutions have been my business for ten years. They told me they were going to have a big one, too."

"Yes," mused Palmer. "A big one."

"Then a little later Knight told me he wanted something carried across the Border to Jamestown in North Texas. I told him no. I was hired for the revolution. And he said, 'Wait—I'll let you know.' Well, he never did. The next thing I know was the letter. What happened to Knight?"

Paul Palmer smiled faintly. "An accident," he temporized. "And now you are here."

"Yes, sir—I am here. Wondering what I'm to do in Texas."

Palmer twisted the cigarette in an ash tray. "Tucker," he said soberly, "I've been associated with men all my life. It's been my business to know them, and I've had to size them up in one look or get the worst of it. I sort of get the idea you'll do."

"I will," said Frost quickly.

"Come on and I'll show you around."

They went out of the room and through the patio to the hangar. Tarver and Merrick were working on a ship. Frost saw there were three inside the building, and that all three mounted cowl guns to shoot through the propeller.

Palmer introduced him to both men, and they laughed and said they'd met before. "Tucker's come to stick around a while," Palmer added.

They idled around the hangar and went off down a dirt trail to a long house about five hundred yards from the hangar. "This is where my waddies stay," Palmer explained. They went inside and were greeted by several men. One of them, dressed in the approved cow-country fashion, stepped out apart from the rest.

Palmer introduced him as Jim Shelburne. "My foreman," he explained. "Tucker here is an old-timer who is going to be a fixture around the place."

"That's swell," Shelburne said. "Pleased to have you."

Frost wasn't highly impressed by the appearance of the foreman. Shelburne wore several days' growth of beard and his chaps exaggerated his natural bowlegs. He looked rather sardonic, Frost thought.

He met the other waddies and Palmer took him back to the house. His final introduction was to Ah Gee, the Chinese jack-of-all-trades. "Mr. Tucker'll eat with us," he said.

The Chinese muttered something, salaamed low, and glided away.

Palmer and Frost sat down in a spacious library. It had

been, Frost saw, done in excellent taste. But purely masculine. Huge built-in bookcases lined the walls, and the furniture was massive and heavy.

"Mr. Palmer," Frost said, "I know I'm more or less a stranger to you, but I'd like to know about the revolution. Maybe I can help. I've had a hand in half a dozen or more."

Palmer thought that over. Frost was playing on a certainty this time. He knew the bigger and more secure they were the easier they were taken in sometimes—and he figured this was the time. It was.

Palmer spread his legs and said, "Well, there isn't a lot to know yet. It should have been under way by now, but some of our guns were captured a little while back and the party was postponed."

"Captured?"

"Yeh—captured. By some Texas Rangers and Secret Service men. At least, that's what they reported to me."

"Rangers, eh. Are they on to the plan?"

"I sometimes think they are. They've been dealing out a lot of hell to me lately. Of course, I'm merely furnishing the money for the revolution. It's no game with me. I've lived in Mexico and I'm convinced they need a change of government. So I'm going to arrange it." He lighted a cigarette. "It's the right thing to do. We'll be doing the people of Mexico a big favor."

So, Frost thought, he's justified himself. The man actually had got to the point where he really believed what he was saying.

"Sure," Frost said, "but those are theories. What are the plans?"

"There aren't any new ones," Palmer said. "But pretty soon we'll have it all arranged."

"I hope so," Frost said. "There's nothing I love better than a revolution."

"Well, don't worry," Palmer grinned. "You'll get one." He grinned again, broader. The grin was infectious. Frost found Paul Palmer wasn't a hard man to like. "As simple," Frost told himself, "as a baby."

But he didn't carry that deduction too far. Frost knew that when the time came Palmer could be hard as steel.

FROST FITTED INTO the life at Los Hermicillos without lost motion. It was a completely new world. It seemed countless miles from any other civilization. And he learned that Jim Shelburne not only was the foreman but the manager of the rancho's business. He seemed Palmer's strongest support, although it was apparent he was taking no part in the plans for the revolution.

In the four days that had elapsed since he had come to the rancho Frost had done nothing but putter around the hangar, take a few test flights and talk briefly with Palmer about his scheduled show below the Border. At first during those meetings Frost was mildly apprehensive of his safety, but gradually this disappeared. Often, though, he got great security out of pressing his arm against his side and feeling his automatic slung in its shoulder-holster.

Palmer would say, "It won't be long now," and that was about all the satisfaction Frost could get.

One day, a week after he had arrived, Palmer called him in and bade him sit down. Before him was stretched a map of Mexico, a businesslike map, dotted with black tacks and red lines.

"I got a little job for you," Palmer began. "You know navigation?" Frost said he did and Palmer went on: "Well, I want you to fly over here at twelve o'clock exactly"—he pointed to a spot on the map—"and meet another ship. They'll signal you with a yellow flag and you'll signal back with a flag of the same color. Then he'll fly over you and let down several packages on a rope. But you needn't bother about that. Tarver'll handle it. All you do is fly. Here's the place." He laid the point of a pencil on the spot he had mentioned. It was near the line between Chihuahua and Coahuila and approximately fifty miles south of the river.

"Think you can manage that?"

"Sure," Frost returned.

"Good. You'll fly one of the Voughts. I've had them arranged a little differently."

Frost subsequently learned that this was no misstatement. Palmer had changed the Vought. He had widened the fuselage between the cockpits and made space sufficient to permit the passage of a body from cockpit to cockpit. But it manifestly was not designed for that. It had been used, Frost knew, for the storage of contrabands.

Tarver climbed in the rear cockpit and Frost pulled at the starter. There was a whirring sound and then he contacted and rolled out to get away.

He circled the rancho in a broad sweep and got away over the tip end of the mountain range, sweeping back on his course like a broad-winged swallow that turns into a spanking breeze. Five minutes later he was above the Rio. He consulted his map, checked his location, and ruddered over.

For twenty minutes he loafed along through the blue, and a

few minutes before the hands of his watch folded together he gave the Vought its head and swung over the meeting place. After a little while he saw a dot in the southern sky that came on fast.

As it drew closer Frost saw it resembled one of those old Sop 1½ strutters which were so common around Toul in July of 1918, but those Sops never could have got the speed this one was making. The fellow at the controls seemed to be racing the crack of doom.

He rushed over Frost, apparently oblivious to his presence, but once out in front he slowed down, banked over and dropped a yellow streamer from his cockpit. Frost threw out a ribbon of the same color and jockeyed beneath him. They were so close together Frost could see the wheels spinning on the undercarriage.

There also was a passenger in the plane above, and he lost no time. He threw out a bundle on a rope and lowered it. The process resembled a refueling operation. Tarver pulled the bundle in. Again the rope went up; again it came down. This was repeated a dozen times, and then the pilot of the upper plane waved his hand and turned back south.

Frost turned and looked at Tarver. He motioned to go ahead.

The plane veered to the right, zoomed to get altitude and its motor soon settled into a purr.

Presently the brown bunker that was the tip end of the Tierra Viega crawled slowly beneath him and he came back to the right and dropped a little lower. Frost thought the mountain would be a bad place to have a crack-up. Never would be found. Flyers steered clear of it. Patrols never got in the vicinity. It afforded a natural screen for the rancho, although it was pretty evident to Frost now that Palmer carried on few operations at his place. He perhaps was too smart for that.

Frost nosed over and went into the landing field. Paul Palmer was waiting, watch in hand.

"Forty minutes," he announced. "Any trouble?"

"Not a bit," Frost replied.

"Fine," Palmer beamed. "Tarver, take that stuff to the cellar."

Frost listened curiously. Cellar. He hadn't heard of a cellar before. He was anxious to see it. So as Tarver took two pouches under his arm and started off, Frost did likewise. He did it as if it were the natural movement of a trusted employee. Palmer looked on, but said nothing.

Tarver went into the hangar and walked to the far end. He went down a narrow flight of steps that led to the storage tanks for the gas and oil, and stopped before what seemed a blank wall. He pushed his hand against it and it swung open. A section four feet wide, evidently hinged with an iron rod through the middle, opened the way into a dark chamber. Tarver pressed a switch and flooded the place.

Frost gasped and stepped back.

He was in an underground vault about fifty feet wide and slightly longer than that, filled with boxes and bundles. He knew at first sight the bundles contained narcotics and contrabands, but the size of the boxes puzzled him. They were small and bulky.

Tarver, unconscious of the surprise of Frost, walked to a stack of bundles and deposited his. Frost did likewise. On the way out Frost said, "What's in the boxes?"

Tarver said, "Ammunition," and came on up the stairs.

Frost reflected there was enough ammunition there to keep a good-sized war going for a long time.

And as he had come upon that secret in the early afternoon, he came upon another later. He came to know that Paul Palmer was the sole directing genius of the proposed revolution. His plan was to install Tento as president, but Tento was to be no more than a puppet.

The following morning Frost came to a sudden decision. He decided he would act at once in some fashion or other. He vaguely felt that trouble was coming. He was not conscious of a definite fear, rather it was desultory, a blending of kaleidoscopic emotions in which caution was the most assertive. Trouble was coming. All right, he'd meet it half way.

And then the lethargy fell away from Los Hermicillos. Something big was in the air. After more than a week's inactivity, the place came alive.

The morning of the eighth day, Frost was walking down the corridor preparatory to his breakfast, usually taken in the patio, when he heard, in the library, voices which he recognized.

At first he thought he was mistaken. These men at Los Hermicillos? Impossible!

Fear of discovery rooted him to the spot. He listened as best he could above the thunder of his heart.

Weisberg!

First lieutenant of the gang, who had escaped from the Eastern Express—his freedom bought with the lives of two Rangers.

Jacobson!

Red-faced, thick-lipped....

Frost felt suddenly as if he had been hit in the stomach with a brick. His head swam as he realized his hazards had increased a thousandfold.

Now he remembered the noise of an airplane motor during the night. It had brought these under-officers, one step removed from the actual leadership.

The executive board of the Black Ship gang. All that remained of the brains of the syndicate. Palmer and Weisberg and Jacobson. José Garza was dead and Floyd Knight was in prison, facing what undoubtedly would be a long term....

Frost had difficulty realizing that the men who had kept the police agencies in such a furor were grouped within the hearing of his voice. And slowly his surprise faded, to be replaced by something like clarity of thought.

He cautiously took a step nearer the open doors and listened.

Palmer was speaking: "Weisberg—you and Jacobson go back today. Right away."

"Everything is arranged," said a voice which Frost recognized as Weisberg's, "but Knight. Floyd is—"

He was interrupted by Palmer. "Knight be damned! He took his chances on those gun trucks and he lost!"

"Nevertheless," Weisberg was saying, "he expects us to do something. The Singleton woman—"

"How in the hell can we do anything?" Palmer demanded crossly. "I tell you, Weisberg, the water is getting too hot. The other business has been broken up, and now you all want to muff the revolution because Knight's in jail. We have got to go on with the revolution or the bottom will fall out!" Frost thought his words contained fire.

"It won't!" Jacobson contributed. "Tento has faith in us. Those guns Frost captured—"

"And that's another thing," barked Palmer in a voice that

startled Frost with its brusqueness. "How you guys ever let him slip out of your fingers is more than I can see!"

Weisberg had an answer for that. "That," he said in a quiet voice, "is because you don't know him. One of your mistakes has been to take him too lightly."

"Maybe so. Just the same, I'll feel safer when you two get back to Rimaya and let Tento know we're striking within the week. I don't suppose the Rangers can stop a shipment of guns from England," he went on defiantly.

"But that drug shipment for Jamestown—"

"Let me worry about that. I've got a hundred thousand dollars' worth of stuff in the cellar. I'll ship it over just as soon as things quiet down. They'll never suspect us if we go in from the north. Our mistake has been in coming from the south."

There was silence for a moment in which Frost started to retreat, so fearful was he that they would hear the clamor of his heart.

Then Palmer went on: "Weisberg, you and Jacobson go on back and keep Tento pepped up. We mustn't let him get down. He has too many supporters. When we get to rule Mexico," he said passionately, savagely, "we'll make him do what we please."

Frost murmured, "Madman."

"Get ready and I'll have you dropped at Rimaya."

There was a light scraping sound as of a man rising and Frost turned and walked swiftly to his room. Evidently the all-night conference was ended. Frost entered his room swiftly, closed and locked the door.

He got into bed with his clothes on, rolled on his left side and took his automatic out of his holster. He anticipated no direct trouble, but he wanted to be ready. It was as if he thought the men knew he was masquerading.

And footsteps did sound in the hall. They came towards his room. Palmer.

There was a rap on the door.

Frost swallowed hard and said: "What is it?"

"Pile out!" came Palmer's gruff command. "I want you to make a hop across the river."

"I'm not up to it," Frost replied through the door. "My eyes are shot. Can't Tarver make it?"

"He's been over once." There was a pause. "Guess he'll have to." Another pause. "Need anything?"

"Nope—I'll be all right in a little while."

Palmer grunted and Frost heard him move down the corridor.

And he lay there, the victim of conflicting emotions. The lieutenants of the Black Ship gang—Weisberg and Jacobson—were about to leave. Frost was seized with an insane desire to stop them—arrest them. First and last he was a Texas Ranger, and it was hard to think that the law should permit two such men to escape its fingers. And yet, he reflected, would not the capture of Paul Palmer assuage that? And if he did make a move would it not be fatal?

His answer was yes to both questions.

He rolled over and pulled back the shade. Presently he saw Weisberg and Tarver emerge from the patio with Jacobson and walk to the hangar where a Vought waited. Neither Weisberg nor Jacobson had any luggage. Palmer spoke to Tarver, and he went into the hangar and emerged at once wearing a flying suit. Palmer shook hands with his lieutenants and they climbed into the same cockpit. He spoke to Tarver again, gesturing expansively. Then Tarver got in.

The propeller jerked, melted into nothing, and the Vought crawled out into the field.

For half an hour after it disappeared Frost remained in his room, desperately trying to evolve some feasible plan from the maelstrom that was his mind. He had to do something, he knew, and do it quickly. He thought it odd how the poles changed. Not long ago he had thought out a plan; now it had slipped into the limbo of the lost. And yet he sensed the drama was rushing to a climax and that he was being driven forward with never a coherent idea of what was happening.

He got up and went out into the corridor.

Paul Palmer was in the library, sitting at a mahogany table and fingering a sheaf of papers. He looked up interestedly as Frost paused at the threshold.

"Well?" he said.

"Better," said Frost. "Much better. I got a whiff of gas during the war and it still bothers me."

"Yeh? Well, I sent Tarver over with a couple of my men." For the first time then he seemed conscious that Frost had not moved. "Come in. I think we're about ready to blast."

Frost went in and sat down. "You mean to start fighting?"

"Yeh. We'll have guns in a week. I don't guess there's much chance of these being intercepted."

"I hope not," Frost said. "How many did you lose in the other shipment?"

"Several thousand," Palmer said vaguely. He swore: "The —— damned Rangers. We had that guy Frost and let him get away!"

"Frost... um... name's familiar. Oh, yes—hero of the Border and all that sort of thing."

"Yeh," said Palmer. "In a month I'll send him my regards from Chapultepec Castle."

"Well," said Frost airily, "I'm ready for action."

Then an odd thing happened. The Ranger captain shifted his position slightly and had started to lay his arm across the back of his chair when his automatic, evidently loosely placed in the holster, fell out of his chamois jacket and clattered to the floor.

For a moment Palmer was nonplussed. His brow wrinkled at the suddenness of it, and his lips came together tightly. It seemed as if he, in that fleeting instant, expected the walls to disgorge his enemies.

But Frost was composed. He picked it up and said carelessly, "When do you think the show is coming off?"

Palmer was frowning. "Never mind the show," he said. "What's the big idea of carrying a gun?"

"Why"—surprised—"I always carry one."

"Give it here!"

"Of course I won't," Frost said. "I always carry a gun. It's a habit."

Palmer melted somewhat, now that the first surprise was fading. He even tried to laugh. "I'm jumpy, I guess. I've been up all night." He stood up, and Frost moved towards the door. At the entrance he turned around.

"I'm sorry," Frost said. "But my gun's as much a part of me as my arm. You never know when you'll need it."

One never did.

ORDINARILY, NOTHING WOULD have been thought of such a trifling matter. But these were not ordinary times. They were loaded with portent. Frost was more anxious than ever that Palmer should not suspect him. He had planned to make the capture within twenty-four hours, in some form or other.

He was in the hangar when Tarver returned with the Vought. He brought it back to the starting line, hopped out and straightened up.

"How's the air?" Frost asked.

Tarver merely glared and strode off towards the house.

Frost smiled amusedly at the schoolboy attitude, and rolled out the service truck. As he climbed up he saw there were two pouches in the compartment between the cockpits—the heavy linen of the U.S. Post office department and easily recognizable from where he stood. He immediately got down and rolled the service truck back in the hangar. He was standing beside the propeller when he saw Palmer and Tarver come out of the house in the direction of the plane.

They stopped beside him. Frost had not the slightest thought that all was not well.

Palmer snapped: "Who the hell do you think you are?"

Right there and then Jerry Frost knew trouble was on him. When he turned his face was grim and cold.

He was looking into the squat barrel of an automatic.

He lifted his hands.

"Good!" Tarver boomed. "Just keep 'em up there!"

He was holding the gun at his hip and Frost saw in a quick glance that the forefinger on his right hand had gone white from pressure.

"What's the ——?" Frost tried to bluster.

"Before you get bumped off," Palmer said, "I want you to know you sucked us in pretty. But now—"

"What's the big idea?" Frost managed.

"What's your name?" Palmer asked.

"Tucker—Tommy Tucker."

"That's a—damned lie! Your name's Jerry Frost. Weisberg got a flash at you through the window—and I've had my doubts for a couple of days. I just wanted to get you dead to rights."

"But—"

"Well, it don't make a damn now one way or the other. I'm gonna bump you off because all of a sudden I don't trust you. Turn around and start walking."

Tarver held the gun up a little. Frost read the light in his eyes. They were glinting like bits of glazed pottery. He was straining to pull the trigger.

Frost's life hung by a thread. The primordial perception of death inherited from countless generations of fighting ancestors gripped his brain. And he did not hesitate.

Like a flash his left arm fell on Tarver's wrist and his leap to one side was but a continuation of that same movement.

The gun snapped downward and cracked. The bullet whistled by Frost's knee and buried itself in the ground.

From above his head Frost's right arm straightened and caught the bewildered Tarver flush on the chin. He staggered back and dropped the pistol.

Frost darted his right hand under his jacket to get his own automatic, but Palmer had recovered by now and was on top of the Ranger, hammering him with blows.

One caught Frost under the eye and drove him a step backwards, and he had a hurried glimpse of Tarver on his hands and knees reaching for the gun. Frost whirled suddenly and kicked him in the throat with all the power he could get in his leg.

Tarver gurgled, his arms turned to tallow, and he melted into the ground, face downward. He was clearly out.

Palmer was beating fiercely at Frost by now, but the Ranger speedily recognized the other's lack of science. Palmer was no fool. He knew he was no scientific fighter, so he rushed in again and grabbed Frost. He was too excited to be careful. He lifted his knee and it knocked a grunt out of Frost. Palmer was made of bone and wire, one of those old-timers who, when not shooting it out, wrestled in the fashion of the wide-open countries. Knuckles had been broken on his skull; he got drunk on his own blood.

He got a powerful hold on Frost's chest and they went down together like a pair of storm-uprooted trees. As they struck the ground Frost got a hold on Palmer's ear, but his thumb slipped within reach of Palmer's mouth and promptly was fastened in a vise of teeth. Frost twisted in agony and drove his knee into Palmer's stomach.

Palmer's mouth popped open and Frost jerked his hand out and clambered to his feet. When he came upright his automatic was in his hand.

Palmer rolled over and yelled: "Help! Help!"

Frost slung his automatic out at arm's length.

"Get up—in a hurry!"

"Help! Help!"

From the patio came voices blending in excitement and anger. The first shot apparently, had seemed nothing unusual. The yells for help were something different.

The automatic barked and a bullet kicked dirt in Palmer's face.

"Next time I won't miss!"

Palmer swore loudly and got up.

"Get in that plane!"

"Say—"

The Ranger's automatic loomed in his eyes.

"Hurry!"

Palmer knew death stared him in the face. He started to get in the plane.

"Get in the front pit!"

He crawled up and by that time Shelburne and half a dozen men who had been sunning in the patio came running out. Palmer hesitated in his motions, for he saw them, too. There was a barely perceptible shifting of weight.

Bang!

The automatic in Frost's hand barked again and a tiny flame leaped out. A white-hot wire stung Palmer's leg; and he groaned and slumped forward—literally knocked into the cockpit by the bullet.

Frost dashed to the plane and yanked at the starter. One... two... three precious seconds... contact... would it?

Crack–k–k–k!

The motor belched and caught....

Frost was over the side and in the pit, his foot on the rudder bar and his hand on the gun. He kicked it open, snapped the rudder bar and the Vought fairly leaped around into the field.

The men were coming closer. Frost looked back and saw the sun glinting off the barrel of a gun. He did not hear the explosion. He did not hear the bullet tear through the linen. He did not hear Palmer groan again. Frost was intent on getting away.

He yanked back on the stick and the bus zoomed; at fifteen

hundred feet it leveled off and turned its nose down the Rio Grande.

Frost stood up in his pit to take a look at his passenger, bracing himself against the slipstream. Palmer was slumped forward in the seat, and then Frost became aware that he himself was in none too good condition.

Sharp pains chased each other through his head, his right eye smarted and stung, his chin was sore and the skin on his right thumb was lacerated from Palmer's teeth.

Still, he managed to smile. He had the leader as well as two pouches of narcotics—enough to put Palmer over right.

"Lucky!" he said to his instrument board. "Another close shave. The old law of averages is catching up!"

Headfirst Into Hell

Captain Jerry Frost and Eddie Giles
bust some clouds in Mañana Land

ALMOST AS SOON as the wheels of his little black ship had touched the landing field at Valbuena, in Mexico City, it was apparent to Captain Jerry Frost that this revolution was not being regarded with the customary Latin indifference. On every side there were unmistakable signs that the Tento uprising plainly was not being taken lightly.

Armed troops were on patrol. The attitude of the field attendants was crisp, so crisp it bordered on hostility. There was a tension that tightened the throat.

Captain Montez hurried into a hangar and conversed with an officer. Presently they returned to the roadway and signaled an automobile. It rolled up quickly. On its windshield was a gum poster—a flag of Mexico and the seal; an eagle holding a serpent entwined in its talons. It was the presidential insignia. Montez nodded and Frost and Giles stepped in. Montez sat beside the driver and Frost and Giles were in the back seat.

They were guest players, these two—temporarily "resigned" from the Rangers, they had been borrowed for a little work below the Border.

Montez said: "We are to meet the President at once."

Eddie Giles frowned and took off his helmet. He ran his fingers through his hair. "Say, I don't want to meet anybody until I have a chance to wash—"

Frost cut in: "You haven't got time to pour perfume on your hair, jellybean. We are now mixed up in a war!"

"Yeah?" Giles said. "I guess the last six months have been a house party!"

Captain Montez felt impelled to arbitrate and half turned to say over his shoulder, "After you see the President there will be time to bathe."

Frost said: "Sure," and nudged Giles. He pointed off in the distance. He said, "Popo."

Giles said: "Who?"

"Popocatepetl—volcano. The smaller one is Ixtaccihuatl."

"Oh!" Giles said blandly. "Volcanoes!"

"Yeah—volcanoes. Nice little places where they dump wise-crackers!"

Giles chuckled and sat back. The car rolled along a road that was like glass, fairly eating up the miles to the city which was now visible through the mauve mists. Occasionally they roared by a surprised *federalista* who, recognizing the emblem on the windshield, came smartly to what Mexican soldiers humor-ously call attention. All of them stared after the car.

Montez leveled a finger ahead. "Castillo de Chapultepec," he said. "Home of the President."

The castle sat atop a rugged, forested peak and it was a cita-del that might have delighted a feudal baron. And, too, it bore a strange resemblance to the lonely fortress the negro Chris-tophe erected a century ago in the Haitian jungles. Nowhere south of Cancer is there similar architecture. Fighting men ever have been surprised and delighted with the strategic possi-bilities of the Castillo de Chapultepec.

Giles sucked in his breath sharply and said, "I could take a machine-gun squad and hold that place against the world!" He leaned over and stared, fascinated.

Frost nodded. "Yea, I guess you could—in the old days. But now somebody would lay an egg on you and whoosh!" He pantomimed the dropping of a bomb.

Two sentries with fixed bayonets approached and saluted. They turned to the interior and shouted:

"*Capitan* Montez!"

Their shouts attracted the crowd and they surged around and stared in undisguised curiosity.

The gates swung open and the car moved through. Inside it stopped again and the gates went to with a clank. Montez and Frost and Giles got out.

They walked into an outside corridor and climbed a wide, thickly carpeted flight of stairs. Two officers passed Montez and saluted sharply.

They moved to an inner door and without ceremony Montez threw it open and preceded Frost and Giles across the threshold. Two men sat behind a massive, hand-carved desk.

One of the men behind the desk stood up. He was small and half bald and wore glasses to which was attached a thin black ribbon. His dress was neat and conservative. He smiled thinly. His name was Manuel Flores and he was President of Mexico.

The other man slowly got up. He was tall and swarthy and wore a double row of campaign ribbons across his tunic. But even without them, even without his pea-green, snug-fitting uniform, you would have known he was a soldier. His name was Pedro Nolanti and he was commander of the army of the republic.

The President said: "Sit down, gentlemen."

The Americans hardly had expected to hear their own language spoken by the President, and they looked at each other in mild surprise. The President observed their expressions and laughed.

"I studied in your country as did Montez. Nolanti also knows your language," the President said.

Frost didn't know exactly what to say, but he said: "That's fine."

The President went on: "Montez' message to us was welcome. Maybe we can help each other, *si?*"

Frost said: "I hope so. Has General Nolanti made his plans?"

Nolanti was a light opera military leader performing for a vast mob. He was perfectly accoutred. A highly polished Sam Browne belt came over a square shoulder and a heroic chest, and his bronzed throat muscles bulged under a collar that was none too loose. His fingers were thin and tapered and on the little finger of his left hand he wore a heavy garnet ring. His forehead was deep and his smile was cold and confident. His eyes struck the only false note in the ensemble. Frost noted they were shifty and darting.

General Nolanti carefully explained the menace of this revolution. He related the insidious methods Tento had employed and told how the country in the north was in revolt. "He has assembled about two thousand men near-about La Salada and Venado."

Frost lifted his eyebrows. He said: "A large number of men to get together in a wild country, General."

Nolanti admitted it. "But," he said, "they are there. Captain," he went on seriously, "the reason other revolutions have caused Mexico so much trouble was because the officers would sit and wonder how a rebel leader could muster an army. Instead, they should have done something about it." He extracted a long black cigarette from his pocket and lighted it. "I do not sit and wonder. I fight." He inhaled luxuriously. "I am moving troops today."

"To the north?"

"*Si*, to the north."

"There will be no trouble in the south?"

Nolanti laughed and said nothing. He regarded Frost in amusement. Then: "Captain, you should know Mexican rebels will not fight where there are no *pulquerias*. They must have tequila."

"They have airplanes," Frost said.

"A few, perhaps. So have we."

Frost said: "How many?"

"Several."

Frost said: "How many are you going to use?"

"Three," said Nolanti. "Montez—you—and you." He indicated Giles.

Frost wrinkled his brow and sat back in the chair. "Only three?"

"That is enough," Nolanti said. "I have good infantry." He said it with the doggedness old-line soldiers usually evidence when modern methods of warfare are mentioned.

Frost bit his lip and Giles looked puzzled. Frost said: "You mean we are going into this revolution with only three airplanes?" His tone was incredulous.

"Porque no?" Nolanti blustered. He repeated: "I have good infantry." His sharp eyes darted about Frost. He had that peculiar sense which warned him of antagonism. He seemed to know that Frost knew he was merely playing a part and, what was infinitely worse, overplaying it.

The President felt something of the same tension for he got up and said: "You gentlemen are here to get two prisoners. If you do get them the revolution—or a big part of it—will be at an end." Abruptly he concluded, "It becomes my privilege, gentlemen, to appoint you *coronels* in the army of Mexico."

Frost said, "Thank you," and looked up. Something in the eyes of the President registered heavily on the American flyer. It might have been pathos… it might have been fatigue. Manuel Flores was involved in deep intrigue… and he was magnificently unprepared.

The look Frost caught prompted the question, "Are the troops loyal?" Later he admitted that was not the proper thing to say. It came impetuously.

The suddenness of the query startled Nolanti, and then he became composed and replied: *"Quien sabe?* One never knows."

Frost said: "Yes." He looked at Giles and Giles nodded.

The President said: "You have had a long trip," and extended his hand, which the Americans shook warmly. "As you *Americanos* say—good luck. Montez will attend you."

On his way to the delayed bath and a change of uniform, Giles remarked to Frost; "The general has got a queer eye."

Frost said: "So you noticed that, too?"

"Yeh—and I don't mind saying I think he's a lousy four-flusher. He couldn't command any army of mine."

Frost regarded his companion with admiration.

"Eddie," he said, "damned if you aren't getting intelligent!"

THE *FEDERALISTAS* FOUND no royal welcome awaiting them in La Salada, which is twenty miles west of Venado on the Mexican National railroad in the state of San Luis Potosi. It is absurdly easy to sit here and write twenty miles in a few motions of the fingers, and in some other country it might have been only a little harder to negotiate. But not between La Salada and Venado. That score of miles which separates them lays through as wild and remote a section as Mexico holds—arroyos and cañons—no roads at all in some places—and crowning it all a terrific sun that was very nearly unmerciful.

Not once during the march—and the march, moving three thousand troops with their provisions and ammunition trains in a single day was not a mediocre military achievement—not once during the march did the Tento *cargadores,* as Nolanti had contemptuously dubbed them, reveal their presence. The official communique had said the country would be filled with them and that sniping probably would be indulged in. Perhaps Tento's men were more clever than the *federalistas* thought. Throughout the march Nolanti's troops expected to be fired on… and mile after mile they trudged, their nerves taut. A brush, a skirmish might have relieved their pent-up emotions. By the time they reached La Salada they were in no mood for frolic. They shed their packs and took up their billets, exhausted. Only a hardy few consorted with the dancing girls in the *pulquerias,* the dancing girls who are, magically, always present on the Latin-American battle fronts before the *soldados.* If the military leaders maintained an espionage system as elaborate as these girls the results would be different.

Unfortunately La Salada was openly hostile to the men of the republic. Weisberg and Jacobson, only officials of the Black Ship gang now at large, unaware that their leader, Paul Palmer, had been captured, executed his propaganda ideas perfectly. They had convinced the somnolent citizens of La Salada, as they had thousands of others in the north, that Mexico's freedom depended on the Tento rebellion. Glorious liberty, they said, could come only from association with his ideals and by helping his men. It is never difficult to sell the ignorant peon a quantity of patriotism. Therefore the name of Tento had been hoisted as a savior.

The day after the federal invasion of the hostile town, three airplanes roared across a molten sky and dropped down on an improvised field almost within the confines of the village itself. One of them was a cabin plane which was totally unfit for battle service and bore, among other precious passengers, the person of General Pedro Nolanti. Another bore the trim figure of Captain Jerry Frost and the third belonged to Eddie Giles. Both Americans were now clad in the green uniform of the Mexican army staff and wore the insignia of *coronels.*

They came into a town thick with the heat of the sun. It was the hour of the siesta. Not even the outrage of a federal invasion, not even Nolanti's pompous proclamation of martial law, could disturb that ritual. There would be plenty of time to worry about the indignities later.

The sun hammered down so relentlessly it brought mirages before the eyes. It was a ghostly and unreal land of cavernous colors and glittering highlights. There even was a drowsiness in the slow clanging of the cathedral bell. The marketplace was ridiculously quiet. Old women slept before piles of unpatted tortillas. The keeper of a shop had gone to sleep sitting in his chair, and his head had fallen forward on his chest in grotesque fashion.

General Nolanti and his men walked ahead and conversed in rapid tones. Behind him was Montez and bringing up the rear were Frost and Giles, regarding the tomb-like village with true tourist curiosity.

Giles mopped his head in a fashion that can only be described as unmilitary and said: "Wham! Am I hot?"

Frost said banteringly: "Come back in the summer. Then you'll find it really hot."

Giles muttered: "It'll have to be a hell of a good show to make up for this."

Then a silence fell between them. Conversation required too much effort. But Nolanti still conversed in that humming tone. He had a lot to talk about. Boots clattered noisily on the cobblestones.

Then from somewhere came the bark of a pistol, so clear and loud and startling that it sounded like the crack of doom.

Frost looked up quickly whence the sound had issued and got a glimpse, through a barred window, of a woman with a pistol in her hand. The silhouette was perfect. And almost immediately that silhouette vanished.

Nolanti and the officer at his side stopped at once. Nolanti said: *"Dios!* Did I not command all civilians to surrender their arms?"

A story-book house disgorged three soldiers. One of them was buttoning his shirt. They saw the group of officers had stopped and went into a meek salute.

"Go in!" Nolanti said. "Arrest the person who fired that shot!"

Before the soldiers could comply, Frost had moved up quickly. He had got a glimpse of the woman... and he would have staked his life she was young. He said: "Would the general permit *Coronel* Giles and me—"

Nolanti frowned at the interruption. The soldiers had not moved.

"We saw her," Frost said. "We know—"

Nolanti said, "Very well." He waved his hand and the soldiers did a clumsy about-face and walked swiftly away. But by then Frost and Giles were crossing the street....

Giles said: "You're crazy! This ain't our fight!"

Frost only smiled. His eyes were sympathetic. His heart was pounding lustily. He was tense with excitement. Adventure! Why didn't someone cheer? He wanted to beat his fists against the wall that surrounded the house and shout: "Adventure! This is adventure!" That was the way it got him. Sudden. Cyclonic. All over.

THE WALL WHICH protected the house was tall and thick, and the house sat back in the yard. At a single glance Frost knew it was occupied by a personage. It was big and formal and aloof in its dignity. The gate was open and they went through it; up the steps and into the hall.

They entered a darkened interior and for a moment they paused to adjust their eyes to the gloom. A man bumped against Frost and he turned and grabbed him by the arm. It was a *federalista*. His shoulder was bloodstained.

Frost said: "What's the trouble, *soldado?*"

"The woman had a pistol, *muy coronel*. General Nolanti ordered—"

"I know. Go get treatment. We'll arrest the woman."

The soldier lamely saluted. Frost saw the red wave of blood had reached to his hand.

Giles said to Frost: "I still think you're crazy."

Frost laughed like a boy at play and they went down the hall and into a room. Despite the brilliance of the mid-afternoon sun a tiny candle burned before a crucifix in a *nicho*.

Kneeling there was a woman. The smoke hardly had cleared from her pistol. She heard them enter and stood up. A vermilion shaft of light hammered through and outlined her figure. In a single glance Frost noted she was young, breathtakingly young, and that the curves of her throat and breasts were superb.

She slowly raised her hand. A pistol gleamed. Her eyes were fearless.

"Pigs!" she said. "Have you no respect for prayer?"

Frost said: "An odd prayer, señorita, with a pistol in your hand."

She said: "You will leave at once!"

"Gladly—after you give me your revolver. No civilian is permitted to have firearms."

Her body trembled with anger. Her eyes flashed. Rage at taking dictation engulfed her. With a visible effort at self-control she said: "One soldier already has been shot. I hope you will spare me the pleasure of shooting another!"

Resolution was written in every feature of her face. Pride is a stubborn master in high-caste Mexicans. There was no mistaking her meaning. In a moment she would fire.

Frost leaped beside her in a sudden bound and wrested the revolver from her hand. He stepped back and looked at her. Her eyes now were coldly contemptuous. Frost bowed slightly.

He said: "My apologies. But this is war. I should arrest you!"

She said between her teeth: "Swine! Fit only to serve Nolanti, the Butcher. Get out! *Andale!*"

Frost nodded to Giles and they walked out. In the street Giles said: "Are all these dames like that?"

Frost said soberly: "Most of them are." He looked at the revolver almost affectionately. He put it in his hip pocket.

"Maybe you should have arrested her," Giles said. "Shooting a soldier, even one of these soldiers, is pretty serious."

Frost shook his head. "No—she doesn't belong in a military prison." He looked back at the house and he thought he saw a form pressed against the window. He could have sworn he saw one. He would have sworn it was the girl.

HOURS LATER, WHEN Nolanti received the report that one of his soldiers had been wounded by a civilian, and a woman at that, he went into a rage. He roared at his officers, he swore at his men, he cursed the American flyers.

He shouted: "Bring her here!"

A little later her identity was established and the general became a dynamo of hatred. The daughter of the rebel Rubiez!

"*Dios!*" he exclaimed. "Must I go myself?"

He stamped the length of his narrow headquarters and recalled that not a great many years before the name of José Rubiez had been one to conjure with in Mexico. Direct descendant of a long line of distinguished ancestors, owner of one of the largest and most prosperous ranchos in the country, he ruled in San Luis Potosi with a kindly hand. Guerrilla invasions had gradually cut his property, for there was no federal protection available. His vaqueros were killed. Taxation had throttled him—and he had died with a prayer on his lips that God speed the Moses who was to bring liberty to his beloved people.

His daughter was not at his deathbed. Only a few of the vaqueros, a *duenna*... the Señorita Rubiez's train, transporting her home from school in the States, raced destiny and, as so often is the case with those handicaps, lost....

"Arrest her!" Nolanti shouted over and over.

And arrest her they did. It was not difficult for she offered no resistance. She made no complaint. It was as if she thought that might cheapen her. She went with the soldiers, but her soul seethed... she walked into Nolanti's headquarters ahead of the soldiers. There was hauteur in the tilt of her head and determination in the ring of her step.

Frost and Giles were unaware of the action taken by Nolanti. If they had known, they would not have invaded headquarters so unceremoniously late that afternoon. They blundered—simply blundered—into the room.

Frost saw her sitting there and his heart looped. She regarded him without so much as a flicker of her eyelids. For all the martial atmosphere she was a regal personage condescending to sit with her inferiors. She felt it. Nolanti felt it. His officers felt it. And they were uncomfortable.

As Frost and Giles entered the room Nolanti frowned.

Frost said: "I beg your pardon. I did not know—" His voice, strangely hard, chopped off the words.

Nolanti hesitated briefly. He cloaked his annoyance behind a mask of inscrutability and said: "Come in." He did it as gracefully as the circumstances would permit.

The flyers entered.

"The Señorita Rubiez," Nolanti said, "is charged with assault on a federal soldier. I suppose," he added, "you are aware that she did shoot a soldier?" He looked directly at Frost and the implication was quite patent. Frost's jaws snapped together.

"Quite, sir. But I saw no reason—"

"Ah, of course not. And since when did you become the commanding officer?" He leered a little. "The Señorita Rubiez is—" He broke off his words as he looked at her. For a long time he feasted his eyes and then he said, suddenly, and in a more dulcet tone: "Perhaps the crime is not so bad, eh?" He smiled. "Every charming woman should be privileged to shoot at least one soldier." He laughed, pleased with himself. His officers smiled. Nolanti, encouraged, went on: "Perhaps the Señorita would appreciate the courtesy if General Nolanti dismissed her?" Everybody in the room but the señorita knew what he meant.

She gave no sign she had heard. She sat immovable. She did dart a swift glance at Frost, as if to make sure he was still present. Frost saw it. His heart looped again.

With no more ado Nolanti decided on his course of action. "Señorita, you may go. I am sorry my men arrested you. They shall be punished. And you would be wise if you could find leniency for General Nolanti."

She did not stir until he had finished speaking. Then she rose and nodded. She murmured, *"Gracias,"* in the same tone she employed to thank her servants, and swept from the room. There was silence in her wake.

Nolanti's expression as she passed out the door was supercilious. It was purely a defensive smile. The sense of inferiority she forced on him was gone. There was a glint in Frost's eye; he experienced a surge of antipathy. His life heretofore had been free of women. He had been a soldier and a soldier has no time for them.

THE FOLLOWING MORNING Montez entered the quarters of Frost and Giles. He was plainly excited. "The general wants to see you," he said.

Frost got up heavily and walked across the narrow room, swimming in heat, to the bunk where Giles lay sleeping in a pool of perspiration. He slapped him on the shoulder and said: "Pile out, soldier."

Giles blinked his eyes and sat up. He observed he was soaked.

"Hell," he said. "Turn off the heat."

Frost said: "Nolanti's sent for us. Looks like work in the wind."

Giles buttoned his shirt and laced his boots. He grunted and said: "What if Weisberg and Jacobson aren't in on this? What if they aren't?"

Frost said: "Well, in that case they just aren't."

"Looks like a hell of a chance we're taking to get 'em." Under his breath he said: "Damn!" He looked up and went on: "Understand, I'm not shaky about it." He jerked his lace through a brass eye of his boot. "I just think it's a hell of a chance to take."

Frost said, "Yeah? Well, you were pretty anxious to get down here."

Giles pulled a crooked forefinger across his forehead and flung the sweat beads to the floor. "Sure—and I'm pretty anxious to get back, too."

Frost let his eyes drift out the window towards the big house where the girl lived.

"Yeah? Well… maybe I ought to agree with you, Eddie. Maybe I ought. But it's different."

"Too different. I hope the next revolution is at the North Pole."

"Sure—but—"

Giles said: "Hell!" He was disgusted. "Let's go see His Nibs."

They found His Nibs red-hot and ready. He hardly gave them time to get in the room before he fired: "How am I going to fight an enemy I can't locate? I want to know where they are! I want information! And at once!"

Frost said: "You mean reconnoiter?"

"Exactly!"

"Very well." Without another word he turned on his heel and left the room, Giles behind.

Giles said, "A swell way to run an army."

"Nix! Don't let it get your goat!"

Later, at the field, Giles said again: "A swell way to run an army."

Frost said: "Crawl in. It'll be cooler where you're going."

"Was that meant for a dirty crack?"

"Take it any way you want to, Duke."

They spun their propellers and the motors thundered in the still air. They got off the field in a flutter of wings and headed north. As they left the field and soared over La Salada they could see beneath them the upturned faces of Nolanti's men, curious at the workings of an airplane in wartime.

Fifteen miles to the north Frost got his first glimpse of the men with whom Tento hoped to march into Mexico City. Over a rolling *finca*, that was at one time a part of the vast holdings of José Rubiez, the flyer caught sight of innumerable forms in the arroyos and cañons, who scurried to cover and resembled headless gnomes.

They looked ready for action. Frost said to his instrument board, "This is no joke!"

He was frankly surprised. He had known the seeds of unrest which the gang had planted in the north had borne fruit, but not in his wildest dreams had he imagined it would be so productive.

He looked across at Giles, who was riding abreast with his neat A3. Frost pointed below. Giles nodded. They conveyed their surprise to each other.

To avoid pot-shooting on the part of the rebels below they remained high, but those rebels evidently had been given their orders. No shots were fired.

Emboldened, Frost swept to within fifteen hundred feet of the ground to better view the surrounding country. Revolutionists were sprawled all about the entire *finca*.

The focal point of this, the enemy territory, apparently lay in a small village which ostensibly had been one of old José Rubiez's commissaries. As Frost and Giles swept over the scene there was great confusion below and they knew they had located the post command. Frost nosed around a spanking breeze and came back at a thousand feet.

Suddenly the chatter of a gun stabbed above the roar of the motor. He looked out. A knot of men manipulated a gun which spat rings of smoke. It was a machine-gun.

Frost said: "Damn!"

He slapped his throttle open and zoomed into what was almost a stall, then he flattened out and had a look through his binoculars. He could make out the forms below.

"Headquarters," he said. "Sure as little apples."

He looked at Giles, rolled his arm and flung it forward. He fell away in a glide and headed for La Salada.

Thirty minutes later he stood before Nolanti.

"Well?" said the general.

Frost said: "They've got thousands of troops scattered about in the arroyos fifteen miles to the north. Their headquarters are in a straight line northwest." He leveled his arm. "They've got the men and there is considerable activity. I'd say they're ready to go any minute."

"Planes?"

"None. But we've had brushes with this outfit before," Frost said soberly. "When the time comes they'll have 'em."

"That's all."

Frost paused a moment and said: "May I be so bold as to suggest our troops be assembled and held in readiness?"

Nolanti said: "No. No."

Frost and Giles wandered aimlessly along in the gathering dusk of early evening, restless and disgruntled but not knowing what they could do about it. They had been hired for the show and were burning with anxiety for action, and this *opéra bouffe* general was cramping their style.

Finding themselves presently before a gaudy restaurant—

the Café Golondrina—they entered by common, tacit consent and killed an hour or so over a hotly spiced meal. There was some stringed music; girls sang and made eyes. The place grew crowded with soldiers and noisier and rougher—but it wasn't particularly amusing to the present mood of the two soldiers of fortune.

Afterwards they walked slowly along the narrow street back towards their billet. The moon had come up full and the world was bathed in ghostliness. A few soldiers loitered along. The only sounds were from the Café Golondrina behind them.

Suddenly Giles said: "Jerry, what about Weisberg and Jacobson?"

"Don't get in a hurry, my boy. I've got a plan all worked out. Tomorrow—"

He cut his speech off short as Giles laid a hand on his arm. They saw a slender form march briskly into the courtyard of the Rubiez home. It vanished in the shadows as if it had been suddenly swept off the face of the earth.

Giles asked: "Get a slant at him?"

"Yeah. And I don't like the looks of it a damned bit. He made a play to her this afternoon—and now he's come to see about it."

They stopped at the gate and looked inside. In the window of the room where Frost had first seen the girl, there was a dim light.

"Come on," Frost said grimly.

They went inside and cautiously made their way to the side of the house. Frost whispered: "Get set for anything." Giles murmured: "Righto!" and they stopped beneath the grated window.

Presently they heard the voice of the general. He was employing his best voice this night. The girl dismissed her *duenna* tremulously.

There was a pause and Nolanti said: "Señorita, pardon the intrusion. I come to warn you. La Salada is no longer safe. The enemy—"

She cut in swiftly: "I do not fear the enemy without. It is the enemy within—the men of Nolanti, the Butcher."

Frost breathed: "Attagirl!"

Nolanti said severely: "That is no tone to take with me. But for me you might have faced the firing squad."

The girl laughed. "I am not afraid."

"I come only to warn you. Still, I am not so hideous. There are women in Mexico—"

"I am not one of those women!" she said acidly. "And now will you go?"

"Not yet," said Nolanti. "Not yet. Since you are so ungrateful I shall show you how Nolanti—"

In a moment there was a resounding slap as an open palm struck a cheek. Nolanti muttered an imprecation, and there were sounds of a struggle. The girl's short cries were laden with fear.

Frost said to Giles: "I'm going in. Gimme a boost."

Giles locked his fingers together to form a step and Frost slid up and reached for the iron grating above with his fingers. He pulled himself up and went through the window.

Before either the girl or Nolanti was aware of his presence he was within the room.

Nolanti snarled and his hand dropped to his hip. "What are you doing here?"

Before he could unbutton the flap of his holster to get his gun Frost was beside him.

He said: "It means, *mi general,* that your attentions are unwelcome."

Nolanti pulled himself erect. He snapped: "You forget your place, *soldado.* I am General Nolanti. *Andale pronto!*"

The girl stifled a sob and fell back a step or two. She lifted her eyes to Frost and he saw, in the dim light of the candles, that the defiance she had earlier evinced, the contempt, was gone from her face. He was no longer to be regarded as an enemy. He saw it and it fired him.

He said: "Beat it, Nolanti. Get out!" He was plainly trying to avert an open break with his superior officer, but his attitude was determined.

Nolanti's eyes glittered. "You are insulting! I shall show you how Nolanti—" His hand went to his hip again. This time the flap was opened: the butt of the gun exposed. This time the general meant business.

Frost recognized it was one or the other. He also went for his gun.

Nolanti had the start of a fraction of a second. Just a fraction. Frost's life hung by that thread.

And then there was a soft *ploomp!* and Nolanti's eyes popped open, he groaned, and folded up on the floor like a Japanese lantern. As his body went down it revealed, directly behind, another form. It was Eddie Giles. He was holding his pistol in the flat of his hand. He put it back in his holster.

"I smashed him pretty hard," he observed dryly.

Frost knelt beside the stricken man. "It was a wallop at that. Where'd you come from?"

Giles said: "Hell—you need a nurse."

Nolanti groaned and turned over on his side. He had been hit hard. Giles had clubbed him over the temple and blood streamed from a deep gash.

Frost said to the señorita: "Get some water and a towel." She whisked out of the room, her nostrils dilated and her hands trembling.

"This is liable to be bad business," Giles said. He looked at Frost and dropped the general's hand. "Women," he said pointedly, "are a damned nuisance. My God, you ought to know that by now."

Frost said: "Cut it! I'm not a bit sorry—not even a little bit."

The girl returned with a basin of water and a towel. Giles propped Nolanti's head in his arms and Frost bathed the cut and tried to bring him back to consciousness.

The girl had dropped on one knee beside Frost. He said: "I'm not sorry I came—"

She didn't say anything. She bestowed a reverent glance on the crucifix in the niche as if it had been responsible for the intervention of the *Americanos.*

Nolanti sat up and blinked his eyes. Giles was holding him.

The girl said: "I should have gone to my brother in Mexico City. But the soldiers—"

The soft candlelight cast exquisite shadows over her face.

Frost said: "Don't worry."

Nolanti placed his hand against his head and looked about the room curiously, desperately seeking to penetrate the fog in his brain. He felt someone holding him and turned around and saw Giles.

"You, eh? From behind." He got to his feet and swayed as if

he would fall again. Frost caught him. Nolanti said: *"Gracias!* I am glad to know how *Americanos* fight." He bowed curtly to the Señorita Rubiez, and wiped away the flow of blood from his eye. "A thousand pardons, señorita. I—"

Frost thought he had never seen so odd a sight. In the flickering shadows Nolanti shifted unsteadily, but vigorously tried to maintain his unctuous manner.

Then suddenly there was a blast of rifles in the street. Shouts and screams of surprise arose. The clarion notes of a bugle rang through the night.

Nolanti stood erect as a tent-pole. *"Madre di Dios!* The rebels!"

He turned and dashed from the room, insensible to his wound.

At every crack of the rifles the girl flinched. Her face was being slowly drained of its color. Outside a pandemonium reigned. La Salada was chaos.

Frost said shortly: "Tento! And he damn' well knew when to come. Señorita—"

"I will remain," she said resolutely, getting a grip on her emotions. "I am not afraid."

"Then we remain," Frost said. "They will sack the town—"

"Viva Tento! *Viva* Tento!"

The shouts were in the hall of the house.

Frost dashed to the door and slammed it. He dragged a table which he shoved against it. Giles grabbed two chairs and together they pulled out a cabinet.

Frost said to the girl: "Go! Hide!"

She looked at him for an instant—seventy-two inches of sinew, flushed in the candlelight, an automatic in his hand and the steel of battle in his eyes. She looked at him and left the room. And unaware of the pounding at the door... of the rifle fire in the street... everything, Frost watched her disappear through a door.

"Jerry!"

Frost turned.

"Gimme a hand!"

Giles was tugging at a huge Renaissance cabinet. They squared it around and crouched behind it.

"Let 'em have it, Eddie!"

"—damned right!"

The door creaked and burst in. Half a dozen swarthy faces appeared above the improvised barricade. Their rifles glinted in the yellow light....

Crack!

Crack!

Twin jets of flame leaped across the space from the *Americanos'* pistols.

A voice boomed curses in the hall.

The soldiers fell away. The doorway became mysteriously bare. The same voice, surprised: "Two men!" And then loudly: "I call upon you to surrender in the name of Tento!"

Frost looked at Giles. Giles looked at Frost.

"The big cheese himself," Giles said. "Well?"

Frost said: "It's the wall any way we go." He raised his voice: "Come and get us!"

It is characteristic of adventurers to discount danger. Even the most extreme moments of peril do not so register. Frost—Giles, too, for that matter—had been in some tight spots. None had ever been tighter than this. Disaster was close. And yet there was little concern.

They should have known their predicament was desperate....

There was a pause broken only by the scurrying of footsteps in the hall. An order was barked in Spanish. A moment later Frost crawled to the window. A dozen soldiers were moving in from the street, their purpose all too plain. He and Giles were trapped. He backed slowly to the cabinet and dropped down on his haunches.

He said softly: "Looks bad. They're surrounding the house. Keep an eye on the window."

Giles said: "Righto! If this is the finish we'll go in a blaze." He laughed shortly. "I was just thinking about that picture show we saw a couple of weeks ago where that Ranger got in a closet and shot it out with the rustlers. Things like that do happen, I guess."

A head appeared over the barricade. Frost nudged Giles. Giles stopped speaking. Frost snapped his automatic up and squeezed the trigger.

The body pitched forward and hung across the top of a chair.

"Three," Frost said.

There was a fervid oath from the corridor in that same heavy voice they had identified as Tento's. *"Madre di Dios!"* It checked itself there and presently another voice was heard. It came from a safe retreat.

"Machine-guns are here, *mi coronel*. Will you come out?"

Frost said: "Nolanti! Eddie, the louse sold out. The—damned traitor. He marched these men into a trap! No wonder he didn't want to fight until tomorrow!"

"Yeah—Nolanti." Giles raised his head and shouted: "Go ——" and Frost clapped his hand over his mouth and said: "Wait a minute!" Then: "We're gone ducks this way. Want to take a chance the other way? We're Americans, you know."

"Yeah—but a hell of a lot of good that'll do you now. We got in with 'em and—"

Frost cut him short with a shout: "We'll come out!"

"Throw your pistols out the door!"

Two automatics went sailing through the air and through the door. A moment later the soldiers cleared a path for Nolanti. He was no longer the immaculate actor. His uniform was bloodstained and bedraggled, and his head was swathed in a bandage. He resembled a desert chieftain.

Behind him came Tento, a hulking figure with fierce mustachios, and half a dozen soldiers.

Nolanti made no effort to suppress his pleasure.

Frost looked at him and said: "You —— damned louse!"

"Ah, yes! But as you *Americanos* say—'All's fair in love and war'— Ah, yes!" He drew himself up proudly. There was a trace of fanaticism in his eyes now. He said: "Tomorrow we amuse you with a court-martial!"

Rifle fire punctuated his speech. The bell in the cathedral kept up its frenzied ringing. It set a mad tempo for the scene in the streets.

Tento's followers had the advantage of preparation and a night move. They knew exactly when and where to strike. The faithful *federalistas*, routed in a surprise attack, went into action with little will and no sort of direction.

The firing was vigorous. Whenever rebels and federals met the streets became narrow battlefields. Neither side gave way until the other had been exterminated. Some combatants, too close for rifles and pistols, closed in with knives....

And above the rifle fire, the confusion, the shots, the ringing of the bell, came the shouts:

"Viva Tento!"

It was a quick and complete rout. By the light of torches Nolanti and Tento rode among the men until the first trace of dawn; the one pompous and confident, the other wounded but clinging to his purpose with a tenacity almost superb... both haranguing the men of the government. Latin-American warfare is largely a matter of oratory, anyway....

By morning the *federalistas* who had survived became rebels—and Mexico City loomed close at hand. It was a wave that gathered speed and size as it went on—the red fires of rebellion....

But the little Flores, unused to governing a republic of such deep intrigue, had placed implicit faith in a more powerful guidance. That very night he got some sort of divine inspiration. He flashed orders from his bedroom in the Castillo de Chapultepec for five thousand additional men to be mustered into service....

Queer? Not at all. History is filled with such premonitions....

ACCUSTOMED AS HE was to military pomp, any court-martial in which Nolanti had a hand would be, of necessity, impressive. The next morning he gathered a small but select tribunal in the wide drawing-room of the Rubiez home, which now was headquarters. There was Tento himself, his barrel chest bulging, his mustachios running wild, like Villa's, who was, incidentally, Tento's military hero. Next sat Nolanti, his appearance slightly more at ease, his head still bandaged; and there were three other officers, nondescript in appearance, who were there to furnish atmosphere for the little drama and background for Nolanti.

Tento, big and gruff and brutal, had roundly complained of the stage setting. He had insisted the formality of a trial was unnecessary. Tento's policy was to shoot them where they stood. He had protested; he still did.

"General, this is the whim of an old man," he said bluntly.

"No," said Nolanti. "Perhaps they can be influenced, *mi jefe*. They could help us. They will see we mean business—"

Still, Tento was not satisfied. "Perhaps. Perhaps. Do you think they will join us?"

"*Quien sabe?*" Nolanti lifted his shoulders. "Maybe."

Tento bestowed a tolerant glance upon him. "You do not know fighting men well, *amigo*. The *Americanos* will laugh."

Two other men entered the room. One was of medium height who walked jerkily, a man past middle age. The other was constructed along sturdy lines and was red-haired.

Tento and Nolanti both rose as they entered the room.

The middle-aged man said, "Where are the prisoners?"

Tento said: "They will be here shortly."

"Damned nonsense! Why all this play?" He snorted. "They should have been killed last night."

The red-haired man put in: "I'm telling you again I don't like this. Bumping off a couple of Americans is no cinch. We are getting into a mess."

Tento said: "Poof!" as the middle-aged man nodded approvingly, Tento held up two fingers. It was the most insulting gesture known below the Border. Tento said again: "Poof!"

There was a sound of boots on the floor and four soldiers escorted Frost and Giles into the room.

The flyers abruptly came to a halt as they looked upon the men grouped around the table. Frost was surprised to see the two men in civilian clothes. He knew them—Weisberg and Jacobson, the two remaining members of the Black Ship gang still at large.

Weisberg smiled. Perhaps smile is not the word. It was more of a smirk. He noted Frost's expression and said: "I see you remember me."

Frost said nothing.

Weisberg went on: "This time there will be no monkey business." His face was bland but there was steel in his words.

Frost looked upon the men with a certain grimness. This was to be no court-martial. This merely was a prelude to murder.

Tento said to the soldiers: "*Vamose! Andale!*" just as a bit of bravado; and they went gladly. There was more fun in the *pulquerias* anyway. Without moving his head Tento said: "You *Americanos* are charged with murder. Have you anything to say?"

Frost grinned. "I'd like to have the rope if you don't mind. I know Mexican marksmanship too well."

Nolanti bristled and a smile played around the corners of Tento's mouth. He shook his leonine head in mock sadness. "What a pity!" he said. "Your sense of humor—" He shook his head again and turned to Nolanti. "You, general, will pronounce sentence."

Frost's heart dropped like a plummet. He said: "You know what this will mean? Uncle Sam—"

"Poof!" said Tento.

Weisberg snapped: "We have waited a long time for you, Frost—a long time."

Nolanti laced his fingers and leaned forward. Before he could open his mouth, a crisp whisper filled the room.

"Hands up, señors!"

Two forms stood in a side doorway. One was the Señorita Rubiez. The other was Captain Montez.

"A single move and you are dead men!"

The girl and Montez both had leveled their pistols.

Montez commanded: "Stand up, señors!" in an excessively polite tone.

The officers got to their feet. Montez said to Frost: "Take their guns!"

Now fully alive, Frost and Giles moved among them and took their revolvers swiftly. When they were disarmed the flyers stepped back.

Tento blustered: "I could raise my voice—"

"And stop a slug with your head!" Giles finished. He covered Tento with Tento's own gun.

Montez said: "And the next time, señors, your men should search the cellar."

Nolanti, almost apoplectic with impotent rage, twisted his heavy garnet ring nervously around his finger. He was an actor and a traitor—and he was frightened. But he was not stupid. He did not wonder how Montez and the girl had hid in the cellar all night; nor why the beautiful señorita seemed so interested in the cause. Nolanti didn't wonder because he didn't care. It had happened. Threats would be absurd. So he said:

"*Capitan,* you should know how helpless you are. The old regime is doomed. Now if you would care to—"

"I don't!" Montez said.

By now Frost had come closer to the Señorita Rubiez. It was no time to indulge in greetings. Yet he said: "How did this happen?"

For an instant a trace of a smile lighted her face. A Japanese carver of ivory might have caught the exquisiteness of her profile and the curve of her lips. She said: "I am a *soldadera*. I owed you a debt. I have tried to repay."

Frost mumbled, "Yes. Yes." He turned away. There were many things to say. He had never wanted to say such things before. But he forced himself to turn away. He was a soldier… a fighting man. What had Giles said… women are a damned nuisance. They weren't really. Not to everybody. But to a fighting man… Frost shut the picture of the beautiful señorita from his mind and remembered his job ahead.

Tento had spread his hulk in a high-backed Spanish chair. He was uneasy. He was restless as an animal. And Nolanti was far from being at ease. The slender traitor recognized the approach of something like his fate. The actor playing the dual role he loved and in which he excelled, and playing it with finesse right down to the finish, sat in this great broad room awaiting whatever was to come. He was like a rabbit in a trap. A life that so long had been conducted for his benefit alone had slipped upside down.

Weisberg and Jacobson looked on through narrowed eyes. They had faced the guns of Jerry Frost before—and they knew the man. Once they had escaped. But they knew they could not again. The next time Frost would say it with lead.

The three other Mexicans were mere puppets and they knew it. They said nothing and sat immovable while the drama played itself swiftly before them.

Montez and the Señorita Rubiez had burst into the room in a moment of sheer impetuosity. He had waited until the soldiers had left the room and gone elsewhere; there were no other sentries. It is doubtful if the gallant officer had thought ahead of that move. What was to happen inside, how he would extricate himself and his friends evidently had been of no immediate concern. Companionships are welded by dangers. Montez's two companions were in danger. That was all that mattered.

Somehow Frost sensed Montez had exhausted his resources. The brave Mexican could think no further. He seemed to have no conception of what to do next. And Frost knew that delay was dangerous—terribly dangerous. His life—their lives—depended on speed.

He said to the señorita: "Get some rope—cord—anything. And some rags! Have you some rope?"

She nodded.

"Hurry!"

Frost gestured with his pistol at one of the Mexican officers. "Stand up and undress!" He turned to Giles. "Eddie, block the door!" He looked back at the Mexican and snapped: "Go on! Pull off your pants and blouse!"

The Mexican slipped out of his blouse and pulled off his pants. He presented rather an incongruous picture there in the room. His comrades looked on puzzled.

"Montez—put on that uniform! Give him yours!"

Montez caught the idea and hurriedly changed clothes.

Two stood guard while the other exchanged uniforms. The fit of the khaki left something to be desired, but no attention was paid to that. When the Señorita Rubiez returned to the room she found Montez, Frost and Giles in the brown of the rebel army. She saw the rebel officers wearing the pea-green of the federal forces and in a moment she knew what had happened. She made no comment.

Frost said to them: "Señors, our position is quite like yours—desperate! It is your life or ours—and we have no scruples against blowing off the top of your heads. The first slip and hell gets turned loose!"

The señorita handed him a quantity of rope and a skirt. She handed them to him with the air of a soldier who completes a mysterious mission successfully and asks no questions.

Frost handed it over to Giles without taking his eyes off the group. "Tie 'em up, Eddie—and gag 'em. Watch the door, Montez! Eddie—all but Weisberg and Jacobson! We'll take them with us!"

Giles went immediately to work. He hummed a bar or two as he tied up the officers.

He gagged them effectually. Nobody offered any resistance. The leveled guns cowed them. Giles stretched them on the floor and admired his handiwork.

Weisberg and Jacobson fidgeted nervously. Weisberg said: "You can't get away with it, Frost—you can't get away with it!"

Frost said: "No! Get this, you—and get it in a hurry! We are going back to the flying field, see? You'll go—and like it! No more chances with you! The next time, I bump you off myself, see?" Frost's eyes were blazing and his voice was hard. He had not forgotten the escape of the Black Ship gang from an express train months before—at the cost of two Rangers' lives.

"Now get up and shove off! We'll send an army back after the others!"

It was a strange procession that emerged a little later from the house of Rubiez—and yet it was not so strange, at that. Jacobson and Weisberg came out first and in the rear were Frost and Giles and Montez and the girl.

Coming through the iron gate Frost said: "Right through the skull if it comes to a showdown."

Giles said: "Righto!"

They walked briskly into the street, into a sun that was brutal in its intensity; and headed for the improvised flying field.

Soldiers stepped aside and saluted mechanically. Not a one of them so much as looked twice. Weisberg and Jacobson occasionally lifted their eyes to the skies. Frost said to Giles, "Black ships are due."

Giles didn't say anything.

Frost increased the cadence. He was nervous. His heart was not normal. He was in a tough spot. The girl complicated the situation. Giles had been right about women.

As they reached the field the guards moved away from the planes. Frost stopped Weisberg and Jacobson beside the cabin plane in which Nolanti and his staff had been transported to La Salada.

Frost said quietly: "Get in the plane. Eddie, you ride with 'em and take Miss Rubiez. And let the lead go at the first sign of monkey business."

"Sure," said Giles. "But I hate to leave my little ship. I hate—"

"Nix!" Frost interrupted. "We're in a hurry. And if anything happens see that these prisoners get through."

Montez got in and sat down at the controls. The starter whirred and then the motor skyrocketed into explosions. Giles and the girl got in and sat in the rear of the cabin. Frost motioned for Weisberg and Jacobson to get in. They did.

As the cabin plane pulled off, Frost stood just clear of the slip-stream and raised his hand.

Montez got away in a rush and Frost went over to his ship

and took his helmet off the accelerator knob. He pulled it down over his forehead insouciantly, and tucked in his ears. He looked behind him at the village of La Salada sprawled in the sun like an ugly wound. Soldiers, tasting a triumph, eager to move. Waiting for orders. But these orders would be late. Frost walked to his plane, wound the starter and got in.

FIFTEEN HUNDRED FEET up he saw that Montez was holding his throttle open. The nose of the cabin plane was up and the ship had gone into a long climb, pointing, roughly, south by east. Its motor was blowing black rings through the exhausts. The swaying of the craft itself in the bumpy channels indicated excessive speed.

Within that plane sat two members of a gang which had given the state of Texas more trouble than any other combine in the turbulent history of the Lone Star State. They had been guilty of murder, robbery, counterfeiting, smuggling, violation of the neutrality act between the United States and Mexico— they had run the length and breadth of the criminal statutes.

As he roared through the air Frost found it difficult to grasp the full significance of his capture. It had gone on so long he hardly could realize it was ended. It was a dream. The two surviving members captured… the others dead or in prison. It had been a long fight. A long, long fight.

Weisberg and Jacobson, the last two….

Montez's cabin plane took a gap in the clouds at six thousand feet and Frost sat on its tail and pulled through directly behind. Above, the sun was shining brightly, so brightly it nearly blinded him. The ground was visible only in smudges of dark brown.

At intervals Frost swept the sky on a level with his eye. Then he began systematically to search in layers. He had an uneasy feeling. For the life of him he could force it into no definite fear. It was just a sort of blend of caution and intuition. Frost didn't stop to analyze it. He merely accepted it and let it go at that. It is possible that the onrush of victory, after so long a fight, might have been predominant in the wave of uneasiness.

He flew on and on. He looked at his air speed indicator. 110. Montez was setting a fast pace. San Luis Potosi unrolled beneath. The white tiled buildings flashed in the sun. The plaza was crowded. Beyond there were tiny settlements which resembled so many dots. Long ago they had been burned into insensibility: and there was no place on the map for them.

Halfway to Mexico City, near Celaya in the state of Guanajuato, Frost's subconscious fears welled into a crystallized mass that chilled him to his ankles. It was like coming out of a nightmare and sitting up stark in a shadowed room. There is nothing so completely unnerving.

The enemy!

It is possible that before he kicked his rudder around he looked back and saw them. Later he said he wasn't sure whether he acted when the hunch hit him or when he saw the planes.

At any rate he perceived two dots hanging on the lower edge of the sun. They hadn't been there a moment ago. It was as if the sun had spawned them.

He did not attempt to surmise how they were so soon in pursuit. He remembered seeing Weisberg and Jacobson glancing upward; he didn't think those two planes were in the northern sky when they took off, but with his attention on Montez' ship, he could not be certain—anyway that was past now.

Other matters of the moment were more pressing.

Frost slid off on a wing and picked-up the bright flash of his pursuers. He loaded his guns methodically. The coldness he had felt a moment ago was gone: in its place had come a comfortable glow.

He opened his throttle and went into a climb—straight into the sun. He put up the ball of his thumb to shut out the blazing inferno. His heart was beating faster but he was not conscious of it. His temples felt tight. He pushed his goggles up. No goggles while firing.

He looked up and around but saw only those two planes. One of them was two thousand feet higher than the other and half a mile away. He had the sun and the altitude. He knew it. He nosed over and came down like a comet.

Frost pulled up sharply, did a quick climbing turn and faced the black ship head on. An old trick. Let him know immediately you've got guts. A big help sometimes. Air fighting deals a lot with the other fellow's psychology.

Frost opened his sight cover and pressed the trigger. Both guns vomited a stream of lead. The black ship's pilot held his fire a trifle too long and in a split-second Frost had driven out of range. The black ship swept by and Frost half-rolled to get on top and went high in the climb.

Montez had observed Frost's predicament. He knew the two black ships were trying to pocket him, catch him on the intersecting line and let go. It was first-grade air stuff and Montez thought Frost was certain to be trapped. He lost speed and his big ship was loafing along at eight or nine thousand feet half a mile away. Frost saw it and swore at his instrument board.

He said: "The fool! Why doesn't he run for it!"

From high above, he saw that the second black ship had spotted the cabin plane and had darted for it like a falcon. Frost waggled his wings in a desperate signal to get away, but it was not seen.

"The fool! Oh, the —— damned fool!" he swore.

He kicked his bus over in a dive—115—120—125—130—140—145—150—160—the wires were screaming so vengefully he could not hear his guns chatter. He knew they were working only because he could see the crank arms moving. He was hammering at the black ship in short bursts of ten. The enemy was visible in his ring sight. The next moment it had disappeared. The pilot had turned in a wild split-air to miss the lead.

Frost stalled and whipped out in a spin. He ruddered out of the spin and ran his stick through a slow ellipse. He leveled off and streaked away: threw himself up and over in an Immelmann turn and came out with his guns barking.

Eddie Giles, peering through the narrow slot of a window in the cabin plane, his face grim and his upper lip in his teeth, muttered: "God! What a pilot! I never saw anything like that before!"

Frost was thinking clearly. He was perfectly coordinated. There was, nevertheless, blood in his eye. They say the ideal ace is a high-strung, impetuous chap who goes wild: a hellion ripping and smashing in brilliant maneuvers. Perhaps. Certainly in this fight Jerry Frost was anything but that. He was cold and calm and deliberate and he knew he had never engaged in a scrap so technically perfect.

He had the wind in his hair and a taste of the clouds on his lip.

He closed in on the black ship and as he rolled over he had a glimpse of the ground—a great, gray scarf that stretched as far as he could see. The other machine split-aired for a frantic second and let go its guns.

A storm of bullets clawed at Frost's plane—and white-hot needles stung him in the shoulder. Something warm trickled down his arm.

He was hit.

"Damn!" he said. "Damn!"

There came that tightening of the throat—that ghastly wound that never quite heals—the fear of men who fly. This was the way it got them—in a flash. For a moment it jumped in every fiber of his body. For just a moment. It was too devastating a force, and Frost knew it. He had to beat it as quickly as it had come.

His hand reached for the trigger control as he pulled up into a half loop, his fabric flaying in the breeze. The black ship flew squarely through his smoky line of fire.

That was all.

It flopped once and a puff of amberish smoke ripped away from it. It stalled madly and side-slipped to whip the flames away from the cockpit. The pilot was up now, with a leg over the side, groping blindly for a foothold on the edge of the lower wing. Then the burning machine slid out of the slip and the flames swept down the fuselage.

The pilot hesitated and then flung himself off into ten thousand feet of space.

Frost thought: Tough to go like that. Tough—damned tough. Mustn't look at him. Might do things to my throat. Won't look.... Funny, how he twists and turns....

Frost blinked his eyes. For the first time he was conscious they stung fearfully. He wiped away the tears on the coat sleeve of the khaki uniform. Then he saw it and remembered it was a rebel soldier's garb. He laughed aloud.

"Funny. Damned funny!"

He looked out and saw the other black ship streaking for the cabin plane. Montez was flying like mad.

Frost opened his throttle and his machine leaped ahead. The fabric ribboned back in the breeze as he eased the stick back and went into a gradual climb.

The pilot of the black ship was unaware of the fate of his companion. He was close beside the cabin plane now, trying to get across some sort of a signal. He knew his superiors rode in that ship.

Inside the cabin plane there was some confusion. They had seen Frost's fight—Weisberg and Jacobson with ominous, brooding eyes and the Señorita Rubiez, slumped in her seat from the excitement. Giles darted swift glances from the prisoners to the ships outside.

Weisberg was sitting ahead of the girl. In the excitement she had laid her pistol in her lap. Weisberg had seen it. He slowly shifted his position, and in a flash he had pivoted quickly. His hand darted for the weapon.

But Giles had seen.

Crack!

The cabin was lighted by a momentary flash, and a puff of smoke rolled by the girl's face.

She screamed and jumped. Weisberg groaned and the reflex jerked his arm back in a convulsive movement. It dangled helplessly beside him. The bullet had smashed his elbow.

"Sit still!" Giles shouted.

Jacobson swore roundly, and the black ship pulled closer. Giles leaned over the señorita and said: "Steady!"

He leveled his arm across her and broke the glass with the barrel of his gun. The air rushed in and tore at her hair. The black ship pilot saw the movement and reached for his own pistol.

Crack! It wasn't a difficult shot, with the two planes side by side and at the same rate of speed.

Giles fired again and the pilot threw up both hands and slid forward like a sack of meal. The black ship dived from sight.

Outside there was another roar—a threnody of victory. The nose of Frost's ship appeared. He looked across and nodded in wide, slow movements. He opened his mouth and slowly formed the words: "O—key!" He threw one arm forward, holding the stick between his knees, and Giles waved his hand. Giles shouted ahead to Montez: "Step on it!"

Giles did not notice Frost sunk low in his cockpit. He screened his shoulder from the eyes in the other plane. His shoulder was badly hit. Blood was streaming from it.

IT SEEMED TO Frost they flew on forever before the snow-capped peak of Popocatepetl emerged from the eternal mists which surround it. He was tired. He had not slept the night before... he had stayed awake in the narrow jail devising an escape....

And his shoulder pinched like the first faint gnawing of cancer. He was seized with a mad desire to close his eyes. The lids were like lead. He laughed to himself. Joke on him. Eyes heavy. Ha, ha, ha. Funniest thing in the world.

There was the field. Right below. Montez down. And Giles was with the prisoners. Good. Old Eddie. Eddie said women were a damned nuisance. Bet no woman ever looked at Eddie the way the señorita looked at him. Going down. Got to hurry. Couldn't keep eyes open. Couldn't fly like this with a shoulder knocked all to hell and back. He chuckled a bit to think of that. Silly to think of flying when a shoulder was knocked all to hell and back.

He yanked his eyes open.

He saw a streak of ground flicker through his struts. Faces. White faces upturned. He yanked back his stick. God, the damned thing was heavy. Must have an elephant on the elevators. Like turning a truck. Never been that heavy before. Something was wrong. Somebody was sitting on the elevators. Get the hell off there. Got to look and see....

He felt a crash and his head shot forward and he remembered throwing up his arm to keep his teeth from being bashed out against the cowl.

IT WAS DARK—VERY dark. Except for a single spot of light way off in the distance. He moved. Something cool touched his forehead.

He muttered: "Everything is okey?" There was a whisper. He saw something. He couldn't make out what it was. "Everything is okey?"

A voice said: "Sure—okey!"

He tried to move. His left side was stiff. Muscles had stuck together. What the hell? He stirred again. No luck. He opened his eyes. He closed them and then opened them again.

"Where am I?" he said. "What's the matter?" Then: "Never mind." He sat up suddenly and winced from the pain.

"Lay down," a voice said. "Be still."

He laughed. "Still? What the hell—still? I'm okey!" He laughed again. "I'm all right." He twisted his head to get a squint at his shoulder. It was taped in bandages. He grinned. "I'm all right."

Then he saw faces. Giles… Montez. A man in a white coat with a stethoscope draped from his neck. Another face, a little round face. He had seen that face before. Now where the devil… sure… sure… the *presidente*.

The face was coming towards him. Montez stepped forward and whispered:

"*El Presidente!*"

Frost said, "Sure. Sure."

The little man was ridden with emotion. He tried to speak but the words clogged in his throat. His hands trembled. He finally managed:

"*Gracias, mi amigo. Gracias!*" That was all he could say.

Frost grinned. "Nix! I want to get up. Hell, I'm okey." He looked at Giles. "Hello, Limey. Everything set?"

Giles smiled and came closer. "Yeah. Weisberg and Jacobson are on their way to the Border with a special guard the President appointed. And say, the troops captured Tento and Nolanti. I've got you an invitation to a little shooting party."

"Heh? How long have I been in here?"

Giles said: "Long enough."

The Señorita Rubiez emerged from the background and Frost again saw the exquisite shadows on her face. His shoulder was throbbing, but not too much for him to think: "I could fall for this dame like nobody's business if I had time. It's too bad I'm a soldier."

The Señorita Rubiez indicated a young man in his late twenties, a young man of proud demeanor. She said: "My brother," and he stepped forward and bowed cordially.

"My thanks, sir. My sister—"

"Nix," Frost said. "Nix."

The Trail to the Tropics

Captain Jerry Frost, flying Ranger,
follows a strange trail southward

A STUPENDOUS JOKE and a big steal had been pulled in the State of Texas.

Three cattlemen, in the south, were not so sure of the joke part of it, but they were very, very certain about the steal.

Incredible as it seemed, a huge herd of cattle had disappeared between two days from the plains that bordered close upon the International Boundary.

Rustling? Yeah—that's old-time stuff. But this was a wholesale proposition. And the old-timers had their inning. What they said about modern methods of riding herd was plenty— no fencing, no proper protection, wonder was they had any cattle left at all.

Somebody said something about planes, and a fellow— not one of the three cattlemen—who looked upon it as just one hell of a joke, said they must have loaded the cows in big passenger outfits and carried them off that way.

But they found broad trails leading to the river, and after a time it became noised around that the bunch had been shipped from Picachos to Tampico and loaded for some republic in the South Atlantic.

But that didn't tell what had happened that night on the south Texas plains, and a lot of people wanted to know about it, including the Adjutant-General at Austin. So he set Jerry Frost of the Air Patrol to snooping around.

Frost didn't get very far at first—and then he did. He found Fred Bennett's diary.

Bennett had been one of the new flyers taken on some months ago by the Air Rangers and a week before had been found dead in his wrecked airplane. He was torn and crushed; there was nothing to indicate foul play.

His plane apparently had come down in a dive from which he couldn't recover. There was an official investigation, but this was pure formality, and it was written off as an unfortunate smash and orders issued that the Air Rangers would do no more night flying except under specific command of Captain Frost.

Bennett's mother had written Frost asking for her dead son's personal effects: photographs, possessions, books and the odd trinkets flying men learn to accumulate and revere. That was how Frost came across the diary.

He had, at first, no intention of looking inside its pages. But when he saw what it was he was overcome with a curiosity to know what Bennett had written before the fatal flight. Did he have a premonition of death? Or was he perfectly normal?

Frost thumbed through the pages and came upon an entry that surprised him—and yet it didn't. He'd half expected to find something.

"... saw four ships near the old Double W, or thought I did. What could four ships be doing out there?"

There was no further entry. That had been Bennett's last message. It was dated under the 12th. His body had been found on the 14th.

Frost whistled softly.

"By——! he went back there. Sure as hell, he did. And something happened."

Frost mailed Bennett's personal things to his mother. All but the diary. He put that in his pocket and took off for Austin.

THE ADJUTANT-GENERAL LIGHTED a cigar and looked at Frost curiously. Frost had something important on his mind. One could tell from his approach.

The Adjutant-General grinned.

"Go on. Get it off your chest."

Frost looked serious.

"I've just found something. Read this."

He laid Bennett's diary on the desk.

The Adjutant-General read it, but he didn't quite understand. He said it was so much Greek to him.

Frost said: "Bennett didn't crash. Something else happened."

The Adjutant-General took the cigar out of his mouth.

"But you went down there yourself—"

Captain Frost nodded.

"I did. There was a crash. I mean Bennett didn't do it. But, by ——! it looked perfect."

"Then," said the Adjutant-General, "how do you know it wasn't an accident?"

Frost frowned.

"Bennett went back out there that night to investigate. He went out there alone and it cost him his life. The Double W is the closest outfit to the ones which lost those cattle. I believe we're on the scent of something big."

"I wonder," said the Adjutant-General, slapping his desk.

"Sure," said Frost. "Four planes he said he saw. There was a rumor that planes were used by the men who drove off the cattle. Somehow, some way, they killed Bennett and made it look like an accident."

The Adjutant-General puffed at his cigar.

"I believe you're right."

Frost nodded.

"I believe I am, too. I don't know much about that business. Did they ever get any dope on it?"

"A little," the Adjutant-General said. "The cattle were shipped to a republic down in the Atlantic Ocean on the tip end of Central America."

Frost pulled himself out of the chair and began to walk up and down.

"I've soldiered from one end of that country to the other. What republic was it?"

"Rigaria."

"Rigaria?" Frost repeated. "Say, I was down there once. I know some big men in Rigaria; rather they used to be big. Is there any way we can find out—"

"Yes," said the Adjutant-General. He pushed a button and his secretary entered. "Get in touch with the press associations and find out the name of the president of the Republic of Rigaria and anything else they can give us."

"If a bird named Maranga is still president down there, I can't miss," Frost said.

He was so enthusiastic the Adjutant-General agreed to give him indefinite leave if Maranga was still president. The command of the Air Rangers would be left to Hans Traub, the former Bavarian ace.

Frost was impatient for the secretary to return with his information. The Adjutant-General once said:

"Sit down and be still. You give me the jimmies when you pace up and down like that."

But Frost wouldn't sit down. When there was a rap at the door some time later, Frost opened it.

The secretary came in. He read off a sheet of paper.

"José Maranga is president of Rigaria. A revolution is reported brewing."

Frost grinned.

"Maranga! The old fat sonofagun."

His voice was soft, his memory went back through the years to a time when he and José Maranga had fought side by side. Only Maranga had been merely a *coronel* then and Frost had been known as El Beneficio, a wild, wild *Americano* who was a master machine-gunner.

He looked at the Adjutant-General and his thoughts were

plain. The Adjutant-General nodded and got up and stuck out his hand. Frost took it and said:

"That's a great country down there."

"Sure," said the Adjutant-General. "Well, be a good boy."

Frost walked out into the corridor. A ghost fell in behind him, the ghost of El Beneficio, the reckless *soldado* who had become a legend in Latin America.

They were going South to the tropics.

AVAZALON, THE CHIEF seaport of Rigaria, is a tired, sleepy town which long ago surrendered to the sun. It is composed of faded red-tile houses which rise from the water's edge and extend back to the heavy growth of the wilderness.

El Beneficio knew Avazalon. Coming across the bay he saw the flat roof of Tomaso's, from which point he once had sprayed a column of advancing, imported fighters with bullets. His mind went back to that day... and he laughed. How Tomaso had prayed to all the saints to preserve his dirty little café, how Tomaso had later kissed his hand and hailed him as a savior, and that star-studded night when he played with the dashing Mayana, she of the dark eyes and crimson lips....

Mayana, the toast of the *cantina*. Now, he reflected, grown old and fat and gone to pipe smoking. Eight years does a lot to a woman, too, in the tropics. El Beneficio shook his head.

His *piragua* groaned against the sides of the quay and he hopped out and tossed the lad a coin. He walked briskly up the narrow street, turned a corner and went into the shadowed interior of Tomaso's place. It was dank and musty and humid, but to El Beneficio's nostrils these odors were myrrh.

Tomaso was asleep, the black boy said. Not even the arrival of the steel boom ship interfered with the siesta. Now would the black boy go upstairs and awake his master? *Non, non.* Maybe one hour, maybe two—

Frost grinned.

"Okey."

He stepped behind the end of the bar and started up the stone steps.

The black boy tugged at his coat.

"Non! Non!"

Frost pushed him away and went up. At the head of the stairs he saw Tomaso. There had been no change in eight years. The fat proprietor was sprawled across a cot, one foot on the floor and one hand drooped over his chest. The other hand held a palm-leaf fan that rested on the floor.

Frost shook the form lightly. But it takes more than that to awaken one of these natives. He finally shook it heavily; Tomaso slowly sat up and tried to clear the haze from his eyes. For a moment his expression was not pleasant, and then as it dawned on him who his visitor was, he grinned broadly.

"Eet ess you, El Beneficio?" he said as if to wipe away the last vestige of doubt.

Frost nodded.

"You didn't forget, eh?"

Tomaso propelled his bulk to the floor and hitched his suspenders. He took both Frost's hands and pressed them.

"Forget? Tomaso forget? Nevair!"

Frost grinned and didn't say anything. His heart was warming; for such friendships, after all, are pretty close to ideal.

Tomaso's eyes widened.

"W'at you do in Rigaria, huh?"

The presence of El Beneficio here meant but one thing to Tomaso—war. Tomaso had a martial conception of the man and never could have had any other.

"Nothing," Frost said. He couldn't explain to Tomaso. He didn't try. "I heard over Guatemala way there was some fighting going on, so here I am."

Tomaso planted his bare feet on the floor and got serious.

"So, you 'ave 'eard."

"Not much. Come on down and tell me about it."

"Sure," Tomaso said, but he nevertheless let his eyes wander to his cot as he prepared to sacrifice his siesta. He pulled on his shoes and they went downstairs.

He went at great length to explain to El Beneficio that what he was about to say was unofficial, and he talked in two languages. Did El Beneficio onnerstan'?

"Yeah," he said.

Tomaso shrugged.

"*Revolucion* not far away. Imlaz still want to win. Beyond the mountains he godder one, mebbe two t'ousand men. Maranga ees worry. *Porque no?* Dere ees gold."

Frost said:

"Maranga's been buying cattle, hasn't he?"

"*Si,*" Tomaso said. "Lot of cattle. Week ago they come."

"How many?"

"Plenty," said Tomaso.

El Beneficio grinned and sipped his beer. He changed the subject.

"Tomaso, remember Mayana?"

Tomaso's eyes lighted and his flabby face broke into a smile.

"*Si!* She go to Havana t'ree years ago."

"Oh." Then: "Does the banana train still run up to Matatic?"

Tomaso bobbed his head up and down.

"Big house there now. Maranga send men to Haiti to copy one."

El Beneficio nodded. Maranga's dream of a castle had been realized. Once he had been able to talk of nothing else but his obsession to erect there in the heart of the jungle a mighty monument to himself.

A shrill whistle cut through the air. El Beneficio jumped up.

Tomaso said: "You wait and go tomorrow, eh. Tonight we have fiesta—"

"Got to go now, Tomaso." He offered him his hand. "Until we meet again."

Tomaso's eyes filled with tears. He held the *Americano* in deep, sincere affection.

"Adios," he said simply.

El Beneficio had little time to spare. The narrow-gauge railway that ran between the capital at Matatic and the seaport of Avazalon waited for nothing. Its conductor, given a little authority, was pompous.

It jerked away as El Beneficio got aboard and took his seat in one of the open cars. It had a canopy above, that was all.

THE LITTLE TRAIN for five hours lurched its way through the heavy undergrowth. The ride was torturous, for this train was not designed for the comforts of modern travel. It was purely a necessity, and had never lost that status.

Eight years before, El Beneficio had been here. He was, or thought he was, on his way home. But fate brought him to the port of Avazalon. He went ashore.

His steps led him to Tomaso's. From there emanated the loudest noise, the greatest celebration, the thin strains of the marimba band. A hastily assembled fiesta was in progress. Rafael Imlaz had been deposed as president. José Maranga was to succeed him. The *revolucion* was over.

To El Beneficio the sight was not a new one. Latin-America teems with them. The accouterments, the habits vary, but the motif is always the same.

He asked somebody what all the racket was about. The fighting man leveled a finger at his *coronel,* an oversized, swarthy man of firm jaw and curiously defiant mustachios. That, he said, was Maranga, the new president.

The eyes of José Maranga and El Beneficio met. Each apparently found something then in each other, some well of sympathy and understanding. Who is there to explain these things? El Beneficio saw no brilliant military leader who was about to assume the dignity of a president's office. He saw instead a pitiable soldier, fatigue written in every line of his face. He saw a soldier with the queer eyes of a patriot, not the greedy eyes of a conqueror. And Maranga saw a clean-limbed *Americano* of lithe carriage with adventure radiating from every fiber.

Camaraderies in the tropics form and mature fast. El Beneficio and the weary *coronel* fell together. Confidences came fast. El Beneficio was going home. The *coronel* said he was fortunate to have a home. But he, a soldier, must always fight.

"I thought the *revolucion* was won," El Beneficio said.

José Maranga smiled wanly.

"Mebbe," he said. "I am told Imlaz has many *soldados* coming on a boat. Mebbe you like to stay wiss me?"

El Beneficio shook his head.

"Nope, I'm going home. I'm through fighting."

Maranga nodded and went on talking. What Rigaria needed, he said, was a *presidente* and not a butcher or a criminal. Imlaz was both. Rigaria had gold mines. Imlaz tried to sell them. That was not right. Now when he, Maranga, took the palace, he would be kindly. He would erect a great citadel that people might know a government had come to stay—a symbol of permanence. He would build schools.

"Well," El Beneficio said. "How could I help?"

José Maranga smiled warmly.

"The fame of El Beneficio has reached even this little republic," he said with an air of pride. "Eet ees not that we want you so much; eet ees that we need you."

The eyes of El Beneficio lighted. He breathed deeply and held out his hand.

"Mio compañero," he said.

Thus the bargain was made. They say it was El Beneficio's reckless courage on a blazing hot day a week later, that swung the tide of the battle to Maranga and broke the spirit and the thrust of Rafael Imlaz and his *federalistas.*

Quien sabe?

But El Beneficio did use his machinegun with devastating effect from the roof of Tomaso's café when Imlaz's troops marched up that narrow street after leaving the boat.

AND NOW, EIGHT years later, El Beneficio reflected, as the train swayed through the verdant undergrowth, Maranga had built his citadel. His ambitions were realized. But was it possible he had sent men into Texas to steal cattle? Hardly. Rigaria was rich, as rich proportionately, as any nation in the world. Why should it have to rustle cattle? No, there was something mysterious behind it. That was what he had come to find out.

Suddenly the train swung into a clearing, coughed triumphantly and rolled down a hill. Beyond was Matatic, the capital, and its cluster of houses. El Beneficio saw a sight then that staggered him.

On the crest of a peak, rising hundreds of feet above the country, was an imposing edifice with massive battlements outlined against the sky. There it stood in the midst of the jungle, eight hundred miles from the white man's civilization, an unbelievable thing.

Unbelievable because the white man's mind cannot grasp the prodigiousness of human labor; unbelievable for the same reason that Henri Christophe's Haitian citadel is, from which this was copied. In the age of machinery one has difficulty realizing such projects are possible. Yet they are there.

A grim fortress was Maranga's citadel. Brutal and defiant, a nightmare come true: a warning fist shot into the air for the world to respect.

Still looking, El Beneficio slowly wandered to the platform of the station. He was pounded in the back and turned. He saw a grinning individual in white linen, bristling mustachios, a sword dangling by his side. He saluted, the blunt gesture of a soldier.

Frost laughed and fell into his outstretched arms.

"Maranga, you old tramp!"

"Mio amigo!"

Maranga's white teeth gleamed, his mustachios waved wildly, and natives stared curiously at their *presidente* locked in the embrace of a stranger.

"How did you know I was coming?"

The *presidente's* grin widened.

"Maranga, 'e know ever't'ing."

He took El Beneficio's arm and walked him to the street where the official car waited. It was a Ford, done in garish colors, but manned by a uniformed soldier. It looked ridiculous, but in Rigaria this was class.

El Beneficio laughed.

"Well, you're red hot with your motor. Last time I saw you you were riding a horse and fighting."

Maranga's face clouded swiftly.

"Mebbe you 'ave come in good time."

"Yeah," El Beneficio said. "But I'm not fighting this time."

"Not fighting? El Beneficio not fighting?" Maranga smiled. "My fr'en', there are but two classes of men—lovers and fighters. You are no lover."

"No? Try me out."

Maranga laughed.

El Beneficio was looking at the citadel as they rolled into the road that wound in a spiral.

"You like it?" Maranga said.

El Beneficio beamed.

"Marvelous," he said. "Marvelous."

As he came closer he discovered it was even a mightier piece of work than he at first thought. The peak and the farness of it had lent an illusion which was false. Close upon it one knew it for an astounding creation.

It was the conception of a fighting man, originally, done forever to keep the black man respectful; and it served something of the same purpose for Maranga. It was not fulfilling its purpose though, for instead of teaching respect it ever loomed as a temptation to the malcontents. Occupancy of this was a glory in itself; small wonder there were plots and intrigue.

Maranga and El Beneficio feasted and went out to a balcony to smoke. It was more than a balcony: it was a room with only the sky for a roof. The sun had gone down with startling speed and the dusk had come on with that welcome *relente* which made life bearable by day.

"Now, my fr'en'," Maranga said. "Why you here?"

El Beneficio puffed long at his cigarette. Then he looked across at the fat *presidente*. In the gathering dusk he could see Maranga's small, black eyes upon him.

El Beneficio said:

"Is there any doubt in your mind how I feel about you?"

Maranga shook his head.

"Ten years I 'ave been beeg man in Rigaria. Ten years they 'ave tried to keel me. Frien'ships for me very dangerous. I geev mine to you," he said without ostentation.

"*Gracias*," El Beneficio said, deeply touched. "Now I'll tell you why I'm here."

He did. He made the story brief; occasionally Maranga's *cigarro* bobbed in the gloom.

"Do you know where those cattle came from?"

Maranga said no.

"Pruitt, 'e buy for me. Two hunnerd fifty t'ousan' dollaire I give him for to buy. I don't ask where 'e go."

El Beneficio sat up a little.

"Pruitt? Who's Pruitt?"

"Another *Americano*. Seex years 'e been here."

Pruitt. Pruitt. El Beneficio nodded. The name was familiar.

It tugged at his memory. A long time ago in France....

"W'at you teenk?" Maranga said.

"Nothing," said El Beneficio. "Nothing."

" 'ow come," Maranga went on, "you know about my cattle?"

"Tomaso told me. He said there was trouble brewing in the north."

Maranga clicked his jaws.

"Tomaso talk too damn' much, 'ow 'e know?"

El Beneficio shrugged.

"It's true, isn't it?"

Maranga nodded heavily.

"*Si*. Imlaz again. I t'ink 'e get money from *Americano* minin' company to start war again. For why they no leave Rigaria alone? Imlaz always start trouble."

"*Revolucion?*"

"*Si, revolucion.*" Maranga laughed. "But zis time I got airplanes. Pruitt bring back flyers to 'elp me."

"Flyers?"

"Shoor. Tree flyers. Airplanes, too. Now I got real army."

"Where are they?"

"In north. They go frighten Imlaz. Intimidate."

"Oh," said El Beneficio. "I see."

Rafael Imlaz again. A corrupt native, former president, whose flaming tongue always held some faithful followers. Since Maranga had deposed him he had hidden in the mountains, harassing the government with petty brigandage. Once or twice Maranga's troops had sought him, and failing, had given up.

El Beneficio was silent a long time, staring into the dark blue of the night.

Maranga said:

"Why you quiet? W'at you t'eenk?"

El Beneficio got up and went over and sat down on the arm of Maranga's deep chair. He rested an elbow on the shoulder of the president.

"You are a great guy, Maranga. You are clever and good-hearted. But I wonder if you know just exactly what's going on?"

Maranga tossed his *cigarro* over the wall. It fell in an arc and then disappeared.

"W'at you mean?" he said suspiciously.

El Beneficio smiled.

"Nothing. I was just thinking how perfect it would be if I could help both of us at one lick. I sort of think I can."

That night El Beneficio lay long awake. A sense of great quiet pervaded the countryside. Occasionally the chatter of a bird or the drumming of a *cigarras* broke the silence. After a while the moon filtered through the matted trellises of interlaced palms and branches: a bright jungle moon, casting black shadows. There was again the silence as of old things weighted down by the pyramiding of many years; a silence such as that which follows the clamor and clang of marching men, whose passing disturbs the dust of ages for a moment and whose footprints are blotted out again by time and dust and forgetfulness.

El Beneficio lay there and watched the moon crawl up on its periphery and thought about his problem and the danger of his friend, José Maranga. But no matter how grave one's problem, one cannot think long on such a night.

COME MORNING, HE had resolved to see Maranga's

cattle, and he was not surprised. They were branded with the marks of the Texas ranchers, and he was not long in reconstructing the plan for the edification of Maranga, whom he found at breakfast.

"Listen," he said, "I'll tell you first about Pruitt, then I'll tell you about the cattle, and putting two and two together we can make a pretty good guess as to what is up."

"*Si*," said Maranga, "you tell it."

So Frost told first the story of Pruitt—Norman Pruitt; he remembered the name now and believed this must be the same man.

Norman Pruitt. That name ought to awaken stirring memories in the mind of many a war-time flying man. During the last summer of the war his name was in headlines about as often as the Baron's or Billy Bishop's. Pruitt was out of the old 90th, a sweet outfit of daredevils, and his name was high on the blackboard of the aces. He had a good score of Boche.

Good air fighters have no illusions about their trade. Life is uncertain; when they work they work and when they play they play. Norman Pruitt lived hard—too hard. He played hard. Sober, he was as regular as they come, but drunk he was a wild man. He was a tough egg when he was plastered. There are paradoxes like that.

One night he got tight and killed a major. Of course he didn't know how it happened. Nobody else did. You would think there might be some justification, some leniency, for he was one of the biggest names in the business. But there wasn't. It was curtains for him unless he could escape. Escape sounds fantastic. It appears incredible. But facing a general court martial and a widespread scandal, Pruitt succeeded. He got out of France while the intelligence departments of the Allied countries searched—and he left not a trace.

If you were over there you may recall the fuss G.H.Q. raised. They were pretty hot. They raised no end of hell. But Pruitt was gone.

One year, two years, then five... then ten. No trace of the once great air fighter named Norman Pruitt. The search cooled as those things do. Newspaper readers and soldiers gradually forgot. But the books of the law never closed. They said that somewhere, some day—

"So, you see," said Frost, "he's been here six years where he wasn't afraid to use his own name. Now about the cattle.

"You gave Pruitt above two hundred thousand dollars with which to buy you a big herd. Well, about what that would represent were chased across the South Texas plains, over the Border, shipped to the coast and brought here by boat.

"You have the cattle—I've seen the brands—but Pruitt didn't leave any money for them; he brought it back with him. You following me?"

"I am wiss you. Go on—"

"Now Pruitt don't mind stealing over two hundred thousand dollars, but he didn't go away with it; he came back. Why? Because he wants a darned sight bigger stake."

Maranga squirmed in his chair but did not interrupt.

"Those gold mines. You won't sell them from the country, but Imlaz would. Therefore, if Imlaz was president Pruitt could put over his deal—for millions probably. And, *amigo mio,* that's where your two hundred thousand went—to outfit Imlaz and put through the revolution. See it?"

Maranga saw it. For two solid minutes he cursed steadily,

scorchingly, calling upon a soldier's full vocabulary. Then, suddenly, he grew cold, ice cold.

"T'at Pruitt," he said. "I kill heem when I see heem."

"No," said El Beneficio. "I want him. Leave him to me. Besides, if he's got three men with him, we'll have to go easy on starting things. You leave it to me, but I'm anxious to meet your flyers," he told Maranga.

Shortly before noon his hope was fulfilled. The drum of airplane motors cut through the hot air and four planes circled the citadel and dropped down to the improvised landing field near the east wing, a landing field cut out of the jungle.

El Beneficio gasped when he saw the planes: they were former ships of the Black Ship gang. They had been shellacked again, but the cut of the wings and the roars of the motors were unmistakable.

He said to Maranga:

"Just as I suspected. Those men are criminals of the worst sort. You are in a bad way, Maranga. I know them." He looked at the fat president, whose face was wreathed in worry. Plainly this sort of treachery was new to him. El Beneficio went on: "You must trust me implicitly. *Si?*"

Maranga nodded.

"*Si,*" he said. "You are my bes' frien'."

El Beneficio said: "*Gracias.* Now get your pistol before we go in and remember those guys are all crooked."

When they went to lunch El Beneficio and Maranga both had their pistols in handy pockets.

Maranga introduced them. They acknowledged the introductions as if they all were strangers—as a matter of fact the three renegades recognized El Beneficio as Jerry Frost at once.

But they didn't know he recognized them. They went slightly pale, but simulated nonchalance. During the lunch they had little to say. Only Pruitt talked, blissfully unaware as to the identity of the newcomer. None of the three men could make him understand warning glances.

Maranga and El Beneficio left the room first and Pruitt and the three flyers stayed behind.

"My——!" said Roy Fulmer to Pruitt. "You sat there and blew off your head all the time. Don't you know who that guy was?"

Pruitt laughed.

"No. Some punk. Who was he?"

"I'll tell you," put in Kirkland. "That's Jerry Frost, captain of the Texas Ranger Air Patrol. I know. I got in a dogfight with him once."

Pruitt's face went slack.

"Frost?" He laughed. "You're crazy."

"Yeah," said Kirkland. "I am like hell."

Dick Clark said: "He's right, Pruitt. That guy trailed us down here. We gotta do something."

Pruitt whirled on him.

"Lissen, you guys are getting scared too early. It'll be no trouble to get rid of Frost. Don't get jumpy."

Kirkland shook his head.

"I ain't jumpy," he said. "But by——! I know that egg. He's tough as pig iron and about as sweet a flyer as there is."

Pruitt gestured impatiently.

"That's the trouble with cheap crooks. Whenever a cop gets near they fall all over themselves to duck. You just sit tight and keep your shirts on. I've waited a long time for this and damned if I'm gonna have my playhouse torn down now."

"Well," mused Clark, "it won't be long now."

"Right," said Pruitt. "It won't be long. Just go on about your business and leave things to me. If the worst comes to the worst we'll get Maranga and this smart Alec at the same time."

Kirkland bit his lip. He wasn't enthusiastic about it at all. He said to hell with the tropics. A flyer didn't have any business messing around such a God-forsaken country.

Pruitt got sore.

"———! you fold up with the works only an hour or two away! We can't lose. By tonight we'll be sitting pretty."

If his plans materialized he would. That was what they had been doing in the north. They hadn't gone there to intimidate the forces of Rafael Imlaz. Not at all. They had gone there to start the march towards the capital. They told him everything was set. Maranga had no idea—

Imlaz and his men hit the trail. With the money he had appropriated Pruitt had outfitted Imlaz's army in great style. They were marching south. The first federal garrison was at Sonoras. Imlaz took it easily, captured a hundred soldiers, executed some and bought the others.

Then the telegraph wires began to crackle.

The news was delivered to José Maranga in the great reception chambers of the citadel and his eyes bulged and his mouth twisted. The message told him that not only had the garrison fallen but that his soldiers had betrayed him.

"——— ———!" he said. "*Mio soldados!*"

Like a wounded bull, he shook his shaggy head and swung his ponderous frame into action. The citadel hummed. The cracked bell high in the tower pealed its somber notes; a shell whistled away towards the mountains.

The *revolucion* was on.

What followed constituted a spectacle that even El Beneficio, a veteran of many of these light opera engagements, had
never seen before. Maranga's officers passed through the halls
in jerky movements, soldiers hurried about, swords rattled and
every face was stern. Dominating the scene was Maranga, a
full-throated figure now, a crafty fighting man back on familiar territory.

Here was a pageant of probably little historical importance,
but one of pomp and color and action. Here was a *presidente*
surrounded by four treacherous renegades, sitting on a volcano
of intrigue, barking orders and issuing commands. To be sure, it
was theatrical. To be sure, it was grandiose. And yet this was an
uncertain stage. There was no telling when the curtain would
fall, and when it started it came down swiftly.

El Beneficio lost no time. He, too, knew Latin-American
warfare. He felt nothing but sympathy for Maranga. He had
been involved in a simple, cunning plot. He virtually was to
execute himself. The deep friendship El Beneficio felt for the
big Rigarian welled, and for the moment his own mission was
forgotten.

He started through the corridor for the flying field, rounded
a turn by a wide, spreading staircase and there was a splitting
crack. A bullet pinged into the wall clipping a hole in the
concrete.

He jumped back and muttered to himself, and went under
the stairs and down below and looked carefully from behind
a colonnade.

Crack!

Another bullet came his way; he could feel the whish of air.

He had narrowly escaped death, but he had located the source of fire.

It was upstairs on the balcony. He pressed himself against the wall, searched all the openings above and waited. After a while he slipped his head out, saw one of the flyers creeping down the wall.

El Beneficio raised his automatic and squeezed the trigger. His aim was much better than his assailant's. The flyer uttered not a sound; pitched forward on his face.

El Beneficio grinned and darted across the corridor below to the huge door. He went through into a room, and burst in upon two of the flyers who were donning their heavy coveralls.

His mind worked faster; he snapped his automatic at them and yelled:

"Get 'em up!"

The man known as Kirkland did, but Pruitt dropped behind a table. Much as Frost wanted him alive, he dared not take chances now, so his automatic barked twice and he dashed around the side of the table in order to get in a shot.

Kirkland jumped out the window, but it was too late to do anything about that.

Pruitt was on the floor in a corner trying to get his gun from inside his coveralls.

"Stand up and be good!"

Pruitt slowly got to his feet, sullenly. About that time Maranga and an officer, attracted by the shots, came running in. Maranga pulled up short and looked from one to the other.

"It's all right," El Beneficio said. "Just get me a guard for this baby."

Maranga rattled some Spanish at the officer and he ran out of the room.

"Get his gun, Maranga," El Beneficio said.

Maranga did.

El Beneficio grinned.

"Pruitt, I don't know whether you can appreciate the honor or not, but you've been frisked by a president."

Pruitt grunted.

"I don't suppose anything I could say would make any difference?"

"You're damned well right it wouldn't. Since I've seen you in that flying outfit I am sure of you. Once upon a time you were a great guy, Pruitt, but you're in a jam now."

Maranga said:

"Are you sure—"

"Hell, yes! Your life wouldn't be safe a minute with this guy around."

The thunder of two airplane motors throbbed into the room. Maranga rushed to the window and looked out.

The guards came in. El Beneficio motioned to the prisoner and they placed him between them. Then he went over to the window.

"Listen, Maranga. I want that guy kept for me. Don't take any chances on your soldiers. And you see that he's locked up and then get out of the way yourself. I'm going to give Imlaz a dose or two."

He clambered over the sill.

"Say, which way is that army coming from?"

The two airplanes got away in a rush and darted straight ahead. Maranga lifted a finger.

"They go north," he said, "the army is there."

El Beneficio dropped to the ground and trotted to the flying field.

Two ships remained there. One was a monoplane of the Black Ship gang, the other was a biplane, a Corsair. Frost went over to the Corsair.

He said to a mechanic who stood there nervously:

"*Buenos?*"

He pointed to the plane.

"*Si, si.*"

Frost wound the starter and got in. He clicked his switch and contacted. The motor caught in a boom; he motioned for the chocks to come out and got away.

He snatched his machine up just in time to miss a giant tree directly ahead. He spent the next fifteen minutes getting the hang of his ship; he put it through its acrobatics, warmed his guns and settled back and grinned. He was satisfied with the performance of his mount.

Fifteen more minutes and the open country swept into view beyond the range of mountains. Imlaz' army was under way. A plodding, typically tropical army with only a few cavalry. And, El Beneficio was willing to wager, the *soldados* already had begun to tire.

He shoved his Corsair over into a long dive and turned loose his guns. The roar of them was lost in the thunder of his motor and the scream of the wind in his wires, but he saw the crank arms jumping and he knew they were working. It had been a long time since he had done any strafing.

He held his dive until within five hundred feet and slowly pulled it up, leveled off and went into a climb. He looked down.

The troops were scattered. Some of them were flat on their backs beside the road, with their rifles trained on him. He saw one or two puffs of smoke and laughed. Then he rolled over and dived again. He held his fire a long time, then he saw them fall like ten pins. It was ludicrous. He could not conceive a lone pilot wreaking so much havoc. It bordered on the ruthless. But it was a ruthless land. One man's life was no safer than his neighbor's.

He zoomed up again and got altitude. El Beneficio was back in a modern battle carriage. The last time he was down in this country—

At twenty-five hundred he banked around and again fell into a long glide. This time he sprayed the entire column, saw half a dozen men in the vanguard of it topple to the ground. Then he fluttered his hand and wheeled about.

A shadow fell across his line of flight. The grotesque patter of bullets sounded against his linen. He looked up through the center section. Two monoplanes were above him; one was bearing down swiftly.

The mist hung above the plateau like the white ruffles from a locomotive's smokestack. A thin wraith groped awkwardly for the Corsair, seeking to pull it down. El Beneficio was in a hole.

He slipped off and turned in a wild split-air and got up and climbed. The plane that had dived at him was now pulling out and circling. The one up above was after him like a hawk.

El Beneficio slipped off on his wing and as the mono-plane roared above, he pulled back on his stick and labored his motor. Height was the one thing that mattered now. The second enemy was coming in fast from the side. El Beneficio Immelmanned and let go a burst, It got the fellow amidships and almost cut him in two. His ship flopped over and began its fall downward.

The fellow above was slipping off for a fatal thrust. Suddenly, the incongruity of the whole thing struck El Beneficio and he smiled. A dogfight like this in the jungles.

He ruddered over and shot the gun to his Corsair. Like a thing alive it responded. He was off in a long steady climb and he got a start because he was on the blind side. At nine thousand he flattened out and a streak of sparklers went by him. The monoplane, if anything, could climb faster. He half-rolled to get on top.

El Beneficio was maneuvering to get his tail up into the sun. Suddenly he looped and caught the enemy in his line of fire. But the fellow cannily realized it. He slipped out and over. El Beneficio veered and peered through his ring sights. He shoved his stick over and the Corsair went into a dive.

The rush of air almost gagged him. A speck slid through the snout of his sights and he lifted his forefinger against the trigger. The enemy zoomed straight up, slipped back and twisted over.

El Beneficio laughed.

Ninety minutes after he had left the flying field he was back. It was a little after one o'clock. He got out of his pit rather heavily, but the broad shoulders of two officers were there to help him.

"Where's *El presidente?*"

They nodded towards the citadel.

El Beneficio found him upstairs on his balcony, his fat bulk spread in that deep chair, an automatic in his hand. In a chair opposite him, tied and his feet bound, was Norman Pruitt.

Maranga got up heavily when El Beneficio entered.

"I thought," El Beneficio said, "you'd be at the head of your troops."

Maranga shook his head.

"You say keep heem safe. I no trust nobody else."

El Beneficio grinned.

"Well, I think the *revolucion* is busted sky high. I killed those other two pilots and gave Imlaz a hot party."

Maranga nodded.

"I 'ave troops on way. I no worry now," he said. He looked at Pruitt. "Not now," he said again.

El Beneficio sat down.

"Well, Maranga, I guess I'll be shoving off. You don't mind if I take a plane back?"

Maranga grinned.

"You take castle if you can carry."

El Beneficio looked at Pruitt. He was quite uncomfortable.

"Tell me all about it," he said.

Pruitt swore.

"You guess it."

"Okey. I'm liable to guess you right into the electric chair, too."

Pruitt thought that over. His face registered his emotions.

"Looks to me," El Beneficio said, "you'd get tired of dodging the law. Here you were, with a perfect set-up and you just couldn't be satisfied. Go on—I want to know what happened." With the shadow of a Federal conviction hanging over him Pruitt weakened. He finally said:

"I framed the cattle business. But I didn't kill that pilot. I swear that."

"Who did?"

"Kirkland. That fellow landed one night—the second night we met, and snooped around. Kirkland crowned him and knocked him out and then got his parachute and took him up in his own plane. He jumped out at five thousand and let the ship crash. That's all I know."

"That's plenty," El Beneficio said. He looked at Maranga. The *presidente's* face was puzzled. He couldn't grasp the devilishness of it.

"Take him away," El Beneficio said. "And have somebody watch him."

"*Si,*" said Maranga. And you would have thought from his demeanor that he was the slave of this *Americano.*

"Now," said El Beneficio, "to hell with war. I'm going to take a *siesta.*"

TWILIGHT FELL IN Rigaria. Twilight with a purple setting of the sun, glowing in crimson and gold that died over the dark hills. In the air was the welcome *relente.* Once in a while came the rise and fall of rifle fire away to the north. It gradually got fainter and fainter. Rare colors melted in the sky. Early stars appeared over the balcony. Two cigarettes burned like fireflies.

"Maranga," said a voice. "You're all set now. No more trouble, no more *revolucions,* no more nothing. Peace has come to you."

"Mebbe. I like peace. I'm no fighting man. Ees jus' I love my countree."

The *presidente* hitched his chair nearer the *Americano.* They sat close together as the day dropped out of the sky and soft shadows stole over the beautiful country. Neither of them said anything.

Friendship. The thing that sends men running from the ends of the earth to the distress of their comrades. Something too high to be caught by cold type.

"Maranga?"

"*Si.*"

"I'm going back tomorrow. I'm taking Pruitt, too."

A long pause.

"My fr'en', you live here long time eef you want. I make you zheneral for life."

"There's Pruitt. I must take him—"

"You forget laws of countries, my frien'."

"Nope. You just look the other way."

THE BELLS OF Matatic were pealing a song as dawn broke and El Beneficio clasped the stubby hand of José Maranga. They were silent: words often are so very inadequate.

Then:

"Some day, you come back, *si?*"

El Beneficio nodded.

"*Si.* I must get back to work. The mines ought to make you a rich man, Maranga."

Maranga smiled.

"Riches ees not all. You onnerstan'?"

El Beneficio turned and walked down the long corridor. He did not look back. He was ashamed to let Maranga see the film across his eyes. But Maranga wouldn't have seen. He too had looked away.

At the field Pruitt was waiting, handcuffed. Two guards loaded him into the front cockpit and El Beneficio strapped him in.

"You're going back, Pruitt," he said. "Any monkey business and I'll drill you through the back of your head."

"I'll be a good boy," Pruitt said.

El Beneficio bared his teeth.

"You damn' well better had."

They wound the starter and El Beneficio ran up his temperature and smoothed the map on his dashboard. There was a heavy line across it from Rigaria to Austin, Texas. He taxied out and took off.

He circled the citadel and looked below. From the balcony a white handkerchief fluttered. El Beneficio held his hand up and roared away. He laid his nose for Haiti, Cuba and the tip end of Louisiana.

He roared along at six thousand feet and with a speed of a hundred and twenty miles an hour. He had taken off shortly after seven o'clock and a little after one he was over Louisiana. Three hours later he was over Houston, then he cut a straight line to Austin. An hour later he dropped his wheels on the landing field after a great flight. He bumped across the field and came to rest at the starting line.

A crowd had gathered. He climbed down and several photographers snapped pictures; then the Adjutant-General came into view.

He thumped Frost on the back. Frost grinned.

Some mechanics lifted Pruitt out of the cockpit.

Frost said to the Adjutant-General: "This is the brains of the cattle rustling. And Bennett was murdered."

The Adjutant-General nodded.

"I know."

He motioned to two gangling men who came up and shook

hands with Frost. They were Bass and Dexter, of the Rangers. They seemed embarrassed.

"Got 'im, eh, Cap?" said Dexter.

Frost grinned again.

"Yeah. We got him."

The Golden Rule

A two million dollar robbery didn't get Jerry Frost excited, but when a poor little Mex boy was kidnaped—well, that was something real

THE STAGE WAS faultlessly set. There was menace aplenty in the late afternoon and the light and sound effects were perfect.

Overhead, a summer rainstorm raged. It had veered in sharply from the Gulf, accompanied by rolling thunder and a howling wind that shrieked madly at its heels, lashing it forward, full gallop. Early twilight had come, a gray presence, and the large, dazzling drops of water banged off the corrugated roof plates like automatics firing at will. Save for a few scurrying pedestrians the streets were deserted and flooded with water, traffic was at a standstill, but the mails were going through.

Twenty-five minutes late, Truck 2446 J, bearing the most important collection of the day, the first-class matter from the banking and bonding houses of Jamestown, backed into the terminal post office substation and was quickly unloaded. An army of clerks who had been waiting impatiently went hurriedly and urgently to work. Speed and accuracy were imperative. The bulk of this cargo was bound for the East, and the Seaboard Limited was due in less than half an hour.

The substation hummed and clattered. Canceling machines rattled. The belt conveyor groaned. Clerks checked the pouches in staccato challenges. Brilliant light shot the scene. Man and machine were synchronized and the result was the high efficiency for which the postal service is famed. Outside, the storm pounded....

This afternoon two and a half millions in mutilated currency had been picked up at the Federal Reserve Bank, consigned to the Washington mint where it was to be destroyed. It had come along with the other first-class matter, a secret shipment under the protectorate of routine mail. Or at least the Federal Reserve thought it was a secret shipment.

Ten minutes before the Seaboard Limited was due, at 5:25 o'clock, a curtained touring car, its windshield wipers furiously swabbing the glass, pulled into the substation loading zone and stopped. Its arrival was unnoticed, the streets still were deserted, and a wavering curtain of water that poured from the low roof hid it from the clerks inside.

Six young women got out and hurried up the platform steps. They walked briskly, intently, as if anxious to get out of the storm. It might have been observed, however, that they were slightly awkward for young women.

Inside the building they were momentarily halted by a clerk who told them, in a somewhat surprised tone, that visiting was contrary to postal regulations. He paid no attention to them except to note they all wore capes and two of them kept their hands from sight. When they continued their march he started to remonstrate. It was not until then he knew what was happening. One of the young women produced her hands and leveled a pistol at his belly.

The command, in a baritone voice, was to stand still, arms down, mouth shut.

Straight to the consignment for the Seaboard Limited went the other five. They knew what they were about. Here, too, was high efficiency, but of another order. This was born of long rehearsal for one performance only.

For the briefest moment those five paused before the mountain of pouches while one of them, taller and heavier than the rest, ran an eye along the seals. Then grabbed one sack from the pile, pointed to three others in swift succession and said almost softly: "There they are."

Four young women, dragging behind them four pouches containing two and a half millions of dollars, started for the door. Then the fifth young woman shouldered aside her cape and backed after them, a submachine-gun in her hands.

Across the room the stamp clerk yelled and reached for his pistol. That yell was his death warrant. The submachine-gun chattered, mingling its explosions with the deep diapason on the roof. The clerk went down, the back of his head blown away, his fingers grasping convulsively for the pistol. Instead they pulled loose a thin drawer and as he sank to the floor a shower of red, green and blue stamps fluttered over his face and shoulders.

The clerk who had first seen the visitors now took a desperate chance. He swung quickly at the jaw of the young woman who held the gun a foot from his body; but she stepped back, firing as she moved. The clerk grabbed his belly with both hands and slowly and grotesquely sat down, a puzzled look on his face.

The rest is hard to tell. Not because the survivors saw so little; they saw everything that happened, but because they had so little in experience to compare it with. They saw two of their brother clerks emerge recklessly from beneath the belt conveyor in the rear, each with a pistol and each firing. But these were men of peace, not men of war; they were excited and alarmed.

The young girl who was covering the retreat of the costumed bandits heard the bullets and saw the clerks. She calmly turned her submachine-gun in that direction and mowed down both clerks much as you would chop sunflowers. Then she went berserk. She turned the gun around the room, spraying lead against the walls and benches behind which the other clerks had now dropped.

At the platform she stuck the gun under her cape and rushed down the steps into the torrent. She piled inside the automobile, a fantastic melange of women's skirts and men's trousers. It looked like a second-rate comedian's exit in a burlesque show.

The automobile jerked away, throwing up a dirty spray from beneath its wheels. It headed for the open country and higher land. Finally, on a state boulevard, it turned into a large cement garage. The occupants jumped out, dragging the pouches. They still were wearing their masquerades.

"It looked clean enough," said one of them to the two pasty-faced mechanics, "but I don't know. Get right to work on the car."

They walked to the rear of the garage and pressed a button on the side of the wall. A flight of stairs descended slowly and they went up to a small room that still smelled of alcohol and sour mash. There were provisions and cigarettes and necessities for a week's hide-away.

"It was a swell job," said the one who had done all the talking, "but I didn't figure there'd be so much killing. But it's done and that's that. We'll burn these dresses and wigs and lay low three or four days. Then we'll blow."

TOMA TOSCA, THIN and brown as the soil of his native Mexico, trotted across the flying field of the Texas Air Rangers at Gentry. He was coatless and hatless. His thin arms worked like flails and his perspiring face mirrored the chaos that swirled within him. He was going to headquarters to Hell's Stepsons. In his hour of greatest distress, Toma Tosca was turning to alien idols.

For three years he had conducted a small gasoline filling station a quarter of a mile from the flying field and for three years he had watched these five guardians of the Rio Grande come and go. He had seen them sail blithely away and return with the fabric of their planes ribboning behind, and he had seen them in laughter and in bandages. Toma Tosca worshiped them with the fierceness that was characteristic of his blood.

Reaching the porch of headquarters where Jerry Frost and

Skipper Hinsdell were sitting in a blotch of shade, Toma pulled up short, panting from exertion and for the moment unable to speak.

"Hello, Toma," Frost said. "What's the matter?"

Hinsdell looked, frowning, in the direction from which Toma had come. He wasn't quite sure what he expected to see, but he knew something was wrong. He saw nothing but the flat hangar, the water tank, two trim battle planes and a multitude of heat waves rolling upward.

"Frank," Toma said, "Frank is gone." Anguish was in his face. "I leave him at pump and he go. Kidnap."

Hell's Stepsons knew Frank, eleven-year-old son of Toma, alert, intelligent and with a mad ambition to become a flyer.

"Kidnaped?" said Frost. "How do you know?"

"The gasoline hose is down," Toma said. "The pump is empty. Frank no leave like that. Somebody make him go."

Frost got up, saying gravely: "You're excited, Toma. Sit down and tell us."

Toma sat down, his hands trembling. He was trying to maintain enough calm to tell his story.

"I go to town at ha'f pas' twelve," he said, "and on way I pass gray car. I do not pay attention to men inside, but I think mebbe they two. It is big car and big car have big tank. I think: How nice if they stop for fill. It be three, mebbe four dollar fill. That is all."

Frost shook his head.

"Toma, that doesn't make sense. What makes you think they kidnaped Frank?"

Toma shrugged with a gesture of futility. He had no words with which to describe his intuition.

"I know, I know," he said. "I keep station clean. Gravel now scattered. Frank have fight and somebody kidnap him."

Frost and Hinsdell looked at each other curiously. The Toscas had no enemies and very little money. Both reasons motivate kidnapings. They couldn't, and for a good reason, comprehend what had happened. To fighting men there can be no greater mystery than the appalling swiftness with which tragedy and disaster descend on a noncombatant.

Frost asked: "There was no robbery?"

Toma sighed. He had hoped they wouldn't ask him this. "No," he said, slowly, "no robbery. Five dollar in drawer not touched." Toma wished now there had been a robbery. That would have been a fact he could have proffered in verification of his suspicion.

He glanced from one to the other quickly and divined their thoughts. They were thinking he was an excited fool. That frightened Toma Tosca.

"I am no excite," he said desperately. "I cannot say very well what I feel, but I know what I know. *Capitan,* you will come see for yourself, please?"

"Toma," Frost said, "there isn't anything we can do. If there's been a kidnaping it's a case for the sheriff. I'll get him on the wire and ask him to come out."

"No, no, no!" Toma cried, his eyes wide.

"Listen, Toma," Hinsdell said, "it's not in our jurisdiction. You understand?" The Skipper gestured with both hands. "The sheriff down here on ground, we upstairs in air. Even if there was a kidnaping we couldn't help. You *sabe?*"

"Yes, yes, sure, sure—damn, I *sabe,*" shrilled Toma, swept away by passion. "Sheriff good man but you men great. You help, *Capitan.*"

Frost bit his lip and shook his head. There wasn't anything he or the squadron members could do officially. Patrol schedules were inexorable and no man could be spared. He liked Toma Tosca, and he was far from blind to the adoration in which Tosca held Hell's Stepsons, but....

"Come on, Toma," Frost said, starting inside headquarters, "and I'll get the sheriff for you."

Toma grabbed Frost by the arm, crying, "Please." He poured his distraught soul into that one word. Frost stopped. *"Capitan,"* Toma said slowly, and with an effort at dignity, "Frank think you greatest men in world. I, too, think you great brave men. I do not know how to speak in English what I feel... but Frank is gone. I poor Mexican but my son mean much to me as Governor or President. Nobody help because I poor Mexican and mebbe I never see...."

Frost stared at the haggard brown face, into the hurt, pleading eyes. As he stared his mind raced beyond Toma Tosca's face into the reckless years of yesterday when he had galloped through Central America, a wild, roistering warrior whose services went to the highest bidder. Those had been stirring, exciting days, for it was guerilla warfare and a man's life was never safe. El Beneficio, they came to call him, and from Chiapas to the turquoise blue waters of Mosquito Gulf they told tales of his prowess.

And Frost well knew but that for nondescript beggars whose names he had never known and whose faces now he had forgotten, he long ago would have rotted on some far-away hill. Once, when he was young and impressionable, a stranger had yanked him down in time to avoid a stiletto thrust. Later—after the would-be assassin had been thoroughly effaced—

Frost had said to the man:

"I don't know how I can ever repay you."

The stranger had smiled and gestured towards the heavens as he said:

"You can't. Just pass it along to someone else."

Frost stared at the haggard, brown face and his blood ran warm again. Toma Tosca was not speaking in his futile, clumsy English now. Toma Tosca was speaking with his eyes in pure diction.

Frost stepped down from the porch.

"Let's go, Toma," he said.

TOMA TOSCA'S COMBINATION residence and filling station was on the Valley Highway that ribbons its way parallel with the Rio Grande from Brownsville to El Paso. The nearest neighbor was two hundred yards removed and the town of Gentry was half a mile east. The Tosca filling station was, in design and appearance, quite like thousands of others in the Border country. No shopkeeper along the Valley Highway has yet retired on his profits.

It was obvious to Frost there had been a struggle. The smoothly graveled floor of the filling station was badly mussed and in some places the dark earth showed through. Two oil cans had been overturned and the pump hose lay on the ground where it had been hurriedly dropped. The pump was, Frost saw, empty. Nothing inside the station had been touched. The five dollars Toma mentioned still was in the unlocked cash drawer.

In the hope that perhaps there had been a witness, Frost took Toma to the adobe house which was nearest. A buxom Mexican woman of fifty, arrayed in a gaudy *camisa* and *reboso*, shook her head sadly and said she hadn't seen anything. She hadn't even seen a gray automobile.

"You're certain about the car being gray?" Frost asked Toma on the way back.

"Yes, yes," Toma said. He pointed to the sky. "It was gray like that."

The sky was copperish gray. The sun was copperish. The whole world was copperish. It was midsummer on the Rio.

"It had maybe two men," Toma said. "I do not know. One man for sure. He had on coat just like you wear." He poked a finger against Frost's chamois jacket.

"And you're sure about that, too?"

"Yes," Toma said emphatically. "I sure automobile gray. I sure they got Frank."

"But why?" Frost demanded. "Why should anybody take him?"

"I do not know," Toma said. "But they take him."

Desperation was clutching at him again. He was helpless in the grip of an emotion which he lacked the equipment to express.

Frost stared studiously at the highway, his lips pursed. He looked at Toma for a minute and said seriously:

"I want to help you, Toma, but I don't see what I can possibly do. There are thousands of automobiles painted gray and thousands of jackets like this. But if it'll make you feel any better, I'll do all I can."

Toma splendidly looked him up and down. There was no mistaking the worship in his face.

"It make me feel very much better," he said simply. "*Capitan* is very great warrior."

Frost blushed and said uncomfortably: "I'll take a look. I'll notify the sheriff to throw out a warning. If anything happens, I'll let you know."

"I go wait at field," Toma said. "I can no stay here now."

They rode back to the field in Toma's dilapidated roadster. Toma felt very proud, in spite of the ache in his soul.

Skipper Hinsdell looked up as they entered.

"Well?" he said.

"We're having a look from above," Frost said. "A gray touring car going west."

He went to the telephone and called Hodges, the sheriff at Gentry. He reported that he wanted held for investigation occupants of gray touring car going west, one man certain, perhaps two. A brown chamois jacket was the only identification.

"License number?"

"No license number," Frost reported.

"Well," Hodges said, "this ain't much data."

"It's all we've got," Frost said. "Scatter it, will you?"

Hodges said he would. Hinsdell got up, shaking his head.

"If there's really been a kidnaping," he observed, "they'll likely hole up by day and travel by night."

Frost admitted the logic of this. "But we're taking a look anyway," he said.

JAMESTOWN NEWSPAPERS SHRIEKED of the big robbery in 96-point Gothic headlines and 12-point body type. The police department, the sheriff's office and even the U.S. Secret Service were unmercifully flayed. The constabulary, punch-drunk from the beating of the press, traveled in a circle.

The Federal Reserve Bank announced that of the two and a half millions stolen less than five hundred thousand was in badly mutilated, or impassable, condition. The remainder could conceivably be passed. Such an announcement did very little to help the situation. The Jamestown Post Office officials proposed to Washington that some dispensation be made to take care of the martyrs' families, which proposal was applauded.

Five days after the Masquerade Massacre, these, and only these, facts were known:

That six bandits disguised as women had killed four post office clerks at the terminal substation.

That they had escaped in a black touring car.

That they had taken two and a half millions in mutilated currency.

That a peculiarly fateful and terrific rainstorm had covered their escape.

These, and nothing more.

TOMA TOSCA PACED the walk in front of headquarters smoking long black cigarettes and looking into the distance that was Mexico and thinking many things.

The Sierra Madre was a long, high serration that rose out of the misty diffusion and crawled away into the south. The copper was leaving the sun and sky now and the mountains were aflame with a curl of purple along their ridges. Somewhere down there, Toma Tosca knew, there was dusky music and flashing colors and laughter and happiness. After all, why had he left?

Maria had died, of course. That had left him with his first ache. And with Maria gone and his mind cataclysmic, it suddenly occurred to Toma Tosca (and for no reason, because his people for generations had lived and died in the south) that his son Francisco was growing ignorantly to manhood. Then and there he decided to rise above the level of peonage. In the north, across the river there was a land....

And so he had come. He had come in spite of the admonitions of his gods and his padre who preached that everywhere else were sorrow and unhappiness... and now he walked in that strange land, arm-in-arm with no one, white-hot anguish in his heart. The advancing years stood before him harshly; and he shuddered. He was not afraid of them, no; but there could be no victory without his son. Suddenly something of the spirit of the actor entered into him, and he flung out his arms towards the mountains, a silent prayer in his heart.

Above throbbed the powerful motors of two battle planes and Toma Tosca, although he had been seen by no one, dropped his arms, embarrassed, and trotted to the flying field.

Frost and Hinsdell dropped their ships deftly and brought them to the tarmac.

"It's no use, Toma," Frost said. "We looked up and down and there was nothing."

Toma nodded without saying anything and walked slowly away in the direction of his filling station. Frost and Hinsdell took off their helmets and watched him go.

"It's a damned shame," Frost remarked. "I'd like to help him."

"Yes," Hinsdell said.

Bob Lunsford, the head mechanic, tall, thin, sandy-haired and thirty-five, came over. His glance was shifty, his demeanor timid, but he had followed airplane motors from San Diego to Warsaw and back again.

The sun was scarlet and an insolent mauve dusk was creeping up.

"Roll 'em in?" he asked.

"Put 'em away," Frost said. He looked into the hangar through the open door. "The others not down yet?"

"They aren't due for thirty minutes," Lunsford said.

Frost and Hinsdell walked slowly across the field. At headquarters the Skipper took off his jacket and boots and stretched out on his bed, complaining that he had a lousy headache.

Frost telephoned Hodges at Gentry and asked him if he'd informed the police and sheriffs along the highway about the car. Hodges said he had and had asked for immediate notification.

"What's this all about?" he demanded.

"Your guess is as good as mine," Frost replied.

He undressed and took a shower, and sat on the sleeping porch, barefooted and in a green Shantung robe, smoking a cigarette and listening to the night come on. Perry and Giles had come in.

Rowdy Perry looked over the top of a newspaper to remark:

"I'd like to have a crack at that Chinese-Japanese thing before it's too late. Bert Hall's over there—"

"Sure," said Hinsdell. "Wouldn't we all?"

Eddie Giles addressed Perry:

"There's big news closer home. I see the police haven't got anywhere with the Jamestown post office hold-up yet."

"Those clucks!" snorted Hans Traub, sliding around in his chair.

"They will," Frost said quietly. "The percentage is with them. Hold-up men who murder just can't make the grade, that's all."

Hinsdell took the paper from Perry.

"It'll be tough on 'em if they're ever caught," he said, "what with pictures in the papers and all. A jury'll know all about 'em in advance."

The paper had used two pictures on the front page of men suspected of complicity in the crime and announced a reward for their apprehension. Hinsdell opened the paper and started reading. The others talked, the way men do when time hangs heavily on their hands.

Some time later an automobile made a fierce racket outside. Frost and Hinsdell exchanged glances. "That's Toma," Frost said.

It was Toma. He was excited. He came across the floor on high. Ignoring the others as if they weren't present, he said to Frost:

"They catch her, they catch her!"

"What?" exclaimed Frost and Hinsdell simultaneously.

"Fifty mile up highway," Toma said. "Gray car. Police find and tell Hodges."

Frost got up, demanding: "How do you know?"

"Sheriff tell me," Toma said. He was more excited now. He was perspiring. The yellow light of the room glistened on his wet face. Hell's Stepsons looked at Toma Tosca but said nothing. Nobody moved. Toma said:

"For God's sake—"

"Wait a minute," Frost said, striding to the telephone. He got Hodges on the wire. Yes, Hodges said, a gray touring car had been located in a garage at Coralles. He said he'd read the telegram.

"Read it," Frost said.

" 'Gray touring car located in garage stop Brought two men and boy stop Am looking for them.' It's signed by MacMaster, the sheriff. I guess that's it, all right."

"I guess so," Frost said.

He hung up the telephone and looked at Toma.

"They're our men," he said.

"Yes, yes," Toma agreed, his lips quivering. "You go, *Capitan?*"

Frost nodded, saying, "Yes, Toma, I'm going."

Skipper Hinsdell laid down the paper and said: "So'm I."

Hans Traub stretched his legs luxuriously and snorted. "Hell, you fellows are crazy. Why get mixed up in something that doesn't concern—"

"I'm going," Frost said. "Alone."

Toma Tosca smiled wanly, nodding his head up and down. Hell's Stepsons scraped their feet and argued, and Traub got up and paced the floor, making a speech about foolishness. Sure, he declared, Toma Tosca was all right, and he liked him, but what the hell?

"Why put yourself in a spot like this for no good reason?" he wanted to know.

"—— ——!" Frost exploded, still irritated over memories that had come to him with the dusk. "Toma's son has been kidnaped! Isn't that a reason?"

"Sure," Traub agreed, "but there's officers to handle things like that. After all—"

"I'm going—alone," Frost snapped. "Eddie, call the airport at Coralles and have 'em give me a light in thirty minutes to get down by."

"Okey," Traub surrendered heavily. "But suppose the Adjutant-General hears about it?"

Frost didn't feel like explaining. As a matter of fact it was doubtful if he could explain. He said again:

"I'm going. If I were Toma, I'd sure as hell want somebody to pull me out."

"Okey," Traub said. "We'll make it a party. We'll all go."

But they didn't. Frost went alone, dressed in civilian clothes and with an extra automatic on his other hip. There was a whish and a roar overhead as he pulled away into the night.

Traub shook his head sadly. "Just one of those fellows who won't listen to reason."

Skipper Hinsdell said to Toma Tosca: "Sit down and make yourself comfortable."

Toma Tosca, at the window, didn't hear. He was whispering a prayer.

FROST PICKED UP the lights of Coralles a little after eight o'clock. Coralles was some sixty miles west of Gentry, a small town in the grapefruit section. It was on the Rio Grande and had a bad name, as did its sister village, Gonzaga, flung on the opposite side.

The landing field was in an embryonic state, but it was lighted and Frost got down safely. MacMaster, the sheriff, was waiting. He was pudgy, wore a black sombrero and a Hickok mustache. Even a native of Tanganyika would have known he was a sheriff. He slapped Frost on the back like he was an old friend and said: "What's up, Cap?"

"Nothing much," Frost said, taking off his helmet and trench coat and putting them in the cockpit. He took out a gray felt hat which he put on. It completed his street dress.

MacMaster said officiously: "Little outta line for you guys to be working on a kidnaping, ain't it?"

"Yes," Frost admitted. "But this happens to be a good friend of mine."

"Oh," said MacMaster, as if that explained everything.

"What about the car?" Frost asked.

"Oh, I've got it tied up, all right. I've tailed the guys that come in it, too. I know where they are."

"In jail?"

"Not yet," MacMaster said, wagging his jowls. "But it won't be long now. They're across the river."

"They might not come back," Frost said.

"They got to get their car, ain't they?" MacMaster said.

"They may not want their car," Frost said.

MacMaster shrugged. "In that case there ain't nothing we can do."

"No," Frost said, "in that case there won't be anything you can do. But you ought to know the officials across the river. Why can't you get them to deliver the men to you—you know how it's done, without a lot of fuss—"

"Won't work," MacMaster said. "They're sore. A month ago we nailed a spig on a stabbing and they tried to bargain. Course, that woulda been all right with me only this spig punctured a friend of a friend of the judge. And I got bosses." He shook his jowls again. "Won't work."

MacMaster drove Frost into town. It was early but there weren't many people about. The buildings were old and in need of repair. Coralles looked like a ghost town that had been rediscovered. Most of the stores were closed. MacMaster drove up a dirt road which ran in back of a garage, and then through the doors.

A man in overalls who had been sitting in front in a chair tipped against the wall got up and came back.

"Joe," MacMaster said," this is Captain Frost. He's come about the gray car."

"Yes," Frost said, looking around.

"It's over here," Joe said, leading the way. "She pulled in a coupla hours ago."

He led them to an eight-cylinder touring car, painted a shiny gray, of excellent make and less than two years old. It showed signs of heavy travel and in front there were mud and dust on the floorboards. Frost peered into the back with MacMaster's flashlight, opening the pockets and lifting the seats. He found something on the rear seat which interested him, large, dark spots. He studied them carefully.

He got out, handing MacMaster the flashlamp. "That's blood," he said.

"Sure," Joe said. "The kid was cut."

"Tell me about it," Frost said.

"They come in a little after sundown," Joe said, "two men and the kid. The kid was Mex and so was one of the men. The Mex said: 'My kid got hurt in the head. He got cut. Call me a cab.' I told him there wasn't no cab, but I'd call a pal of mine, Charley Barlow, who runs a jitney. Charley and me are brothers-in-law. Charley came and got 'em. Then the other fellow handed me a dollar bill and said: "We'll be back in the morning."

"You don't know where Charley Barlow took them?"

"Yes," Joe said.

"Across the river," MacMaster said. "He took 'em to a Mex doctor and left them. When they come back across the river, we'll nab 'em."

"They had two valises, too," Joe said.

"I'd like to talk to Charley Barlow," Frost said.

Joe went out and came back a few minutes later with his pal, Charley Barlow. Charley was a jitney driver, but said he had a combination trucking body and occasionally he hauled grapefruit out of the valley. Frost asked him about the two men and the boy, and Charley substantiated Joe's story. He took them to a doctor in Gonzaga.

"Who suggested the doctor?" Frost asked.

"Why," Charley said, "the little guy did. The Mex."

"That proves something," Frost said. "Did either of you ever see them before?"

Nobody had. Frost asked what they looked like.

Joe said the fellow who was driving was pretty young, about thirty, he guessed; heavy-set and wearing a brown leather jacket. He needed a shave. The Mex was about the same size, only he wore a blue suit and a sort of dark cap. They had two valises.

"Did the kid say anything?"

Joe said he had not heard him. Charley said he talked a little on the way to the doc's, but he couldn't make out what he said.

"You didn't know it was a kidnaping?" Frost asked.

"Lord, no," said Charley Barlow. "Was it?"

"Yes," Frost said, "I think so." He turned to Joe. "You got a good description of the men. Do you pay that much attention to all strangers?"

"You bet I do," Joe said heartily. "We have a lot of devilment in this town. Ever since I read in a magazine about that truck driver in Missouri who caught Fred Burke, you bet I keep my eyes open."

Frost smiled, then said to MacMaster: "I won't have any trouble getting across, will I?"

MacMaster said not as long as it looked like he had money to spend. "But you'd better hurry," he said. "The bridge closes at nine."

Frost laughed.

"But I'm told," he said, "the Rio is almost dried up here and a man can step across."

"That's right," MacMaster said. "I never thought of that."

"Take me to that doctor's," Frost said to Charley Barlow.

THE TOWN OF Gonzaga was a brown adobe warren of chrome-yellow lights, foreboding and hostile with the deadly hostility of indifference. Ghostly mountains rose in the distance. The tinkle of music ascended, mixed with boisterous laughter and conversation. Furtive-eyed men slunk in doorways and wore long serapes that hid sharp blades. If Coralles had a bad name, then there was no adjective for Gonzaga's. It was off the beaten path, where men made their own laws, and where the police judge had the power to condemn a man to death for petty crime.

The jitney stopped in front of a flat building in the heart of town and Charley Barlow said: "Here she is. You want me to wait?"

"No," Frost replied, "you may go." Charley Barlow seemed relieved. He offered a bit of advice.

" 'Course, you know your business better'n I do, but I know these parts. Been around 'em, man and boy, for thirty years. It's pretty near nine o'clock, and I'm tellin' you a stranger ain't safe—"

"I'll be all right," Frost responded. He walked up the dirt approach and knocked on the door of the adobe house. An old Mexican woman swung open the upper half and peered out.

Frost addressed her in Mexican, saying he wanted to see the doctor.

She swung shut the door and disappeared. Frost could hear voices inside. In a moment the door was opened again, wider, and not a bad-looking man invited him inside.

Frost went into a room with whitewashed walls which were given a lot of color by a profusion of shawls and rugs.

The doctor bowed stiffly and said: "Perhaps you would prefer to speak in English?"

Frost nodded, saying, "Thank you."

"What is your mission?" asked the doctor.

"I'm trying to locate a young Mexican boy you treated this afternoon for a scalp wound," Frost said.

The doctor's eyes glittered suspiciously and for a moment Frost thought he was about to deny he had had such a patient. Then he smiled and said:

"They came and went, I do not know where."

"Did you know either of the men who brought him?"

"No," the doctor said. "One man was Mexican and one man was American. I do not know either, but the Mexican knew me. He called me by name."

"Well," Frost said, "he must have known you."

"Yes," the doctor replied, "but it is not uncommon for a doctor to be known by men he does not know."

"Yes," said Frost. "Did they offer any explanation about the wound?"

The doctor shook his head.

"Nor did I ask for one. Scalp cuts are not rare."

"No," Frost said. He was silent for a moment, then said, preparing to go: "Thank you very much, doctor."

"Not at all," the doctor said. "May I ask who you are and what is your business?"

"I'm a member of the Texas Rangers," Frost replied.

"Oh," said the doctor. "Well, good night."

"Good night, doctor."

THE CAFÉ WHICH Frost entered, was crowded, but there were few whites. Being far removed from the tourist trade, Gonzaga had no censorship of morals and no false front for camouflage. Gonzaga, in short, could be itself. It took full advantage of that.

In one brightly lighted corner was gambling paraphernalia and a few swarthy men sat stoically at the tables, corn-husk cigarettes dangling from their lips. They played on, paying no attention to the noise in the room.

Around the walls were tables and in the middle was a space reserved for dancing. The music jerked and clattered. Glasses clinked.

Frost picked a table on the side and sat down against the wall from which point he could command a view of the entire room. He looked slowly around and was aware of someone standing beside him, of something inimical. It was a waiter.

Frost ordered beer.

Cigarette smoke hid the ceiling. It lay in thick blue billows. The ventilation was bad and the place reeked with a multitude of odors. But nobody seemed to mind.

There were upwards of a hundred people present, the majority of them men, dark-skinned and slouchily dressed. Frost sank down deeper in his chair, half-hidden by a quartet in front at a table. He was glad of that. His dress stamped him as a stranger, and perhaps a prosperous one, and Gonzaga was filled with brigands who thought nothing of bashing in a strange skull for a few dollars.

For two hours Frost sat there, the beer bottles piling up on the table. But he was drinking but little. His hat was down over his eyes, but not enough to obscure his vision, and he appeared to be slightly drunk and interested only in his beer.

He had his eyes on a corner near the bar.

Here sat two men and a native woman. One of the men was American in cast of countenance and wore a chamois jacket, and the other was Mexican and wore a dark cap and a blue suit.

It seemed to Frost that these were the kidnapers of Frank Tosca.

They did not rise from the table until after eleven o'clock. They seemed anxious to be rid of their female companion, who was unashamedly plastered. However, all three started for the door together.

Frost summoned the waiter and, paying his check, followed them into the street.

He was unaware that he, too, was being followed. Two youths who had kept their eyes on him for an hour padded behind.

AT THE CORNER down the street Frost saw his quarry separate from the woman and continue their march. They edged into a crowd at a cock fight, which was large and noisy with excitement; and Frost stopped, lounging against a column that supported a wooden awning above the pavement. Two hundred feet behind him the two Mexicans also stopped.

After a few minutes the two men Frost was trailing backed out of the crowd at the cock fight and continued down the street. They seemed in no particular hurry, yet Frost had observed them in the café scanning a watch numerous times.

They turned into a gloomy street. Frost turned in behind them, pressing himself close against the wall when he realized that should they look around he would be perfectly silhouetted by the light from which he had just emerged. There was nobody else in the street. Frost felt the warmth of the bricks which had not yet cooled after the heat of the sun.

In a moment he heard footsteps and pressed closer against the wall, his hand clutching the butt of his automatic. The two youths who had been following him came around the corner, but when they saw him prepared for action, they bolted and fled to the rear.

Frost went ahead slowly and saw the two men he had trailed turn into a house next door to the corner. He walked by and looked at it without stopping. It was a plain, adobe brick of the middle-class laborer, and a light shone through a barred window. After Frost had passed it he turned and retraced his steps. He paused a moment at the window but heard nothing.

Fearful lest he be discovered here, he walked briskly around the corner and into an alley at the rear. He passed a window from which emanated shrill screams and the deeper overtone of a man's voice, rumbling Spanish imprecations and calling down the wrath of the heavens on his unfaithful wife. In a more frolicsome mood Frost would have looked in; but now he kept going.

Vaulting a low, four-foot wall, he went into the patio of the adobe house. A dog growled somewhere in the darkness, and Frost stopped, nerves taut. The dog stopped growling. After a moment Frost crept ahead.

He reached the stout back door and listened, trying the knob. It turned but the door wouldn't budge. He moved down the wall to a window through which appeared a chink of light. The window was closed, but not locked, and he dropped to his hands and knees and waited.

Hearing no voices or movement of any kind, he straightened up and looked in. The room was dark, the light came from a crack in the door of a room adjoining.

Carefully he pushed back the shutters and climbed inside. He could see nothing of the interior, knew not whether it was inhabited, so he drew his automatic and tiptoed across the floor.

At the open door he paused, flat against the wall, and listened. Now he could hear voices, but the words were indistinguishable. They were coming from a room ahead.

He pulled at the door, half an inch at a time. It responded silently; and when it had opened sufficiently to permit his entrance he slipped through sidewise. Now he was in a hallway of some sort and there was enough light for him to see his way about.

The voices were coming from the direction of the street, so he moved swiftly in that direction, pausing before another door which was closed. He could hear what they were saying now.

"The plane'll be here at midnight," one said. "They don't know who we are, so there's no damned use getting jumpy. After we leave, then he can take care of the kid."

"We must hurry," said another, with a trace of an accent. Frost judged this was the Mexican.

Then a third voice put in something in rapid speech of which Frost was able to translate only, "…it will be done."

"Well," he said to himself, "there's no damned use standing here and taking a chance on being found."

He worked the knob of the door and felt the latch unbolt. He opened the door, making a crack through which he looked. He saw the American sitting on a bench beside an aged Mexican. They were looking at a wall. Frost opened the door a little more. And then his heart lurched. There was a shadow on the floor. Someone was behind that door, waiting for him to enter.

HE TIGHTENED HIS grasp on the pistol and kept opening the door. When he had opened it three-quarters way he made a motion to step inside, a definite motion which he checked almost at once. The man behind the door, thinking he was coming, stepped out. Too late he realized his mistake. It was the Mexican in the dark blue suit.

Before he could utter a sound Frost had slugged him with the barrel of his gun. The Mexican sagged and went down.

The two men in front wheeled around. Surprise was etched into their faces, with fear in the aged man's and anger and bitterness in the American's.

"Put your hands up," Frost commanded quietly.

They did.

"Where's the boy you kidnaped?" Frost asked in that same monotone.

A groan from behind him answered. Frost backed against the wall, looking. Frank Tosca lay on a rude pallet, bound and gagged.

Frost's eyes narrowed. Waving his gun, he said: "Untie him. And be careful."

"Look," said the American, "you got us all wrong—"

"Untie him," Frost repeated.

The man did. Wide-eyed, Frank Tosca sat up. His head was bandaged and his clothes were muddy, but his youthful jaw was square and determined. He grunted at the man who unloosened the ropes and slapped him hard as he sat up.

"That's him," he said quickly. "That's him."

"I know," Frost said. "Put those ropes on the old man, Frank. Tie him up just like they did you."

Frank flexed his arms and muscles for a minute and then took the ropes to the aged Mexican. Nobody said anything while Frank bound him. The only sounds in the room were of the men breathing.

When Frank had finished, Frost said: "Take this gun and keep them covered. If either makes a move, pull the trigger."

"Yes, sir," Frank said, taking the gun. Frost stooped over the Mexican he had slugged. A trickle of red slid down his temple. Frost searched him, taking a pistol from his coat pocket; and then searched the American. He got a .38 Police Positive from him.

"This ain't gonna do you any good," he growled. "We haven't—"

"Shut up," Frost snapped.

He dabbed a towel in a jar of water and bathed the wounded man's face. Pretty soon the Mexican blinked his eyes and sat up. He looked into the barrel of his own gun.

"Come on," Frost said, "we're moving."

Without taking his eyes off the American, Frank said:

"Get the bags, Cap. That's where the stuff is. In the bags. I saw it."

"What stuff?" Frost asked.

"The money," Frank said.

"What money?" Frost asked.

He looked at Frank, puzzled. In that instant the wounded Mexican flashed his hand to his belt and it came out with a gleaming knife. Frost saw him just in time. He saw the yellow glint of the blade and pulled the trigger at the same moment.

There were two sharp explosions and the Mexican went backward, two holes in his forehead.

The American cursed and bellowed.

"They held up the Jamestown Post Office," Frank cried. "This one's Riker. I knew him from his pictures. I knew him this afternoon at the filling station. He saw it; that's why they took me."

Then it dawned on Frost.

"My God!" he ejaculated. "Get the bags!"

Frank dashed into the next room and came back lugging two valises.

"Grab 'em," Frost barked at Riker, "and move!"

His face contorted, Riker picked up the valises and Frost prodded him out the front door. People were beginning to be roused by the mysterious sounds within the house. They were standing in their doors looking out. The shots had startled them. In the distance sounded a police whistle.

"Run!" Frost yelled.

They trotted down the street, Riker ahead with the two valises. Of a sudden he stopped, dropped the bags and cursed loudly.

"Shoot me, you ——!" he gritted. "I'm not moving another step!"

Frost pulled the trigger. A pencil of flame reached out and burned Riker's left shoulder. He swore and grabbed it fiercely with his right hand.

"The next one," Frost said, "is through the eye. Go on—"

Frost grabbed one valise and Riker took the other. They moved on down the street to the bank of the Rio. Riker halted.

"Go on—" Frost yelled.

Riker stepped down in the sandy bottoms. The river was narrow and shallow. They went downstream for three hundred feet until they found a spot where they could almost jump over. They waded through, and came up, panting, on the other side.

They moved on to a hollow, where they stopped.

"Frank," Frost said, pointing, "that's Coralles. Get MacMaster, inform the sheriff, and bring him back."

Frank dashed off. Frost said to Riker: "Here, let's see how badly you're hurt."

MACMASTER AND TWO deputies arrived in a Ford, highly wrought-up.

"MacMaster," Frost said, "this is Riker, one of the men who stuck up the Jamestown Post Office last week. Remember the case?"

MacMaster simply whistled.

"Put him in your jail, give him a doctor, be good to him—but don't let him get away."

"Don't you worry none," he said.

"But don't get rough with him," Frost said. "We've been having a talk and I think maybe he might tell the District

Attorney some facts about that case. He's not anxious to get the chair."

Riker, sullen, but saying nothing, was loaded in the back seat with MacMaster and a deputy. The third deputy drove the Ford. Frost held Frank in his lap in front and the two valises were crammed between the fenders and the hood on either side of the car.

They went to the jail and locked up Riker, leaving a guard and summoning a doctor; and MacMaster and the other deputy escorted Frost to the flying field.

Frost loaded the valises into the front cockpit with Frank and donned his helmet and coat.

"Remember, Mac," he said; "keep an eye on Riker."

"Don't you worry," MacMaster said again. "That's a big break for me and I'll watch him."

"It certainly is," Frost said. "Mac, they'll have your picture in every paper in the state in a week's time. This'll make you famous."

"Yeah," MacMaster said. As Frost started to climb up, MacMaster caught his arm and drew him aside. He said: "Cap, I don't know how to thank you for throwing this my way. It ain't exactly my case, but if you ever need anything around here—"

"Forget it, Mac," Frost laughed, putting his hand on the other's shoulder.

Frost wound the starter and said to Frank: "All set?"

Frank nodded, too thrilled to speak.

MacMaster watched the plane get away.

WHEN FROST FIRST went over the field at Gentry there was no illumination save the moon, which would have been enough for him on this field, but before he could get down, the landing lights poured on and bathed the field in a ghostly white. They had been waiting for him.

Hell's Stepsons and Toma Tosca were at the line. Frost cut his switch and got down, and Frank looked out. Toma Tosca saw his son, shrieked something in Spanish, and rushed to the fuselage to embrace him.

Skipper Hinsdell, in felt sneaks and pajamas, said:

"By God, it must be a gift or something. How the hell and where the hell did you get him?"

"That's not the half of it," Frost replied. "Eddie, get those bags out of the front cockpit."

Eddie Giles took out the valises.

"There's a big part of the Jamestown robbery," Frost said. "One bandit is dead, another is in jail—and willing to turn state's evidence."

"But—"

"But—"

"They were the kidnapers," Frost said. "Frank recognized them from their pictures in the paper, and he tried to stop them when he had filled their gas tank. They kidnaped him. They were getting away by plane tonight for Mexico City—"

Perry and Hinsdell smiled proudly. Traub grunted. Giles was looking down at the valises, trying to understand they contained a fortune. He said: "Well, this ought to be worth a raise—"

Toma Tosca came over and touched Frost's elbow. Tears were in his eyes.

"*Capitan*—" he said, "I never forget—"

His shoulders arched with emotion. His chin trembled.

"Nix, Toma," Frost said. "You don't owe us anything. We owe you. See what happened? We catch bandits."

Toma bit his lip and tried to say something. Instead he put an arm around his son's shoulder.

"You give us Mexican dinner some time, eh, Toma?" Frost asked.

Toma Tosca nodded.

Wings Over Texas

A story of Jerry Frost, fighting, flying Ranger

RAIN STRADDLED THE blue norther at midnight and together they marched across the flatlands, stinging and freezing. They beat down in thin sheets, whispering at doors and making music on the windowpanes. The lyric was comforting but the melody was awesome.

Jim Cavanaugh, III, great shaggy Governor of the great State of Texas, up to his neck in a bitter campaign for re-election, sat in the bedroom of his hotel suite, pulling at a panatela as thin as he was broad and staring through the frosted glass of the window. His gray eyes were thoughtful and his forehead was creased. Eruptions of smoke were synchronized with the soft pat of his bare foot on a carpeted floor. With the inside of his fingers he nervously caressed the nap on the arm of a luxurious chair. He was clad only in shorts. His body was thick and hard and hairy.

He laid back his head, stared at the ceiling. For thirty seconds he was motionless. Then he suddenly got to his feet and went into the adjoining room.

A thin man was protesting into a French telephone.

"There must be a way... it's the Governor calling. Yes... yes... I understand. Thank you."

He replaced the telephone and faced the Governor, palms spread upward.

"The wires are down on the trunk south of Waco," he said. "The operator can't get through."

The Governor nodded, dropped his bulk into a chair beside

the telephone stand. "Dan Hughes'll know. Get me Dan Hughes."

The thin man thumbed the directory, asked the operator for an Avondale number. A gust of wind reached for the window with icy and noisy fingers. The thin man shivered slightly and said over the telephone: "You ought to have on your robe, sir."

The Governor grunted and twisted the panatela into a corner of his mouth.

"Hello... Mr. Hughes, please.... Yes, very important.... Governor Cavanaugh calling...." He looked down and said again: "Governor, you ought to have on your robe."

The Governor grunted and shifted the panatela into the other corner of his mouth.

"Hello... Mr. Hughes.... Just a moment...."

The Governor got up and took the instrument.

"Dan, I've got to be in Gentry by dawn and I've got to have a car that can take the punishment. Who's got one?"

"What's the matter with mine?"

"It's not fast enough."

"It'll do seventy—maybe seventy-five."

"That's not fast enough."

"In that case... I think I know what you need. I'll call you back."

"Hurry, Dan."

"Sure, Jim."

When the telephone rang fifteen minutes later the Governor was wearing a maroon silk dressing-gown and oversized felt slippers and the panatela was still in a corner of his mouth. Now it was soggy and unlighted.

"I've got you an Italian car that nobody's had the nerve to

open up. It'll be down in twenty minutes with a chauffeur."

"Thanks… but I'm leaving the chauffeur here. I'll drive it. Thanks, Dan."

"Briggs," said the Governor, "rustle up a thermos of coffee, sandwiches and get me some cigars. Fix it through Oak Cliff and out the Waco road. We're going like hell."

The thin man moved to the telephone and the Governor yanked off his robe.

"IT'S SLEETING," BRIGGS said.

"November in Texas is wild enough," the Governor said.

"Yes," Briggs said. He leaned forward, his eyes seeking the speedometer in a maze of dimly lighted dials and gauges.

"Sixty," he said.

They were roaring across the Trinity river bottoms to Oak Cliff on the longest concrete viaduct in the world.

Two screaming wails, coming from nowhere, suddenly shrilled above the noise of their motor. The Governor eased over to the right and two motorcycles with uniformed riders slid ahead.

"We'll have them all the way now," Briggs said.

"A tribute to power," the Governor said.

Briggs lighted a panatela, got it to drawing and stuck it between the Governor's lips. The big car slewed around a bend in the street. The Governor twisted the wheel and grunted. When the car had been straightened Briggs sat back heavily.

"You hold on," the Governor said. "This bus is going through."

They struck the open country, made two turns and swung due south on a black paved highway that paralleled the railroad. A searchlight on the running-board stabbed a long lane of white out ahead.

A sudden red glow in the sky on the left was torn away and left behind.

"The Houston Express," Briggs said.

Two tiny crimson lights on the rear fenders of the state highway motorcycle police shone out in front.

The Governor turned a knob on the dashboard and a pulse-stirring roar beat upon the night.

"There goes the super-charger—and two hundred and fifty wild horses," the Governor said.

"Seventy," Briggs said; "...seventy-five."

They were overtaking the tiny crimson lights so the Governor sounded his horn. In a moment they pulled away.

"Remember the names of those boys," the Governor said. "They've got guts."

Briggs said nothing, pushed harder against the floorboards. The sleet had gone back to rain and the windshield wipers swabbed the glass furiously. The body and framework of the automobile were vibrating as if built of taut strings. The Governor, motionless, stared out over the wheel as the metal comet catapulted through the night.

"Ninety miles an hour," Briggs whispered hoarsely.

The Governor clamped his cigar in a fresh grip. For uncounted heart-beats they were silent. Only the prodigious clamor of the motor, only the fingers of white light jutting ahead, only the crimson dots holding their distance. At a turn, the car slowed to fifty—forty.

Came a sharp explosion like the bang of a gun. The big car lurched to the right. The world rocked about them. Metal screamed on metal. The Governor's right hand swung to the emergency, jumped back to the wheel, which was yanking with demoniac power to free itself from human control.

They went off the road and swerved to a stop. The motor was turned off.

The fingers of Briggs' right hand were buried deep in the softness of the polo coat on the Governor's left arm.

"All right, sir?" he asked shakily.

The Governor got to the ground.

"A blow-out," he said. "Three minutes and we're off."

Four minutes elapsed before they were roaring through the night again. The highway police were coming back to look for them, but when the Governor blew his horn they turned around and showed their crimson lights again.

Briggs glued his eyes on the speedometer and when the needle crawled past eighty he said nervously: "It's pretty slick. The road's like a piece of glass."

The Governor grunted.

"You just hold on," he said.

ON THE SOUTHERLY fringe of Waco they picked up a new escort of highway police and the black car ground to a stop under the canopy of an oil station. It was still raining and cold and save for the lights of the machines the countryside was a world of blackness.

Briggs roused the attendant and while high-test gas was being pumped into the tank the Governor was thanking the police who had led the way from Jamestown.

They were wet and cold and half-frozen, but they didn't mind, because they were sitting in on drama.

One of the new policemen jerked his head at the car and said: "Better let me shaft 'er the rest of the way."

"I'll push it through," the Governor said.

DAWN BROKE AND an orange sun shot into the sky, splashing the world with color. Storm clouds, rulers for a night, scattered and fled before the fiery invader from the rim of the universe. The earth was wet and fresh and smelled with the dampness of an early fall morning on the Border.

The Governor sat at the head of the table, hunched down in a wrinkled camel-hair topcoat, his gray hair stringy and his face red and raw because he had driven the last fifty miles with his head out the side.

Beside him was Briggs, tall and thin and wearing an air of

injured dignity because the wild ride had been made against his advice, and next to Briggs was Captain Frost in pyjama pants and no coat. Frost's torso was naked and in the early morning light it had a pinkish bronze sheen.

Across the table were Hell's Stepsons, hair disheveled, not fully awake yet and all in pyjamas but Eddie Giles, who had hurriedly jerked on a worn green Shantung robe over bare skin. The flyers were waiting for the Governor to speak. Four hundred miles through a storm in six and a half hours was proof he had something to say.

He did have something to say. He had plenty to say. He pushed back the collar of his camel-hair coat and lighted a panatela. He bristled with a belligerency that had no outlet because he couldn't understand his enemies. Fights he had known before, hundreds of them; but they were toe-to-toe, hammer-and-tongs, may-the-best-man-win fights where you could feel your fists hitting something. This wasn't. His enemies were swinging in the dark, below the belt, any-way-to-win. The great bear of a man was just a little puzzled. He was swinging but he was swinging on empty air.

Through narrowed eyes he looked out at the guardians of a thousand miles of Border country. Their faces held a nominal curiosity, but he intuitively felt they understood his predica-ment; and he was willing to risk his intuition. It had been a prize heritage; his grandfather, relying on it when all else failed, had blazed a trail through an unknown country long before the great State was born. He had that same spirit.

He told himself, looking at Hell's Stepsons, that here were men he could trust, were his to command; and a keen thrill of pride surged through him.

He looked at Frost and said: "I'm in a jam. I need a hell of a lot of help."

Frost nodded but didn't say anything.

The Governor went on: "A great many things are about to happen. And the future of the State, as well as my personal honor, is involved."

Hell's Stepsons listened gravely. They might have smiled, listening to anyone else speak of honor, for a year and more of Border patrol had taught them something of the viciousness and intrigue of big-time politics. But they had a tremendous respect for Big Jim Cavanaugh and when he spoke of honor they listened.

He was saying: "The job I hold is worth ten millions a year, maybe more, to a man who sets out to collect. That's exactly what Fred Myers is planning to do."

Fred Myers was in a run-off with Cavanaugh for the office.

"I know the man is crooked and that his machine is crooked, but I can't say that from the platform because I've got my own ideas of what a campaign ought to be like. Myers' organization is high-powered and will stop at nothing to elect him—and unless something is done damned quick he will be elected." He paused and something like a shiver ran through his ponderous frame. In an undertone he added: "There's no doubt of that.

"Politics," he went on, "is a crazy business. Until a short time ago I was perfectly willing to step down and let somebody else worry about being governor. I've been in two terms and that's a long time not to do a few of the things you'd like with your own life. Until a few nights ago I didn't care whether I won or lost."

Briggs passed around a pack of cigarettes and Traub and Frost lighted up. The Governor puffed reflectively at his panatela. The flyers were attentively quiet.

"But now," the Governor continued, "it's different." The dull gleam went from his eyes as he snapped: "By ——! they've got a battle on their hands! They couldn't let well enough alone! They were afraid to gamble, they couldn't take a chance." Looking up suddenly, he asked: "You heard about the bank at Salada?"

Frost nodded, saying: "Yes, sir," and moved to the table. He scattered some papers around and picked out a Secret Service broadcast containing a man's picture and an attached mimeographed list of serial numbers on currency of various denominations.

The Governor held the broadcast in his hand and looked at it, his lips pressed tightly together. It was headed "$2500 REWARD" and contained a close-up picture of a man's head and a description.

It was the Governor's brother.

Slowly the great man let the picture and the paper flutter to the table, looked out the window, removed his panatela and said a little fiercely:

"There's monkey business in this! Bob didn't skip with that million." He pressed his lips together again as if to dam back the resentment. "Our grandfather founded that bank," he said, "and for three generations the integrity of the Cavanaughs has kept it going." He beat his left fist up and down on the table, a dull obbligato to his duller words. "Somebody has done away with Bob. Myers' gang, that's who it is—Myers' gang. For the last two nights Myers has publicly insinuated a Cavanaugh skipped with the money. In another week he'll be making flat charges. You see, that's the way they're striking at me, the way they're trying to ruin me. Pretty soon it'll be all over the State and it's too close to election to wonder what can be done. Somebody's got to do something damned quick. I can't. I can't leave my campaign now."

Frost tossed his cigarette out the window and asked, scowling:

"Any suggestions?"

"There's something wrong at Salada," the Governor said. "I don't know what it is. Nobody there seems to know. You'd think in my own home town I'd have friends—but I haven't. I can't take chances now with detectives and police and men who may, for all I know, be my enemies. I've got to have the help of somebody who'll go the limit. That's why I'm here."

Frost said: "——!" softly and looked at Hell's Stepsons. They were affected by the Governor's frank confession. Their faces were hardened into expressions that said they were ready to go.

"We're ready," Frost said.

The Governor nodded and looked at his aide. "Briggs," he said, "you drive the car back to Dan Hughes. Captain Frost'll fly me back to Jamestown."

"Yes, sir," said Briggs, "but you've got a noon address—"

"——it, I know that," the Governor said. He pitched his half-smoked panatela out the window. Briggs stood up, pouting like a schoolboy. The Governor grinned and slapped him good-naturedly with his open hand. It was a sharp blow in the rear. "Shake a leg now, you old woman," the Governor said affectionately.

Briggs smiled and went out. The Governor said to Frost:

"I swear I believe I could sleep now."

A SILVER-WINGED MONOPLANE, mounting

two cowled guns, dropped out of an azure sky over James-town shortly after 11 o'clock that morning. The ship was no stranger to Winters Field. The orange longhorns' heads on the wings and fuselage told that it was a fighting craft of the Border patrol and the thin red streamer ribboning back from the fin told that the commander of the Air Rangers was in the saddle.

It swept down to a feathery landing and pulled around to the rubber stop signs that marked the field limit opposite the hangars. The propeller whistled to a stop. A bulky figure in a voluminous tan coat crawled down, smoothed his hair with the fingers of his right hand and fitted a rumpled felt hat on his head. A moment later a slender man in flying clothes vaulted clear of the control pit.

They shook hands. The Governor said: "I've got to hurry. I'll fix it with the Adjutant-General. And good luck to you."

"Good luck to you, sir," Frost replied.

The Governor walked across the roadway and rolled through the narrow door of Operations office. Frost raised his hand, signaling for the gasoline truck. A phalanx of hangers-on and mechanics started for the plane; in the foreground was an undersized man in greasy coveralls and a greasier canvas helmet. He was eating a sandwich with gusto, but he rolled a hunk of it into the corner of his mouth and called:

"Hi, Cap."

"Hello, Rusty," Frost said. "How's the weather west?"

"Perfect through to El Paso. Got business in the West, Cap?"

"Yeah, Rusty—business in the West. Take a look at my No. 4 plug while I give the boys my autograph."

Rusty held up his sandwich and made a wry face.

"Jeeze, Cap," he said; "you pick out the ——est times to drop down. In a hurry?"

"One hell of a hurry," Frost replied.

SALADA'S POLICE HEADQUARTERS, the Bureau of Detectives, the office of the Chief....

Martin Thomas swayed back in his chair, looked up at the uniformed secretary and growled: "My ——! another one! The next thing you know I'll be getting 'em in my hair." He was fifty, robust, with a shock of iron-gray hair and heavy jowls. He wore a number sixteen collar, a number twelve shoe, had fought his way up through the ranks and showed it. He looked exactly like what he was—a copper. He looked like a copper even in a bathing suit.

The uniformed secretary said in a throaty whisper: "——! he coulda fooled me. He's the last guy in the world I'd take for Jerry Frost. He looks like a damn' college boy. Whaddya want me to tell 'im?"

Martin Thomas gave him a nasty glare. People who got a kick out of anything annoyed him. His twenty years in a hard-boiled school had made a professional stoic out of him and he couldn't understand or forgive enthusiasm in anyone else. He didn't believe in anything or anybody. To him Waterloo was in the bag for Wellington.

"You tell 'im nothing," he snapped. "I get paid to do the telling around here. Let 'im come in."

When Frost came in Thomas didn't get up. He didn't even indicate a chair. He mumbled an unintelligible something that may or may not have been a salutation and played his eyes up the gray-tweed form of the Ranger with cool insolence. In a minute he said:

"Well, Captain, and what can I do you for?"

Frost sat down and crossed his long legs.

"If you aren't too busy," he said, "I'd like a few facts."

"Oh, no, I'm not too busy," Thomas said sweetly. "Why should I be too busy? I've been a reception committee and an information bureau for every damn' dick who's hit town yet. Where do you think I'd better start, Captain?"

"The beginning," Frost said evenly, "is usually a good place."

Thomas mumbled something else and said: "I guess you're right." He moved his jowls around and went on: "All right, at the beginning then. I'll tell you the same thing I've told everybody else. Robert Cavanaugh is missing and so's a million dollars of the Trail National's money. That's all I know."

"All?" said Frost.

"All," said Thomas gruffly, disliking the Ranger intensely.

"Everybody in the State knows that much. After a week on the case and—"

"Well, what do you expect *me* to do?" Thomas bawled, jerking himself upright in the chair. He slapped the table and went on bawling: "I'm getting damn' sick of being wet nurse to a lot of small-town Sherlockos. Every time I turn around I step on a new cop. It was bad enough before, but now the Rangers have got to stick their noses into—"

Frost got up from the chair and said:

"Stop yelling at me. I don't give a damn if you're the chief or who you are. I don't like people to yell at me. I'm not after the reward and I'm not here because I like the town. So stop yelling."

Thomas didn't answer. It was a new experience for him, meeting somebody he couldn't bully. He moved his jowls around again and said in a lower register: "Well, by ——! there's a limit to everything. The town's cluttered up with detectives. They've knocked my department cuckoo. It looks like everybody knows more than I do."

Frost let it go at that.

"And nobody seems to know a hell of a lot."

"There isn't a hell of a lot to know," Thomas said. "A little more than a million dollars is missing in big bills, but I still don't see how anybody could move a hunk of dough like that without being seen. Cavanaugh is missing. When the news leaked out we hadda lot of excitement and the bank was in a bad way until the Federal Reserve at Jamestown came to bat. There are a lot of people in Salada who don't think Bob Cavanaugh took the money. I'm one of 'em."

"The Government agents think differently," Frost said.

"I believe what I believe," Thomas declared doggedly. "You can't beat blood. Blood'll tell. The Cavanaughs have got the right blood in 'em."

"A million can do a lot of things to good blood."

Martin Thomas scattered a little profanity around the office. Then:

"All right, where's the motive? His business was in shape, his personal life clean, he had thousands of friends. He had plenty of money and his brother was Governor of the State."

Frost asked: "Where'd he go?"

"—— ——!" boomed Thomas, getting profane again. "If I knew where he went I'd pinch him! But I don't. All I can do is dig—and I'm digging. Railroads, bus lines, airways, everything." He paused to light a cigarette, glared and went on:

"And all these correspondence school dicks aren't helping the situation any."

"I should think not," Frost agreed.

"And now the Rangers come in," Thomas said, getting back to his pet peeve. "It's a reflection on my department."

"It looks," Frost said bluntly, "as if you might be able to use a few Rangers."

"By——!" Thomas cried, hoarse with pent-up rage, "anybody who thinks they can do more than me is welcome to try!"

He gripped the desk until his knuckles went white. It looked for a moment as if he might get up and start something. Frost moved a little closer and got set to crack him the minute he left the chair.

"I'm going to give it a whirl," Frost said grimly.

"That's okey by me," Thomas snorted. "I wish you luck— loads of it. But lookout some of these jealous guys don't step on you."

Frost said he'd try not to get stepped on.

"I'm just telling you."

"Thanks."

"That's okey. Don't mention it."

Thomas got up and stood behind the desk, wanting to say something else but not knowing what. When Frost had gone his face darkened and he snatched the telephone.

"Get me Fritz Compton," he bawled to the operator.

Fritz Compton was the District Attorney.

FROST MADE A half dozen visits where he thought they would do the most good, but he learned nothing Martin Thomas hadn't already told him, scant as that was. Friends of

Robert Cavanaugh couldn't or wouldn't talk; so he gave up and at five o'clock, after cutting a lot of red tape, he was in Cavanaugh's apartment on the third floor of the Salada Athletic Club.

It was a neat and tastefully furnished three-room suite that had about it an air of occupancy. Everything apparently was in its place, awaiting the return of the master. Books were scattered over the tables and in niches, the humidors were filled with cigarettes, the single Winthrop desk was orderly and on it lay a small stack of letters.

Frost sat down and went through the letters. They told him nothing. They were mostly current bills, there was an embossed entry card and an invitation to the Houston Country Club's annual tournament, and two brief notes from personal friends in the East. Frost left them as tidy as he had found them and gave the room a look-see. He worked diligently for thirty minutes without exactly knowing what he was looking for.

But when he found it he knew this was it. He found it in the side pocket of a kit bag in the closet, a narrow little box no bigger than his forefinger. He snapped on the light, shoved one end out, and fell back in astonishment.

It was the business end of a hypodermic syringe.

Looking at it, he felt better. Now, he told himself, he was getting somewhere. Thus encouraged, he dropped it in his pocket and began another search of the room, much more minute than the first. He turned the bathroom upside down. The living-room came next. He ransacked the desk, the book niches, the humidors, looked for false bottoms in the tables, held up the books by their covers and shook them vigorously. He took the pictures from the walls, examined their frames, looked under the rugs.

He lifted a Samoan wood-pulp print from the wall to look behind it and found the handle of a vault and a small combination lock in the wall. He tried the knob. It wouldn't budge.

He went downstairs to the boiler-room and borrowed a ball-peen hammer and a chisel without having to answer funny questions.

He came back and in a moment he had knocked off the knob.

Among other things in the vault were four tell-tale white papers, decks of morphine. "Here we are," Frost said to himself. He put the four decks in his pocket and pulled out an account book. On one of the pages was what appeared to be a notation of sums paid to somebody by the name of Glavell totaling sixty thousand dollars.

Frost tore out the page, replaced the book and went downstairs.

The lobby was ablaze with lights and crowded with men and women in evening dress. The manager was busy because it was a formal party, but when he got word Frost wanted to see him he came at once.

Frost handed him the key to Cavanaugh's apartment and said: "Don't let anybody know I was up there."

"Is there anything wrong?" asked the manager, worried.

"No. Only just don't let anybody know I was there, that's all. It might cramp my style."

"Oh, sure, Captain," said the manager, relieved. "Sure."

AT 10 O'CLOCK the next morning Frost was in the Federal Building, in the office of Louis Plant, head of the Narcotic Squad, who had grown gray in the service. Frost asked him if he'd ever heard of a man named Glavell.

"Plenty," Plant said emphatically. "Is he mixed up in the Cavanaugh thing?"

"Not so fast," Frost said. "Tell me about him."

Well, Plant told him, Dr. Jonathan Glavell was a capable man, a very clever man. He got started on the road to affluence about ten years ago with a cancer cure and some way or other had got a contact with the underworld. It was pretty generally known that Doc Glavell was a right guy.

He treated patients who had been injured on steps, who had turned their ankles on loose bricks, skinned their fingers in motion picture theaters, and the like. His reports always contained serious personal injury to his patients; and in every case the insurance adjuster was referred to Jonathan Glavell, M.D. When the settlement was effected the doctor retained half the proceeds.

It was not generally known, but he operated a sanitarium across the Line in Coahuila, "The Poplars," worked under a concession from the Government of Mexico in which charity cases were treated. Few people in Salada knew of his connection with the sanitarium in Coahuila. Recently, too, the doctor had opened another office in the Trail National Bank Building. During office hours one could count a dozen women filing in and out.

"Personally," Plant said, "I think the guy is a genius. Ever see him?"

Frost said he hadn't.

"Looks like an ambassador—all but his eyes. They're little and sharp as diamonds. I think he's messed up with the dope racket on a big scale—but I can't get anything on him. I've given up all hopes of landing him by working hard. To get a guy like that you have to get a break first."

Frost took the decks of morphine out of his pocket and the sheet he had torn from the ledger.

"Look at these. From Cavanaugh's apartment."

Louis Plant looked and whistled.

"——! Then Cavanaugh *was* mixed up with him?"

"It looks like it," Frost said. "It sure as hell looks like it."

Plant grew serious.

"This is enough to crash Glavell on."

"Wait," Frost said. "I got an idea. I want to take a look at him first."

"Okey," Plant said slowly. "Okey. But you better wear your cannon."

"I'd be undressed without it," Frost said, grinning.

DR. JONATHAN GLAVELL permitted Frost an immediate entry to his inner office. He was a distinguished personality, tall, ruddy, more than fifty, but erect and active. His hair was thin and brown, his forehead high, and he wore professional horn-rimmed spectacles. His mustache was clipped, his goatee trimmed and he was immaculately dressed. He might have just stepped from a potentate's entourage.

"How do you do, sir?" he said, rising and offering his hand. "Won't you sit down?"

He had a pleasant voice and his manners were polished.

"Thanks," said Frost, sitting down.

Dr. Glavell took the lid off an inlaid humidor and held it out. Frost took a cigarette and lighted it. So did the doctor. It was then Frost got his first sensation: Dr. Glavell's eyes. Small, too small, black and hard—and fiery. Frost wrestled with himself to maintain his indifferent pose, but Dr. Glavell smiled and said:

"I am rather surprised. After all I had heard and read I expected a much older man. You're almost—legendary. And you don't look as if you needed a doctor."

"Thanks," said Frost. "My business here is professional."

The doctor's "That so?" was polite.

"It's about the Cavanaugh case. I suppose you've heard?"

"Lord, yes," Dr. Glavell said, letting the smoke roll from nostrils. "Hasn't everybody? It's quite puzzling, isn't it?"

"Quite," said Frost dryly. "Did you ever treat him?"

A thin smile hovered between the mustache and the goatee.

"Not exactly," he confessed. "Bob was susceptible to colds; I wrote his whiskey prescriptions. That was all. Why?"

"Just curious. I happened to hear your name in connection with his"—he saw the doctor's eyes narrow almost impercep-tibly—"and I thought maybe you might be able to help us out. I don't suppose you ever heard him mention a—trip?"

"Why, no, no," said Dr. Glavell, his forehead wrinkled. "As a matter of fact, we weren't close enough for that. I'm afraid, Captain, I won't be able to help you much."

"I'm afraid not," Frost said, getting up. "Well, sorry to have disturbed you."

Dr. Glavell rose.

"That's quite all right," he said, his eyes beady. "It was a plea-sure to see you—an honor. If there's anything I can do—"

"Thanks," Frost said.

When he had gone Dr. Glavell reached thoughtfully for the telephone.

"Get me Fritz Compton," he said to his operator.

FROST WENT BACK to the hotel at 3 o'clock and the clerk handed him his key and a memorandum that Mr. Briggs at Denton had called.

"When did this come in?"

"An hour ago," the clerk said.

It sounded urgent, so Frost went to his room and placed a call. He got Briggs in twenty minutes and Briggs put the Governor on.

The Governor was more upset than ever and asked him what he'd learned. "Nothing," Frost said. "This is a hell of a mess."

"We've got to hurry," the Governor said. "It's all over this end of the State."

"I am hurrying," Frost said; "but there's nothing to work on. We've got to be patient."

"Keep bearing down."

"I will. Do you know anything about your brother's private life?"

"Nothing that would help," the Governor said. "I haven't seen much of him for four years."

"Do you know a Dr. Glavell?"

"Yes, but I don't know anything good about him. When I was practicing law in Salada he was almost nabbed for performing criminal operations. Fritz Compton saved him. Does he figure in the case?"

"I can't tell yet. You know Compton?"

"He's been my bitterest enemy for years. But no matter who is involved—give them the works."

"No matter who is involved?"

"No matter who is involved," the Governor repeated solemnly. "I don't give a damn about anything but justice and the future of my State."

"Very good, sir," Frost said.

WHEN HE EMERGED from the elevator downstairs a
bulky man who wore a gray felt hat snapped down over his
eyes tossed away a cigarette and nodded to two men who were
sitting in a rakish blue touring car at the curbing. The younger
of the men, under the wheel, started the motor, smiled and
winked at his companion. They seemed happy. They were. This
was a great break for them. They had expected to wait at least
three hours.

When Frost stepped from under the marquee the spotter
in the gray felt hat moved directly behind him, nodded again;
then walked up the street. Frost walked down the street.

The rakish blue touring car slid out into the traffic and
crawled along behind him.

Three blocks away he stepped from the pavement to cross
the street when the traffic bell rang. He stopped and stepped
back. In that fraction of a second the blue automobile raced by.

Had Frost kept going he would have been hit.

It missed him by an inch and the suction that trailed in its
wake tugged at his coat.

For a moment Frost was too astonished to move. Then he
realized this was no chance episode, but a deliberate plot with
him as the intended victim. He jumped out in the street, trying
to catch the license numbers. But the blue car had put on added
speed, was bouncing and swaying over the narrow, uneven
street and this was impossible. Almost automatically Frost
started after it; of a sudden he saw the car slew around, heard
the scream of brakes and a crash. It had collided with the inevitable truck at a blind corner.

Gun in hand, Frost started running between the street-car tracks. Two men slid out of the car on opposite sides, the one on the right leaping to the curbing and disappearing around the corner. The other kept straight on across the intersection.

With a fresh burst of speed Frost went after this one. Pedestrians were loudly jabbering and a couple of motorists were frozen to their horn buttons. There was a lot of excitement, heightened by the occupants of the damaged touring car abruptly deserting their posts.

Frost kept on going. Several times he had his man in the open and was about to wing him when a pedestrian interfered.

Suddenly the man turned into an alley between two whole-sale houses, Frost piling in behind him, twenty-five yards behind. He ran head-first into a flash of crimson, there was an explosion that rocked his ear drums and a bullet plunged into a wall beside him.

He fell flat on his stomach against the wall, turning on his left side to leave his gun arm free. The man who had tried to kill him jumped out from behind a box and ran across the alley into an open door. Frost took a shot at him as he jumped, but it was no good.

He got up and went forward. The door frame, set deep in the brick wall, seemed a rear entrance to a commercial house of some sort, for the alleyway nearby was cluttered with empty boxes, packing crates and warehouse rubbish.

The door was open, the interior was dark, so Frost stood quietly, listening for some movement within that would betray a presence. He risked one eye but could see nothing; the place was sepulchral. Behind him, from the alley, floated the rumble of traffic.

Footsteps padded into the alley. The sounds of the shots had been located.

Hearing people behind him prompted Frost to a sudden decision. He quickly stepped inside. No sooner was he across the threshold than he felt something prod him between his shoulders. It felt like a pistol. Frost turned slowly, hands high. It was a pistol. And behind that pistol was a youngish, clean-shaven man with sharp features and a thin, cruel mouth. It was the driver of the blue car.

"Stand still," he said, "or it'll be just too bad."

Frost stood still. The driver kicked the door shut with his foot and called into the darkness in a voice vibrant with excitement:

"Hey! Cholly! Cholly!"

Ahead a door squeaked and a yellow finger of light fell out. A man followed it, making a grotesque silhouette on the floor and wall.

"Who the hell is it?" he asked quickly.

"Me," the driver said, and that evidently was sufficient identification, for the man called Charlie left the door open and came down the hall. Frost could hear Charlie's footsteps, the slightly noisier babble outside, but above all these came the driver's breathing, sharp and asthmatic.

"What the hell?" said Charlie hoarsely.

"Get 'is rod."

Charlie took Frost's gun and slipped it in his pocket. The commotion outside grew louder. Somebody said: "They came in here somewhere," and Charlie realized what it was all about.

"My ——! Johnny, you two wasn't shooting at each other in the alley?"

Johnny grunted a profanity and ended with: "You don't think

I'm going to let a guy plug me first, do you?"

"The whole damn' town's at the back door," Charlie snapped. "Get going, you," he said to Frost.

With the pistol still between his shoulders, Frost got going. Both men were behind him. Johnny steered him through the open door into a small room which contained an iron hospital type bed, some chairs, a table, a few magazines and a long, clerical desk of ancient vintage which stood in a corner. The only illumination was from a single shadeless globe that S'd from the wall.

Charlie shut the door. Johnny said:

"See if he's got another rod stashed on 'im."

Charlie frisked Frost and shook his head negatively, but Johnny wasn't taking chances. He said: "Take this cannon," and slowly and carefully felt over Frost from head to foot. When he had finished he said: "Go over there and sit down."

It was when he sat down that he had his first good look at the two men. Johnny was slender, youngish, dressed not too shabbily, but with a haunted, pinched look in his face. His voice was staccato, his movements sharp and jerky and occasionally he jabbed both lobes of his nose into the crook of his elbow in violent fashion. His full name was Johnny the Hop.

The man called Charlie was short, stout, with long arms and an unshaven face. He looked like a gorilla.

"This is the guy," said Johnny with a touch of pride.

Charlie's face wrinkled but he didn't say anything.

"Frost—the Ranger."

Charlie's face revealed his thought processes. He slowly broke into a smile, saying:

"Yeah? It's a shame he's such a good-looking—"

They both glared at him. Frost said:

"You won't have any luck this way, brother."

Johnny the Hop winked at Charlie and said in his jagged voice:

"He says we won't have any luck, Cholly."

"Oh, the hell with him," growled Charlie. "How'd you get 'im in here under his own power? I thought—"

"So did I," said Johnny, "but what the hell? We was supposed to hit him and then pick him up for the 'hospital.'" He leered and said: "Hospital," again. "I missed him but a couple of blocks away I crashed a country —— —— in a truck. This mug followed."

"You left the car, hunh?"

"Sure—it was hot. The Old Man can fix anything."

"Maybe even murder," said Charlie broadly.

"Maybe even murder," said Johnny.

Frost bit his lip and began to feel uncomfortable. There was a peculiar, slightly chilly feeling at the base of his spine. He had never in his life minimized a situation and he didn't now. He was in a bad way and he knew it; but he didn't grow panicky and curse himself for rushing into it. He was here and that was that. To escape was the problem.

He took a quick look at the door and then at the window to his left.

Johnny the Hop saw his eyes traveling and read his mind.

"Cholly," he called softly, almost amorously, "this guy's getting ideas."

Charlie cocked his head towards the window, listening for a moment to the voices outside. Then he nodded and said: "Uh-hunh." He pulled down the window shade and looked at Johnny.

"Well," he said, "let's let him have it."

"Damned right," said Johnny.

They closed in on him. Frost jumped up and squared off. Johnny the Hop, getting close to action, couldn't control himself. He paused and sneaked his gun from a wide coat pocket. It was a blue-barreled .38.

He bared his teeth and said:

"Right in the kisser for you, Pretty Boy."

Before the gun fired, Charlie swung his body around and viciously slammed his doubled fist across Johnny the Hop's wrist. The gun rattled on the floor.

"You crazy ——!" he snarled.

Frost saw his chance and wasted not a second. He pivoted, shot a quick left and right to the thin face of Johnny the Hop, sacrificing punching power and timing for speed. Johnny the Hop staggered but fell back only a few steps, and Charlie swung a long right to Frost's temple. The blow moved Frost a couple of feet nearer Johnny the Hop and he let go two more—a left and a right.

The left brought a puzzled look to Johnny's face, started him downward, and Frost turned loose the right again. This time there was nothing wrong with it. Johnny sagged, and before he hit the floor Frost had cocked him three or four more times.

The force of the blows carried Frost across the body.

Grunting and drooling, his head low, Charlie came on like an animal. He simply bored in. Frost smacked him with a right and a left but they cracked harmlessly off his skull, and Charlie flailed his long arms out and embraced the Ranger.

The arms were like steel bands, but Frost brought his knee up suddenly in a move which would have ruined his opponent, but fighting at close quarters like this was right up Charlie's alley. He twisted his body and Frost's knee slipped off his hip. Charlie laughed shortly and bear-hugged Frost, putting his head under his chin and slowly forcing him back to the wall. They went to the wall in that shape. Frost kept trying to fall to the floor, hoping he could maneuver towards the gun Johnny the Hop had dropped.

He did manage to get away from the wall, tearing and swinging, but he failed to hear the door open.

In a moment a voice said:

"Step back away from 'im, Cholly." Charlie looked up but kept Frost's arms locked against his sides.

"He's tough, hunh? Step straight back away from 'im, Cholly."

Frost got a glimpse of Charlie's ugly face. There was a smile on it. Charlie stepped back and Frost started to turn around.

He never made it.

Something, everything, crashed into his head; the walls, the ceiling, the roof, the sky above and all that it contained. Debris showered him. It was the splinters of a chair's legs.

The floor was sliding up on its end fast and he tried to clutch it. He couldn't. His muscles wouldn't respond. He remembered how ridiculous it was to have muscles which wouldn't respond.

But before the lights plopped out and his mind went black he thought to cover his face with his arms so his chin and nose wouldn't be broken.

HE SAT BOLT upright in bed in a swimming sea of darkness. His stomach was doing loops and his head was splitting.

He tried to remember what had happened but his brain was

a lighted pinwheel and he couldn't get a thought through. He tried to hurl the thoughts through the spokes of the wheel, tried to time it properly, and once or twice almost did. But inevitably they were cut half in two.

He lay down again, shut his eyes tightly and fought hard.

Pretty soon he became aware of voices. They were coming from somewhere at his right.

He sat up again, gave his eyes time to adjust themselves to the darkness, coaxing them with: "Come on, Baby; come on, Baby," and patting them softly as he often did his motor when he needed another mile or two an hour. In a little while he could make out he was in a small room.

Before him was a window and staring hard he could see the sky outside. He twisted around and swung his feet to the floor. He sat like that for some time, straining to hear what was being said on the other side of the wall. Men were talking but their words were faint and indistinguishable.

He got up and walked to the window, but made sure he was in good shape before he looked out, three stories below into a narrow channel of blackness which contained oddly-shaped islands of gray. He had seen them before; they were the packing crates scattered in the alley.

He turned his head and glanced down the building. It was a great dead surface in the night, like a lake turned on its end. Looking along the wall he saw a blob of light that kept going on and off. This confused him until he realized a flapping shade was permitting the light to escape.

He thought: That is the room where the voices are. Men are in there talking. The light is on and the shade is down. That breeze against my face is moving the shade. Moving the shade permits the light to escape. The shade makes funny noises when it hits the window facing.

A few inches below the sill was a ledge that jutted twelve inches out. It had once been a cornice; the building once had been three-storied. New stories now had been added but the cornice remained. He tested it with one hand, with both hands and decided it would hold his weight.

He crawled carefully across the sill and straightened up.

Pressed against the wall, his fingers wedged in between the bricks, he inched along. The voices became plainer. He was thankful for the flapping of the shade, because it covered the light scraping of his feet on the stone ledge. He twisted his head, looked over his shoulder at the metallic sky.

He was close enough now to hear what was being said. At least four men were in the room and all of them were trying to talk at the same time. They were having a heated discussion; and tiny electrical impulses traveled along Frost's arms and legs as he recognized three of the voices.

Dr. Glavell was there, quietly interrupting; Martin Thomas was still gruff, trying to overpower the others with his tones, and the bass of the man named Charlie was ringing and booming.

"Lissen, lissen," said a baritone voice Frost had never heard before; "—— it, pipe down!"

It had an authoritative timbre and the others piped down.

"Doc," the baritone went on, "the best thing for you to do now is take a long vacation. You may be needed elsewhere."

"I'm making plans, Fritz," Glavell said.

Frost's heart pounded its way into his throat. Fritz! Fritz Compton, the District Attorney. Big Jim Cavanaugh's bitterest enemy!

"It may be a few days before any action is taken," Fritz was saying. "My tip was that Frost had linked you with Cavanaugh, but he told Plant to lay off for more evidence. You'd better get to Coahuila. How about your accounts?"

"It won't take me long. I'm converting everything into cash. I was prepared for emergencies."

"Well, it's not an emergency. It's a crisis. If you stay away from Cavanaugh too long—"

"He'll be all right. What about the—er—money?"

"—— it!" Fritz barked. "Stop harping on that! We'll take care of it in its proper place. *Stop harping on it now!*"

"Pipe down yourself," growled Thomas. "They can hear you at the court house."

THERE WAS SILENCE for a moment. Frost turned loose with one hand and flexed his fingers, then the other hand.

"How much dope came across on the last trip?" asked Fritz.

"Three hundred and fifty pounds," Glavell replied.

"How much did you pay?"

"Twelve dollars an ounce. About fifty grand, all told."

"That goes ten grains to a deck, eh?"

"Right."

"Ten grains, two bucks. Sixty grains in a dram, eight drams in an ounce. That's ninety-six dollars an ounce. Sixteen ounces is a pound; that's $1536 a pound. Three hundred and fifty pounds at $1536 is $537,600. Sweet profit on a fifty-grand investment."

"——!" boomed Charlie.

"But get this," Fritz went on; "and get it straight. This is the last trick. There's too —— much in the balance to gum things up now. It takes a smart man to know when to quit—and we're quitting. If we use our noodles we'll be sitting in France in four years with a coupla millions apiece in the sock. We've got to be patient—and follow orders. You're getting 'em now. Doc, you're beating it to Cavanaugh. Charlie, you're taking a long trip somewhere after you get through here. Everybody lays low until Taylor gives me the word."

"But we're gonna win the election, hunh?"

"You never knew me to be wrong, did you?"

"Right," said Glavell.

"And now," Fritz said, "about Frost. What I wanted was to get him out of the way until after the election. Doc, you sure that shot you gave him won't kill him?"

"I'm positive. He'll be unconscious for another day, perhaps—but it won't harm him."

"But you can't work any black magic on him?"

"No," said Glavell. "He would not be receptive. If he were in a weakened mental condition, yes. But he isn't. I'd say he has rather a powerful personality. With Cavanaugh it was different. It's too bad I can't write a paper on that. I'm satisfied the case is practically without precedent.

"He was an important figure with what I can only call an 'exhibitionist' complex. He liked to impress people, but his personality was dwarfed by his brother's. It was the Governor this and the Governor that; it ate at him, but subconsciously. When I explained what the trouble was, he agreed with the analysis. From then on, it was simple. I think the picture of turning one brother against the other is remarkable. Induced, of course, by proper administrations of narcotics and certain treatments known only to specialists."

When he finished there was a round of laughter. There was no doubt that Dr. Jonathan Glavell was a smart doctor.

But Frost was startled… and he became acutely conscious that his fingers were stiffening and that his position was far from healthy. Any moment they might discover his escape….

Hoping to find a fire-escape, he hurried down the ledge with as much safety as he could possibly manage. There was none. He paused before a window, tried to raise it. He had no luck. There was but one thing to do now and he did it.

He put his foot through the glass, it parted with a snap as sharp as the rip of torn silk and tinkled to the floor inside. Frost reached under the frame, snapped back the thumb lock and jerked the frame upward. He jumped inside and crossed the office.

He opened a door in the hall, peered out. Silence and solitude. He moved swiftly to the staircase behind the elevator and went down to the first floor. It was fifty feet to the street, the big double doors of the building were closed. He strode across the foyer, swung one of the doors open and stepped into the street.

Inside he heard the elevator bang and a loud voice yell: "Halt!"

Frost kept going. He picked a corner a half block away as his objective and broke into a run. Behind him came two more sharp cries of "Halt! Halt!" which reverberated through the canyons of the wholesale district.

He got all out of his legs he could but before he reached the corner the night lighted in three lurid bursts of crimson and orange, so close they seemed to hover above his head. The explosions sounded like three quick bursts from a seventy-five.

The first bullet shattered the plate-glass of a store front, the second flattened into a wall and the third whined past Frost's head on an angry, rising note. Even above the heavy noise of the falling glass he heard that third bullet singing.

He breasted the corner, ducked around it and kept going. This was a short block; in a moment he had come to Franklin, the main street, but he did not lessen his speed until he came to an all-night cab stand.

He flung open the rear door of a cab, fell against the seat and yelled to a startled driver:

"Let's go! Let's go!"

The cab started with a lurch, jerked from first to second and then to high and stretched out.

"Where to?" asked the driver as soon as he dared.

Frost's stomach rumbled again but he disregarded it.

"The airport," he said.

AT SIX-FIFTY O'CLOCK the next morning the owlish-eyed night clerk of a little hotel in Denton, which is in the north of Texas, stirred himself and gazed at the apparition before him.

It was a hatless, wind-blown man in a rumpled and stained gray tweed suit, whose face was red and wild and splotched with oil and a dark substance that might have been mud, but was really blood. He looked like an innocent civilian who had somehow been caught in the tail end of a war.

The clerk stared hard and said: "Yes, sir," because he could think of nothing else.

"I want to see the Governor," the apparition said. "My name's Frost."

The clerk wagged his head.

"You can't see him. Nobody can see him. Orders are—"

"The hell with orders. What room's he in?"

He lost his words and some of his brusqueness when Frost reached across the desk and grabbed him by the coat lapel.

"Phone him. Go on—phone him."

The clerk shook himself loose, hissed a couple of times and telephoned. In a minute he said: "It's 201. I'll take you up."

They went up in the elevator. The clerk slid back the door, pointed and said: "It's down thataway."

Briggs was waiting for him with his head out the door. "Come in," he said in a whisper. He buttoned his pyjama coat, shut the door, wondering what was up but not asking any questions. "The Governor's asleep," he said. "Please let him sleep unless it's important. He had one hell of a time going to sleep."

"Worried, hunh?"

Briggs nodded.

"Okey," Frost said. "Later. I want to wash. Fix me a tub, will you, Briggs?"

"It's a shower," Briggs said.

The door behind him opened and the Governor came out. He was wearing faded pink flannel pyjamas, what little hair he had was disheveled and his face was haggard. Frost could tell the way the race was going by his face.

"What's happened?" Cavanaugh asked.

"Plenty," said Frost. "Sorry to rush in on you like this, but it had to be done."

He started undressing. The Governor went to the table and selected a panatela. Briggs struck a match and held it out, but the Governor shook him off.

"Come on in while I take a bath," Frost said.

The Governor and Briggs trooped into the bathroom behind him. The Governor sat down on the commode and Briggs stood by the door. Frost got the shower going and stepped under. It was warm and soft and caressing.

He said luxuriously: "This is so grand it almost evens things up."

"That's a nasty cut in your scalp," the Governor said.

"It's beginning to sting now. The water hurts it. Do you know a man named Taylor who's in this campaign?"

"Phineas Taylor," the Governor said. "Myers' manager. He used to be Assistant District Attorney at Salada under Compton."

"That's the one," Frost said.

He told the story, omitting nothing but references to the Governor's brother, Robert. The Governor twisted the unlighted panatela around in his mouth, grunting occasionally but saying nothing.

When Frost had finished he asked: "But what about Bob? Do you think Glavell had anything to do with it?"

"It's not impossible," Frost said. "Glavell might have used friendship as a decoy. I'm going to get the boys and have a look at that sanitarium in Coahuila."

"By ——!" said the Governor; "they must have him locked up or something. Bob's not one to give up. He's a fighter. He's a Cavanaugh."

"Has he ever used morphine?"

The Governor pursed his lips, slightly taken aback by the suddenness of the question.

"Yes—a long time ago," he said finally. "But he's been off the stuff for years. Who told you?"

"Nobody. It was a case of adding. Your brother and Glavell were such good friends."

"Not exactly friends," the Governor corrected. "Just sort of business partners. They owned the South Plains Airways until a short time ago."

Frost nodded. The case was beginning to clear up. He judged, and rightly, that the principal business of the South Plains Airways was trafficking in drugs.

The Governor said bitterly: "This is Fritz Compton's work. He's pitched in with Myers and Taylor to beat me. They are the ones who got away with that money. I know it. Bob was kidnaped or framed—one of the two. He was a Cavanaugh," the Governor said again. He shook his head morosely and went on: "What's the plan now? We can't let 'em get into office. What's the plan?"

Frost hooked the bath towel over the shower and went out. He crawled into Briggs' bed and turned his face to the wall.

"Call me at noon," he said over his shoulder.

TWO DAYS BEFORE election it appeared that nothing could save Big Jim Cavanaugh from defeat. Newspapers in the State editorialized vaguely, but most of them were just so many words, because the press, as a whole, lacked courage.

Even his staunchest supporters saw shadows on the horizon. They believed the charges brought against his brother were false and they denied them vehemently, but their voices were weak as opposed to the clamor of a mob and therefore were lost. They begged and pleaded with the Governor to snap out of his lethargy and tell the people the truth.

But Big Jim Cavanaugh stolidly shook his head.

"Nope," he said laconically; "that's not my idea of a campaign. But"— and here a flash of the old-time warrior came into his eyes—"if I'm beaten I'll settle with Myers personally."

Texas is a vast State and a gubernatorial candidate who hopes to meet voters in its many sections must hump to get around. Jim Cavanaugh spoke morning, noon and night. Sometimes it seemed to him that he was merely a speech-making robot; when at the end of his talks, he had finished letting people wring at his hands his Frankenstein hauled him off to a train or an automobile for the next jump. He did not complain, though; and sat alone, apparently resigned to his fate.

Frost's last words to him had been: "Keep banging away and leave everything to us. Don't worry."

That was easy enough to say but not so easy to do. He was worried, he did want to fight back; instead he fought himself to maintain the placid exterior. But the struggle was distorting everything, blotting out everything.

WHEN THE FIRST rays of the sun crawled over the horizon the following morning, five flyers were grouped at the open doors of their hangar, in earnest conversation. Four of them were booted, wore chamois jackets and helmets, but the fifth, who was Eddie Giles, clung to his white drill pants, tennis shoes and the blue sweater he never ventured aloft without. All of them had automatics strapped at their hips.

Mechanics were trundling their ships windward.

"Stick close," said Jerry Frost.

They crawled up, revved their motors; and in a moment they had bounced into the air, headed for Mexico.

Their destination was Vinamo, in the State of Coahuila, seventy miles from Gentry, headquarters of the Air Rangers. They made it in forty minutes, following Frost, who traveled straight as a homing pigeon. He had made the trip yesterday.

They put their ships down in a wide spot on the fringe of a little adobe town that lay sweltering under a sun already terrific.

Pedro Sansovar, former Mexican customs collector at the bridge-head, was waiting as per arrangements. He flashed his white teeth in a wide smile and greeted Frost with some demonstration. Frost introduced him, saying:

"This is Pedro—the one I was telling you about."

Pedro nodded and began a rapid-fire conversation with Frost in Mexican. It was sprinkled with idioms, but Frost understood. He had soldiered from Juarez to Quintana Roo in a half dozen armies.

A few natives wandered over. One of them was tall and gaunt and wore a battered U.S. campaign hat, khaki shorts and a nondescript coat. A double cartridge belt was slung over his shoulder, but his only weapon was a short billy. He moved with a certain majesty characteristic of minor Mexican authority. Pedro introduced him as a cousin, Vinamo's *alcalde,* the only law in the district.

Frost told the *alcalde* he would give him twenty pesos to keep the curious natives away from the planes. Pedro said: "Twenty pesos is too much for that bum," but he kept a smile on his face so the *alcalde* wouldn't understand.

"But he's a cousin—" Frost said.

"He's a bum," Pedro said, "and I got plenta cousins—"

Hans Traub growled harshly in his throat and said: "How about getting somewhere?"

Frost asked Pedro if everything was ready and Pedro said yes. Hell's Stepson's fitted their Tommy guns with drums as they crossed the field to Pedro's car, a three-year-old flivver.

They got in and said little as they bounced along the road and left Vinamo behind, an ugly splotch on the Coahuilan plateau.

Ten miles away Pedro suddenly swerved from the road and drove across a field, finally turning into a wide trail that led down an arroyo to a river bed long since dried. He stopped under a ledge which was crowned by mesquite stubs.

"It's back up there," Frost said, pointing.

"The lousiest country in the world," said Skipper Hinsdell, getting out.

"Check," said Rowdy Perry.

"Double-check," said Traub.

"Come on," said Frost.

They crawled up the side of the arroyo and poked their heads above the level of the plateau. It was a wild and barren country; it stretched to the hazy mountains in the distance, a sea of chaparral and sage serrated by the hairy fingers of cholla and sauhara. The sanitarium stood in a grove of scrawny poplars, old and feeble, but fiercely proud as is the way with once great haciendas when they fall into evil hands.

The heat rolled upward in shimmering waves and the sun was emperor of all.

Hell's Stepsons reached the place before they were discovered. A swarthy, unkempt native who was dozing on the porch in a chair tilted back, American fashion, awoke to face five Americans whose faces were set and tense.

Frost prodded him out of the chair with the barrel of a machine-gun and in Mexican told him to lead the way to Dr. Glavell.

He did. They trooped through a shadowy hall and emerged into a patio of wicker settees and canvas deck chairs. An awning on wires across the top was partly opened. The house broadened and stretched back.

Hans Traub saw the glint of a rifle muzzle in a window, yelled: "Look out!" and fired at the same time.

His machine-gun chattered sharply and across the patio a Spanish blasphemy arose. A rifle slid through the window and fell into the patio.

"Hurry up, Jerry," Traub cried. "The —— couldn't miss us out here if they tried!"

Frost urged the Mexican forward with the muzzle of his gun.

"That was swell," Giles said to Traub. "Glad you came."

"——!" growled Traub.

Somebody inside screamed: "Ramon! Ramon!" and a couple of doors slammed. Footsteps pattered and then died. A brown face appeared in a window but disappeared before Giles could heft his gun.

Hell's Stepsons passed into a long, coolish corridor in the rear wing. The Mexican had stopped before a door and they grouped around. Frost heaved a boot against the bolt and the door popped open like tinder.

They piled in.

Before them, at an ornate desk, with a tight smile on his face, sat Dr. Jonathan Glavell. He sat very stiff and very straight; he knew he was in a hell of a hole, and his eyes, resting on the sweaty, formidable group of flyers, contained a hint of fear, but the expression on his face never changed.

"Get out from behind that desk," Frost said.

Glavell half-sneered, but he got up and stood facing them,

his hands at his side. Quietly he said: "So we meet again."

"Right," said Frost.

"And this time," Glavell went on with some heat, "you take the laws of two countries into your own hands."

"You got a lot of guts to talk to me about law," Frost snapped. "Where's Cavanaugh?"

Glavell's slender body quivered a little.

"You'll never know," he gritted.

Footsteps padded again in the hall outside and across the tile of the patio. Loud, excited conversation arose. A thin, almost feminine scream cut through the tension.

The rear door popped open and a thin, wild-eyed man hurtled into the room. He was disheveled as if he had just awakened from a sleep and his lips were working convulsively. He looked like a madman.

"Stop it!" he bellowed. "Stop it!"

Dr. Glavell grabbed him, saying:

"Get out! Damn it, get out!"

Rowdy Perry laid his gun across the desk and separated them.

"Who are you?" Frost asked.

The disheveled man faced him, panting, defiant.

"I am Robert Cavanaugh," he said; "and you are the Rangers. I knew you would come sooner or later." He faced Glavell and went on hysterically: "I told you to leave. I told you to take me away." To Frost he said: "But it won't do you any good. I'm not going back—"

With a cry of rage Glavell leaped and struck him on the side of the head.

"Shut up," he yelled. "He's crazy—crazy—"

Traub caught Glavell and flung him back. He half-fell on

to the desk, groped for its edge, missed and caved to the floor. Traub yanked him up with his left hand.

Cavanaugh shrieked: "I'm not crazy! I'm sick—only —— knows how sick I am. But I'm not going back. You hear that? I'm not going back!"

"Sure you are," Frost said. "The Governor—"

Robert Cavanaugh's voice swelled.

"Damn him!" he shouted. "I hate him! 'The Governor, the Governor'—that's all I've heard for four years! That's what has made me sick as I am. Don't say that any more! I hate him!"

"Shut up," yelled Glavell, getting excited. "You ——! Shut up!"

"Oh, I'm sick," Cavanaugh groaned, slumping in Giles' arms. Looking at Glavell, he said in a whining tone: "Why don't you do what you promised? Why don't you? Just a little—"

"Where's the money?" said Giles.

"I don't know," Cavanaugh said. He pointed to Glavell and shrilled: "He's got it! He's got everything! He took everything! He cheated me, made me steal—" He was whimpering like a child.

"He's a no-good ——!" Frost said. "The lousiest —— I ever saw."

There was fire in his eyes and steel in his voice. Hell's Stepsons jerked with excitement, their blood pounded. They knew their skipper. They knew they were listening to Jonathan Glavell's death warrant. When Jerry Frost swore like this somebody died.

"I'll get you a shot," Frost said to Cavanaugh. "Tell us about it."

Robert Cavanaugh, his face contorted in anguish, looked at

Glavell. Glavell returned the look through narrow-slitted eyes. The lines began to leave Cavanaugh's face, his lips fluttered, his eyes were stony.

Frost realized what was happening.

"Stop it!" he yelled. He swung his fist into Glavell's jaw and the doctor almost went down against the wall.

The hypnotic spell broken, Cavanaugh sobbed and relaxed.

Frost dropped his gun to the floor and dived on Glavell. The doctor was struggling to get something out of his pocket. Frost socked him with a left and then drove a short, straight right into his throat. Glavell grunted, flung both arms upward and sagged. His shoulders struck the wall and he slid to the floor. Quickly Frost had moved down on him, had taken a nickel-plated .38 from his pocket.

He flung the gun into a corner and went over to Cavanaugh.

"Hurry," Frost said. "What's the rest of it?"

"Take your hands off me!" Cavanaugh cried, hysterical again. He was going through hell. "Damn you, I won't tell you! I hate you! I hate everybody! We'll ruin him; then we'll go away. Nobody will ever mention *him* again!" He broke off in a peal of shrill, wild laughter.

Frost shut his eyes tightly, his soul in revolt. This pathetic thing was the progeny of Jim Cavanaugh, the giant who had flung the frontier of a civilization forward. It was devastating!

"Set him down, Hans," Frost said. "Try to keep him quiet."

He went back to Glavell. The doctor was sprawled on the floor, his head against the wall, blinking his eyes. He was not a pretty picture; he was mussed, his hair was awry and a tiny trickle of blood crawled down from his cheek from a tear under the eye.

"Get up!" Frost said, roughly jerking him by his coat collar.

A panel in the wall behind Frost slowly swung open, inch by inch. Eddie Giles saw it, grinned and lifted his gun. In a moment a face appeared, then a hand, holding a pistol, emerged from nowhere.

Giles turned loose his machine-gun, spraying the face.

The panel swung open as the body wedged through to the floor.

Robert Cavanaugh screamed. Jonathan Glavell cursed. Frost retrieved his gun as Hell's Stepsons swung sharply, their noses and eyes stinging from the acridity of the gun smoke.

"In there," Cavanaugh cried suddenly; "in there! Get my money!"

"Through there!" Frost barked.

Guns high, Skipper Hinsdell and Rowdy Perry stepped over the lifeless body and went through the opening.

Frost looked at Glavell, his face grim.

"Get started talking!" he said. "You've got five minutes to live!"

Robert Cavanaugh pleaded: "Don't kill him, don't kill him. What will happen to me then?"

Dr. Glavell turned his eyes off Cavanaugh on to Frost. They burned and seemed bottomless.

"What," he asked, "is your price? I've got a million—I'll give you half. I'll walk out and never come back."

"You'll go out in a coffin," Frost said.

"Half a million," Glavell repeated, licking the words.

There was another scurrying sound in the patio. Frost looked towards the noise, then at Giles.

"Watch 'em," he said.

Giles went to the window.

"Now," said Frost to Glavell, "start talking."

"If I talk," said Glavell, "do I go free?"

"You talk or else."

"I'll else," said Glavell.

"You promised me—" Cavanaugh began.

"I'll remember," said Frost.

"I'll ruin you, too," Cavanaugh screamed.

Frost said to Glavell:

"I'm going to kill you, but before I do I'm going to turn the house upside down. You're in a staggering plot to get control of a State, but it won't work. You struck at Texas through this weakling, and somehow or other you made him steal a million dollars. Only a madman could have got away with that, Glavell—only a man made mad by hypnotism and dope."

Glavell shrugged his shoulders and said evenly:

"It has worked. Tomorrow night Myers will be Governor. You can kill me but you can't stop that. You can kill me"—he gloated over the words heroically—"but the thing's too big to stop, Frost. We force a president to rob his bank, we elect our own Governor. You can't change that, Frost—no matter what you do."

Cavanaugh looked from one to the other in bewilderment. Slowly he repeated: "You force a president to rob a bank of a million dollars." And then he went on dramatically, as if the facts were just now becoming known to him: "Why, he's talking about me! Yes—yes, he did! That man and Compton. They ruined me to ruin my brother. I hate him—kill him—kill him—kill them all—" He calmed a little, looked at Glavell and whimpered: "I didn't mean it, Doctor. I didn't mean it. Please do what you promised."

Rat-tat-tat-tat-tat-tat-tat! Rat-tat-tat-tat-tat-tat-tat!

A Tommy gun was barking; the tones were muffled as if it were shooting in a barrel. They were coming from the passageway behind the panel.

"Hey!" yelled Perry, his voice ringing.

Traub rushed into the opening. Frost took a couple of steps backward to cover Glavell and Cavanaugh. Glavell was standing motionless, his beady eyes never still for a moment; and Cavanaugh sat in a chair, his face buried in his hands.

In a moment Traub came out of the opening, followed by Perry and Hinsdell. They were carrying a heavy leather pouch as big as a dunnage bag.

"There's the dough," Perry said. "It was in a little closet down there. We shot the lock off."

Glavell was smiling easily.

"That's the element of chance, Captain," he said. "Ramon was the only man who knew of the tunnel—and he used it to come to my rescue. Instead he is killed, exposing our secret. The element of chance, Captain."

Giles called from the window: "Jerry, come here, quick!"

Frost swiftly strode across the room and looked out. A score of natives, armed with rifles, had gathered in the patio.

Jonathan Glavell laughed.

"You don't suppose, for —— sake, I'd be simple enough to leave my flanks unprotected?" he said. "You're surrounded on all sides."

"Tell 'em," Frost hissed, "to put down their rifles!"

Glavell laughed again. Robert Cavanaugh lifted his head. He slowly got to his feet. He said: "I'll tell 'em," and moved feebly to the window, shouting: *"Andale! Andale!"*

Jonathan Glavell dived for the gun in the corner, lifted it. His face was rimmed with frenzied hatred and his eyes were rolling in their sockets. He fired three shots into Robert Cavanaugh's body at such close range the bullets tore through and banged into the wall behind.

Robert Cavanaugh never murmured. He did not move backward or forward, his feet were anchored. His body simply melted to the floor.

Glavell turned and pointed the pistol at Frost, not hurriedly or swiftly, but slowly and deliberately, as if contemptuously.

Frost kept his eyes on the pistol in Glavell's hand, tense and taut, his mind and muscles keenly co-ordinated with that synchronization peculiar to fighting men the world over.

A moment before the pistol barked, Frost swayed; crimson flame and lead hurtled over his shoulder. He fired his machine-gun from a half crouch. The burst caught Glavell full in the chest and face, he snarled a short cry and staggered back. Blood stenciled his shirt and face and he made a tremendous effort to right himself, but nothing human could withstand that hail of death.

Bullets drove him back to the wall and crushed him.

Frost kept his gun open until Glavell had fallen to the floor, the bullets eating at the stuccoed wall. Glavell rolled over dead and an avalanche of plaster shrouded his face.

Rifles cracked in the patio and bullets whistled through the window.

They shattered the dramatic spell in the room of death.

"——!" shouted Giles, making for the window.

"Stay away from there!" Frost bawled.

Outside there were cries and shouts and more gunfire. It

crackled like a war-god's holiday. Another wave of fire rolled, topped by shriller shouting.

Frost risked an eye at the window and drew in his breath sharply.

A legion had come to his rescue—headed by Pedro Sansovar—but what a legion… a dozen tattered savages in brown, some astride horses, some afoot, but all heavily armed and with the lust of battle on their oily faces. The rifles, Frost took time to note, were modern pieces.

His legion in undisputed control, Pedro Sansovar, a magnificent figure, with a six-shooter in either hand, lifted his head and shouted, the sun glinting off his teeth:

"*Capitan! Capitan* Frost!"

Hell's Stepsons crowded to the window.

"It's Pedro," Frost said. He framed himself in the window and said: "Here, Pedro—here!"

Pedro saw him, laughed again, spread his arms and shouted: "*Capitan!*"

He came trotting over with a fiercely mustachioed man at his side, a paunchy, ill-kempt man who carried a rifle in his hand, a .45 automatic in a worn holster on his right side, a small machete in a sling on his left side, and who was grinning from ear to ear.

"This ees Laudo Cimarosa," he said, indicating the paunchy man so thoroughly accoutered. And to Laudo Cimarosa, Pedro said something in rapid Mexican that caused that gentleman to salaam with a grace astonishing in one of such bulk. Pedro was saying in his richly flavored American:

"I am chatting with Laudo, we hear shots and I think maybe you need help. So we come."

"*Gracias,*" said Frost, bowing to Cimarosa and thinking: "Well, I'll be damned! To my rescue comes Laudo Cimarosa, successor to Pancho Villa, the bandit for whose death Mexico is offering a fortune. Laudo Cimarosa. Well, I'll be damned!"

He turned to Hell's Stepsons and said:

"Cimarosa."

"You need no help?" asked Pedro naively.

"Not now," Frost said. "But it was pretty hot for a while before you came. *Gracias.*"

Pedro and Cimarosa looked at each other and laughed.

Giles whispered: "Let's scram! We got dough to worry about—the bloody stuff!"

Cimarosa turned to his men, barked a command and he and Pedro came inside. Pedro stared at the bodies, open-mouthed. Cimarosa smiled understandingly. It was nothing new to him.

Pedro said: "Laudo and I take you back."

Laudo grinned and bowed again, clanking his artillery and pushing his machete back with the palm of his hand. He said:

"It will be great honor. *El Capitan* is a great soldier!"

Frost nodded his head courteously and replied:

"Laudo Cimarosa is also a great soldier!"

Cimarosa smiled, pleased, but he knew what the other flyers were thinking, so he spread his hands and said: "Cimarosa fight only for poor peons who government tries to starve."

"*Si,*" Frost agreed.

Laudo Cimarosa was not, he told himself, a bad egg; not a bad egg at all. *If* he happened to be your friend. But there was a pillaged trail from San Luis Potosi to Piedras Niegras that told what kind of an egg he could be *if* he didn't like you.

"Let's go," Frost said aloud.

"Leave everything," Pedro said. "You cannot move nothing. My cousin—*El Alcalde*—come back to take charge. For long time he teenk everything not so good here dis place."

"Everything," Frost said, "but that body and this sack." He indicated Robert Cavanaugh and the pouch of money.

Cimarosa poked the pouch with a curious toe. He darted a swift glance at Frost and said: "Thees ees money."

"Two million pesos," Frost said evenly.

"My men," said Cimarosa without batting an eye, "will carry dead man and two million pesos to your airship."

Hell's Stepsons instinctively gripped their machine-guns. But Frost smiled and said:

"Gracias."

Thirty minutes later Hell's Stepsons were bouncing back to Vinamo, escorted by the nondescripts of Laudo Cimarosa, the bandit killer whose maraudings were legendary.

A few miles from town Cimarosa wheeled his horse and came alongside the car.

"Good-bye," he said. "We leave you now."

"Adios," Frost said.

Cimarosa stood in his stirrups and flung his arm towards the mountains. In that moment he reminded Frost of pictures he had seen of that Confederate gallant, Jeb Stuart.

Eastward, across an inferno of wasteland, the band of Laudo Cimarosa galloped towards the mountains....

Pedro jogged the car along.

"Cimarosa is picturesque," Frost said.

"A great man," said Pedro, nodding soberly. "Those he hate, he kill. Those he love, he give all."

"You know him long time?" asked Frost.

"Laudo Cimarosa my cousin," said Pedro somewhat proudly, and Frost, of a sudden, could understand that pride.

IT WAS NINE o'clock election eve night. Tomorrow the citizens of Texas would name their Governor. But the procedure itself, the choosing of the highest executive in the State, was considered only a formality. For one of the few times in history a candidate apparently was riding on a landslide. Throughout the State he had finished in a whirlwind fashion, arousing an antipathy which seemed certain to sweep Big Jim Cavanaugh into the political scrapheap and which also struck at his status as a man. The integrity of the name of Cavanaugh was crumbling fast.

Nine o'clock. In the drawing-room of a hotel suite in San Antonio were six men. On a Jacobean coffee table in the center of the room stood ginger ale bottles, four fizz water bottles, a silver bowl of ice cubes, two quarts of Scotch whiskey and two ash trays heaped with cigarette butts. The room was warm and close, the windows were shut: outside a norther whistled.

Three of the men sat on a lounge: Fred Myers, sleek and trim and, in the glow of victory, not looking his forty-five years; Phineas Taylor, his campaign manager, bald, hatchet-faced, thin-lipped, holding a sheet of typewritten paper; and Fritz Compton, the Salada District Attorney who was paying an indiscreet visit to get in congratulations early. In a chair opposite sat a lieutenant named Cason; and they all were looking at the man, standing beside the coffee table, who had interrupted their celebration ten minutes ago. Beside him stood a younger man in gray, square-jawed, wearing a heavy gray overcoat.

"And that, gentlemen," said Frost, "is the alternative. Myers, you will sign the statement Taylor holds or Mr. Newhall here will release tonight over his press association wires a complete story of the whole affair. It's what's known in newspaper circles as a 'red-hot' yarn."

Into Fred Myers' face there crept a look of concern. He glanced at Taylor, but found no comfort there.

"We could say," he declared, "this was a frame-up. Who'd believe your story?"

"We have the body of Robert Cavanaugh and the original letters written by Taylor to Jonathan Glavell from Jamestown two years ago in which the whole plot was hatched. I took those letters from Glavell's desk in the Coahuila sanitarium after the fight. They are now in the possession of Governor Cavanaugh. It looks like the finish, Myers."

Myers grunted.

"And you, Compton," Frost went on evenly, "tried to have me murdered. I've got a lousy disposition; I don't like people who try to have me killed. This afternoon Louis Plant, narcotic man at Salada, landed Martin Thomas—and Thomas squealed. Yeah, big, bullying Chief Thomas squealed. So when I leave here, Compton, I'm taking you with me. I'm arresting you, Compton, and holding you for Plant. I hope you make a break for it—because I'd like to let you have it right in the back."

Fritz Compton twisted nervously in his seat, looking nervously about the room, worrying a handkerchief between his palms.

"This is the finish, Myers," Frost said again. "You sign that paper, which finishes you in State politics, or we'll take you all to jail and crack the story and tomorrow this State will be on your tail. You ought to go to jail—thank Jim Cavanaugh for the mercy."

Myers looked thoughtful. He said:

"If I resign, do I get the letters?"

"Jim Cavanaugh probably will deliver 'em in person," Frost said.

"No, no, not Cavanaugh," said Myers. "Somebody else. Here, Phin,"—he snatched the paper from Taylor—"gimme that."

He slid forward in his seat, cleared a place for it on the coffee table. Newhall stepped forward, held out a pen and said sweetly:

"Here you are, sir."

Fred Myers scratched his name. Newhall took both the paper and the pen and shoved them in his pocket.

Fritz Compton realized what had happened. With a startled cry he leaped out of his chair, rushed to the French window and flung it open. The icy wind swept past him. He stood looking out for a fleeting second; then, without a word or a backward glance, he dived over the four-foot railing into space.

Frost reached the railing in time to see the body strike the pavement, nine stories below.

Somewhere a woman screamed. A police whistle rattled in the night, was lifted by the gale and rushed upward to the roofs. People were pointing up to the window and in the rich red glare of the thick neon drug-store sign their faces looked skinless and horrible.

Inside the room the wind rushed and raced and sucked Fritz Compton's handkerchief from the arm of the lounge and flung it into a corner.

DEEP NIGHT HAD come to the Border country. A myriad of low-hung stars blinked watchfully over a tired and weary world.

And of all the people under those stars none was wearier than Big Jim Cavanaugh, who sat now, deep in an enormous leather chair—Jerry Frost's own—in headquarters room of the Air Rangers, in Gentry, on the banks of the Rio Grande.

Tonight Big Jim Cavanaugh could have been any one of a thousand places, but he had chosen this narrow room, plain, barely furnished, with only a single globe... and inhabited by five fighting men. Chosen it in preference to all else....

From the corner of his mouth dangled an unlighted panatela, his eyes fixed on the console radio against the wall. Hell's Stepsons sat around, smoking, saying nothing, half dressed.

"... WFBB bringing you the result of the history-making run-off, by special arrangement with the Texas Election Bureau....Here's Bosque County... Myers, 1,151; Cavanaugh, 6,403....That's the way it's going all over, folks....It looks like Big Jim is going back to Austin by a four to one majority.... Last night, as everybody knows, Myers resigned from the race, giving ill-health as the cause, too late to put a substitute on the ticket.... And here's a flash from San Antonio that might interest you: 'San Antonio—Justice of the Peace Dyer today returned a verdict of suicide in the case of Fritz Compton, Salada District Attorney, who was killed in a fall from the ninth floor of a local hotel early last night. Compton was formally charged, earlier in the day, in Salada with violation of the Harrison anti-narcotic law....Just a minute now, folks, and we'll have some more returns...."

Jerry Frost said quietly:

"Well, sir, it looks like you're in."

Big Jim Cavanaugh nodded and said:

"You boys—"

"That's okey, sir," Skipper Hinsdell cut in.

"Did you," Big Jim asked, "—see Bob—die?"

"Yes, sir," said Frost promptly. "We cut him loose from his ropes in the dungeon and took him upstairs. He was weak and suffering and kept swearing at his kidnapers. When the fight started and he saw the odds against us, he grabbed my pistol and jumped out in the patio before anybody could stop him. Well, that's all there is to it, sir. Before he went he dropped Glavell and three of the enemy. Then your brother sagged and—"

"Go on."

"That's all, sir. Really. He was dead when we reached him."

Frost looked at Hell's Stepsons. They nodded vigorously.

"That's the way to go—if you've got to go," murmured Big Jim; "that's the way—giving 'em hell right down to the finish."

"Yes, sir," Frost said. "You can well be proud of him."

"I am," the Governor said softly, drawing a deep breath. "You boys delivered the goods. The people of this State owe you a great debt. I owe you a great debt. We won't forget."

HE LOOKED OUT the window into the night. Somewhere out there a rugged giant, an earlier Jim Cavanaugh, with the scars of Cherokee arrows in his back, pressed onward with the conquistadores of other years, rocking the uttermost isles with his cry:

"Hai-ai-ai-ai! Here's one more outfit that's going through!"

Flight at Sunrise

*Eddie Giles flies east at sunrise, and
Hell's stepsons ride a lost trail*

RAIN FELL SLANTWISE over the Rio Grande country, striking the windows of Border Patrol headquarters softly, then running slowly down, like tears. From the flying field outside came the sharp rise and fall of airplane motors, thin stabs of sound, blurred by the damp air, as the planes settled for landings. They were coming in to report—no success. The search for Eddie Giles, flying Texas Ranger, missing four days, was seemingly of no avail.

Jerry Frost leaned on the table and stared with melancholy eyes at the rain running down the glass. Through the small window, whose sill was on a level with his eyes, he could see a patch of cloud-swept sky as the airplanes dropped out of it, one by one, obliquely, like crippled birds....

He thought of Giles, a lump rising in his throat.

Four mornings ago the tall, ruddy Britisher, an incorrigible romanticist, had raced away into the dawn on a flight at sunrise. It was not the first time he had raced away; it was a daily ritual, probably suggested by something Rupert Brooke had written, but it was the first time he hadn't raced directly home.

Frost recalled the beginnings of uncertainty of that first morning.

Eight o'clock... nine o'clock... ten o'clock....

The sun was well up the bowl and no Giles. Still, even then, Hell's Stepsons were not really alarmed. This was his late-trick day; he had probably dropped into some señorita's backyard for a brief, hurried visit. Galahad in goggles, Giles once had said of himself.

Eleven o'clock... twelve o'clock... one o'clock....

He was now late for duty. This was something that had never happened before, not even when, he had gone on a Brooke debauch. Frost, slender and tall, commander of the patrol, began to fret a little, squinting his eyes at the sky more often, wondering what could have happened.

Two o'clock... three o'clock... four o'clock....

A sudden premonitory pang shot through Frost. The uncertainty was becoming something more real. Impatiently he stamped into the radio-room and cut in the transmitter.

"Frost—to the patrol. Giles still missing. May have fallen. May have been attacked by smugglers. Perry and Hinsdell swing south into Coahuila. Traub meet me over Del Rio in twenty minutes. I am worried—"

A short-wave radio hound, fumbling around with his dials, tuned in on that. He stiffened in his chair, his heart pounded and he listened, not daring to breathe. This was drama. When the message was finished he turned excitedly to his broadcasting set....

It was inevitable, then, that the newspapers would get the story. In 96-point Gothic they shouted their pessimism:

Border Patrol Ace Missing: Fear Giles Met with Violence: Think Giles Dead Somewhere in Mexico: Hell's Stepsons Mourn Loss of Comrade.

Searching parties were formed in almost every section of the Border country; private flyers volunteered and from Kelly Field

the Army had sent a couple of observation units. But none of these agencies discovered the slightest clue to the disappearance. At the end of the fourth day they were no nearer a solution to the mystery than they were on the first. It was as if Giles and his plane had straddled a moonbeam out of a Brooke quatrain and ridden it into another world.... And now it was getting on in the fourth day. As Frost sat, staring moodily through the small window, the rain lessened, the sky lightened with promise of early clearing; but Frost hardly noticed the indication.

Abruptly the door of headquarters fanned and Rosenfield, the dumpy little mechanic, entered, bringing with him from the outside the reek of wet rubber and castor oil.

"Austin's on the line," he said. "I think it's the governor."

Frost got up and went to the phone, across the patio to the office. The governor it was, Jim Cavanaugh himself, his great voice booming through the wire, calling Frost to Austin immediately. Frost frowned at the wall. He was tired, worn out; for almost the entire four days he had been in the saddle leading the search. He was in neither physical nor mental condition to fly the four hundred-odd miles to the state capital.

So he argued he couldn't come, and had rather definitely made up his mind he wouldn't go when the governor said: "This is about Giles!"

"I'll shove off now," Frost said.

DYING TEXAS SUNLIGHT spilled into the governor's office in a cone of gold, limning that great man against the toneless gray wall in sharp silhouette. The silhouette was big and burly and leonine. Jim Cavanaugh himself was big and burly and leonine.

He moved forward in his chair, handing Frost a folded sheet of paper. "Read that," he said.

Frost opened it. It was a letter, neatly typed and spaced, bearing the characteristics of a job done with a portable typewriter:

Your Excellency:

This is to inform you that we have captured Ranger Giles, of the Border Patrol, for the sole purpose of effecting the release of Franz Weisberg, now held in the state penitentiary. Release Weisberg, who will contact us, and Giles will be set free, unharmed. If we do not hear from Weisberg in five days Giles' life will be taken.

Do not badger Weisberg for information as to the senders of this note. He knows nothing except where to go when he gets out. We do not want

to have to send you one of Giles' ears or one of his hands to prove we
mean business. Ask Jerry Frost.

Friends of Weisberg.

Frost finished reading the letter and looked above it to a portrait of Sam Houston on the east wall. His eyes were not focused on the portrait; they were not focused on anything in particular. His face was grim and thoughtful. *Friends of Weisberg.* He knew who they were: Border traffickers in aliens and contrabands, renegade pilots, long ago demoralised, most of them captured by Hell's Stepsons and sent to prison for long terms. *Friends of Weisberg.* Did this mean a new menace was rising?

Frost turned and looked into the sunshine, passing now in deep, reddish effulgence. It felt warm and friendly to his face, and brought out a refinement and a spirituality which were, in a fighting man, oddly moving.

"They probably mean business—if they've got him," he said finally. "But how do we know this isn't a bluff?"

"It's no bluff," the governor said. "Here—this came with the letter." He dropped into Frost's outstretched hand a silver identification bracelet, the kind flyers wear. Frost looked at it, his hopes fading.

"It's Giles', all right," he said slowly. "But what a nerve they've got to bargain with you—the governor!"

"That's exactly why they came to me," Cavanaugh said. "They know as governor how I depend upon the Border Patrol. At least, I suppose they know it. Everybody does."

Frost looked at him, a sudden suspicion forming in his mind. He tapped the letter. "You're not thinking of doing this?"

"Why not? I haven't forgotten… and anyway, who gives a damn about this convict Weisberg? Why shouldn't I turn him loose?"

"That's ridiculous," Frost said. "You can't afford—"

"I know." The governor lifted his hand wearily. "Precedent; Position. I mustn't forget my position. Well, to hell with all that. This is a matter of life or death. If Weisberg isn't released they'll kill Giles."

"They probably will," Frost said. "But that's a risk he takes. I take it. You take it. We all take it."

Cavanaugh shook his leonine head belligerently. "If you think I'm going to let this man die because of a silly conception of honor, or because I'm afraid of what the public will think, you're a—damn' fool," he said doggedly. "All that matters is getting Giles back again. He has risked his life too many times in my behalf for me to hold back now."

"He wouldn't want to come back that way," Frost said, so sharply the governor glared across the desk at him.

"No? Well, that's the way he's coming back—and you'll be the one to pick him up. You go back to the Border and stand by for orders from me"

His lips were pressed tightly together, his eyes were narrowed and his whole face was determined. His mind was made up and nothing could change it. Come hell or high water or impeachment, he was going to see this through.

Frost realized it was useless to argue further.

"All right," he said, getting up. "But this is probably the worst mistake you've ever made."

"I wish all my mistakes were as profitable," the governor said. "This one is going to save a man's life."

WHEN FROST EMERGED from the capitol building and started down the long, wide steps, the street lights were on and before him electric signs glimmered brightly. You had a swell view of Austin from the capitol steps. Frost walked down the steps, slowly. The legislature was in late session, which accounted for all the taxis parked at the curb. Frost paid no attention to the cries of the chauffeurs, preferring to walk.

"The governor is getting himself into a spot," he thought, "a hell of a spot. He can pardon Weisberg, but he'll never get away with it. Sooner or later it will come out. Yes, and then disgrace will come. Cavanaugh can never stand disgrace. It will kill him as surely as a shot through the heart. Honor, to him, is everything. Yet he is determined to go through with this. I've got to stop him. But how?"

The shrill cry of a newsboy hammered suddenly in his ear: "*Statesman! Statesman!* Giles Still Missing!" Frost nodded. There was how.

WALTER HORNBEAK, SENIOR correspondent at the state capitol of a half dozen newspapers, looked shrewdly at Frost from under bushy eyebrows. He had been a long time in the business; twenty years a reporter.

"Now that the applesauce has been concluded," he said, "just what in the hell is the big idea of calling me over here?"

"Don't be so suspicious. Sit down," Frost said. "Maybe I just want to visit with you a while."

"Nerts," Hornbeak said. "You been here plenty of times before and you never visited with me."

"Stop squawking. Sit down."

Hornbeak sniffed, but sat down. "Of course," he said airily, "I am greatly flattered that you called me here because you are a great man and you are a pal of the governor's, but just the same I'd like to know what the hell you got on your mind, because I got a story to file."

"I'll give you a story to file," Frost said. "I'll give you a story that'll knock your ear off."

"Yeah?" Hornbeak was a little more conciliatory now, but he didn't want to seem too anxious. "Well, it's been so long since I had one I probably wouldn't know what to do with it. These farmers in the legislature—"

"You'll get this one exclusive," Frost said. "But I invoke the rules—you'll have to protect me on it."

"I never divulge a news source," Hornbeak said solemnly, trying to appear a little injured. "I'll lose my job first."

"You'll probably lose it about this story," Frost said. "There'll be plenty of hell raised. The governor'll hit the roof and he'll put the pressure on you—"

"Wait a minute," Hornbeak said, dignified. "Is this story true? Will it stand up?"

"Absolutely. My word."

"To hell with the trimmings," Hornbeak said. "That's all that matters. It's true. What is it?"

"We've found Giles."

"Dead—or alive?" he asked, trying to make his voice sound casual.

"Alive—so far as we know. He's been captured."

"Snatched? You mean he's been snatched?" He couldn't keep the excitement out of that one.

"Yes—and they are holding him for ransom."

"They? Who is 'they'?"

"Remember Weisberg? One of the Black Ship Gang?"

"I remember him. He's doing fifty years in Huntsville."

"Right. They grabbed Giles to effect the release of Weisberg—" And Frost explained about the rush trip he had made to Austin at the bidding of the governor and of the letter he had received from the men who held Giles.

"Where's the letter?" Hornbeak asked.

"It's on Cavanaugh's desk," Frost said. "But I can tell you substantially what it said—" And he did, Hornbeak writing rapidly on a wad of folded copy paper.

"Holy hell!" the reporter exclaimed. "That is a story! A gang of crooks negotiating with the governor for the release of their leader. Holy hell! That is a story!"

"I thought you'd go for it," Frost said. "But leave me completely out of it—remember that."

"Trust me," Hornbeak said, twisting around in his chair to pick up his cap. He was no longer indifferent. He got up, his eyes dancing. "I'll protect you." He took a couple of steps towards the door, then turned and said:

"Why are *you* giving this out? Why not the governor?"

Frost shrugged.

"You get the story, don't you?"

"Sure. But look. Printing this is liable to mean Giles' death, isn't it?"

"Maybe. *Honor virtutis praemium.*"

"What?"

"Nothing," Frost said.

Hornbeak looked at him blankly for a second, then shrugged and went out with the story. In a few minutes teletype machines would be clicking in a thousand newspaper offices and tomorrow that story would be on a thousand front pages. The eyes of the state would be on the governor....

Frost smiled, satisfied with himself, and looked at his watch. Six-fifteen. Dinner would take forty-five minutes. He'd have to shake a leg to get back to the Border before midnight.

HORNBEAK WANTED THE story for himself, but it was much too big for that. He might as well have tried to keep an earthquake exclusive. All the news agencies grabbed it, and where it didn't go through as a flash it went as a bulletin. It was a red-hot piece of news.

Around eleven o'clock that night the telephones in the executive mansion at Austin started ringing, and reporters descended on the governor. Big Jim Cavanaugh had never been hard to see and had never refused a statement. The press was taking advantage of this now.

"What's your answer?" they demanded to know.

For a long and awkward instant, in which he thought of many things, the governor was silent. Then he said:

"The sovereign State of Texas does not bargain with criminals...."

Which was exactly what Frost knew he would say—if it was put to him that way.

TOMA TOSCA OWNED a small filling station at the north end of the Border Patrol flying field, on the state highway. He was a cadaverous, almost ageless Mexican with a deep respect for the flying Rangers, even if they did, once in a while, play hob with the roof of his shack by bouncing their wheels off the shingles.

On this morning—the fifth morning of Giles' disappearance—he came to patrol headquarters, highly excited. He was so excited he had difficulty in talking. After a couple of futile efforts to get the words out, he pulled something from under his coat and handed it to Frost.

"Look," he managed to say.

It was a flyer's helmet. It was Giles' helmet. There was his name, boldly printed on the inside of the crown.

Frost was so startled that for a moment his head swam. He grabbed Tosca by the shoulder. "Where'd you get this?"

Slowly, in agonized tones, Toma Tosca related the story. His brother, Munoz, wanted by the police of San Antone, was in hiding there at the home of a woman, a widow with a nine- or ten-year-old son. This boy, digging around the backyards of the neighborhood, had found the helmet half-buried in a trash box. The G-I-L-E-S printed on the inside of the helmet meant nothing to him, so innocently enough he took it home. To Munoz, who read the papers, that name meant plenty, but for obvious reasons he couldn't go to the police. He realized something should be done about it pronto, but what? Then he remembered his brother, Toma, knew all Hell's Stepsons, so he had driven all night to bring him the helmet.

"Where is Munoz now?" Frost asked.

"At gasoline pump," Toma replied.

"Let's go see him."

They started across the patio. Behind them a screen door slammed and Skipper Hinsdell overtook them. His eyes were bloodshot from worry and lack of sleep.

"The governor's on the phone, Jerry—sore as hell."

Frost stopped.

"How many times do I have to give an order around here?" he demanded irritably. "I told you every time he called I was in the air."

Hinsdell bit his lip and his eyes flashed. His nerves were jagged, too, and that sharp tone dragged across them like a rasp. For just an instant trouble threatened; the Skipper had a blazing retort on the end of his tongue, but he bit it off.

"It's the third time this morning," he said quietly. "If I were you—"

"Lissen, Skip," Frost said, a little desperately. "I can't talk to him because he'll fire me. He'll fire me because I gave the newspapers that story. I don't want to be fired yet, because I've got things to do. Now, for ——'s sake, will you cover me up?"

"Sure, Jerry. I didn't understand...."

"Come on, Toma," Frost said.

They went hurriedly across the flying field to the filling station.

Munoz Tosca was a slightly overdressed young man and wore a thin strip of a mustachio in the swaggering fashion of a Chihuahua barber-shop dandy. He was nervous at the sight of Frost, and was reluctant to talk for fear of involving himself.

Anger clouded Toma's face and he spoke rapidly in native dialect. "You are a fool, Munoz! This man is our friend!"

Munoz was unimpressed; the look of doubt remained on his face. "Perhaps he will surrender me to the police!"

"Ah! He is the police! But he wants only to find Giles!"

"How can I be sure?"

"Ah!" Toma raised his skinny arms in a storm of fury, maddened by the obstinacy of his younger brother.

"Have no fear, Munoz," Frost said, speaking the same dialect.

Both Mexicans looked at him, greatly surprised. "I will not surrender you to the police. I will help you with them."

Munoz had a long moment of indecision, staring into Frost's face. Frost smiled slowly. Munoz smiled slowly.

"*Bueno,*" he said.

He was perfectly willing to answer the questions, but he didn't know the answers. No, he had no idea where the helmet was found. José, the son, might remember.... No, he didn't know the address of the house in question. No, he had said nothing about this to anybody.

"That's something," Frost muttered grimly. "Look here," he went on, speaking in the dialect again, "you'll have to go back to San Antone with me—"

"The police—" Munoz whined.

"I'll go with you to the chief—"

"They will put me in prison—"

Frost's teeth clicked as his jaws came together. He wasn't going to waste any more time in conversation.

"If they don't, I will," he snapped.

Toma Tosca drew himself up to his thin six-feet-two and murmured something about pride and ideals, reminding his brother that the Toscas were directly descended from the ill-starred Montezuma.

These words had a magic effect on Munoz. His apprehension instantly vanished. His shoulders straightened and his lips went into a thin, determined curve.

Having been associated with Latin temperament for years, Frost knew no further persuasion was necessary.

"Let's go to San Antone," he said.

THOMAS RYAN, THE chief of police, was a huge man, over six feet and weighing about two hundred and twenty pounds, with grizzled gray hair and a grizzled gray mustache. There was a long L-shaped scar on the right side of his face, inscribed by a Mexican sadist, and the ring finger of his left hand had been shot away by a blackamoor murderer. Ryan was probably the best chief of police in the State of Texas.

He lowered his eyes from the card that contained the police record of Munoz Tosca. He looked slightly disappointed.

"From what you told me over the telephone," he said to Frost, "I imagined this guy must have killed seven or eight people. He's wanted because he hasn't paid money to his ex-wife."

"He only told me he was hiding from the police," Frost said. "I didn't ask him why."

"Unless"—Ryan leveled his eyes ferociously on Munoz— "you've been up to some other monkey business."

"No, no," Munoz replied nervously. "I been up to no monkey business. I help Capitan Frost."

"You better help him," Ryan said sternly.

"*Si, si,* I help."

"Thanks, chief," Frost said, getting up to go.

The chief spat in disgust.

"You're welcome to him," he said, scowling. "But a lily like that'd never be much good if the going got rough. You better take some of my men."

"This is probably another false alarm," Frost said, shrugging. "Giles may not be within a hundred miles of here."

"And then again he might be," Ryan said. He glanced suspiciously at Frost. "You figuring on doing this job alone?"

Munoz sank back. Frost lit a cigarette without answering. Ryan construed the silence to mean what he wanted it to mean.

"I don't like for the Rangers to come in here and pull stuff like that," he went on in a quarrelsome tone, wagging his head from side to side. "It gives the newspapers the idea my own boys can't handle the situation; it makes me look bad personally." He scowled. "I don't like that. I have to live here. Maybe Giles is stashed away in town somewhere and maybe you will find him. I hope you do. But I wanna be in on the pinch and don't you forget it. If I ain't—"

The chief's voice was a coarse bass; it filled the room, and the pictures on the wall vibrated; his whisper could be heard across the corridor.

Frost saw his eyes narrow and sensed his antagonism.

"I've got to find him first," he said, motioning to Munoz, who got up and followed him out.

MUNOZ'S WOMAN, DINAR, was a big, handsome, flashy Mexican woman, thirty-one or -two, with big shoulders and breasts and slender legs which she displayed prominently. She looked like a Riviera peasant brought up to date; her face was sharply aquiline, her smile was warm and likable, and she was very striking in a dark, bold, predatory way. She had had a few temporary marriages; the result of one of these was José, ten years old, the boy who had found the helmet.

Frost asked him if he remembered where he had found it.

"Sure, I remember," he said, leading him to the front window and pointing to a disreputable one-story house diagonally across the street. Frost saw the number was 930. "I found it in the trash box back of that house."

Frost looked at the house a moment, then turned back into the room.

"Know anything about the people in that house?" he asked the woman.

"I know nothing," she said, ill at ease, a little frightened.

"Ever see anybody go in or come out?"

She said "No," in a slightly apologetic tone.

Frost looked at José.

"I've never seen anybody around there either," José said.

"Is there a garage? Ever see an automobile?"

"There's a garage," Munoz said.

"Did you ever see a car there?" Frost asked José.

José said "No."

"I think nobody lives there," the woman, Dinar, exclaimed.

"What else was in the trash box?" Frost asked José.

José didn't understand.

"Any cans? The kind food comes in?"

José smiled.

"Sure—lotsa those."

"Somebody lives there, all right," Frost said, walking back to the window.

The house didn't look lived in; there was no sign or indication of life. This was strange, he thought; the newspapers had printed the story and by now the snatchers should have realized their plans had failed. Why; then, if they were there, weren't they getting out?... A sudden pang of horror struck him. What if they had already gone, leaving Giles....

He shuddered. There was no time to lose. He just had to get into that house.

He called Munoz to one side. "Don't say anything to

anybody," he said in dialect. "And keep that boy inside the house. Don't let him out; He might talk."

"He will not talk if his mother tells him not to," Munoz said.

"I can't take chances now," Frost said. "Keep him inside. I'll see you later," he said, nodding to the woman as he went out.

KELSEY, THE SUPERINTENDENT of the power and light company, said: "I've been reading about it and I think it's a damn' shame. We'll do anything we can to help, Captain."

"You can help me get into that house without arousing suspicion," Frost said, "which is the only safe thing to do—if Giles is still there. It occurred to me I might go in as a meter reader."

Kelsey pursed up his lips. "That's a good idea," he said, "but whether it works or not depends on when our man was there last. Just a minute." He picked up a telephone and asked for the service department. "Hello. Kelsey. When was the last meter reading at 930 South Mendoza Street?... Thanks," he said, hanging up.

"That meter hasn't been read in three weeks," he told Frost. "It's supposed to be read only once a month, but I think you can get away with it."

Frost nodded vehemently.

"I can get away with it if you'll be kind enough to give me some paraphernalia and show me how to act," he said.

Kelsey thought that was very funny. He laughed boisterously. "Just what I was going to suggest," he said. "Come on with me to the service department; we'll teach you in a jiffy. Hey, that's not a bad idea—then if business gets bad on the Border, you'll have a trade to fall back on."

He laughed again. Frost went out behind him.

It was then twenty minutes until eleven o'clock.

At noon, that same day, Jerry Frost turned off Southern Avenue on to Mendoza Street in the nine hundred block. Now he wore the neat uniform of a service department employe of the power and light company: dark green whipcord riding pants, dark green shirt and cap, and black leather puttees. Under his right arm he carried a small ledger; the accounts of one man's district. Under his left arm, inside his shirt, he carried a .38 automatic, slung in a leather holster.

Number 930 Mendoza Street had no front fence and very little front yard. A portion of the curbing had been chopped down to make a crude automobile entrance; the driveway, unpaved, ran alongside the house. Frost walked down it towards a frame garage with the doors closed. It may or may not have contained an automobile.

Frost paused before a rear porch, screened in. The screening was rusty; old age had worn holes in it. The screen door was not locked. Frost pushed it open and stepped on the porch. The light meter was inside the kitchen, to the right of the rear door as you entered. The regular meter reader had rehearsed him....

Frost crossed the porch.

At the kitchen door he paused momentarily and listened, his ear close to the crack. There was no sound from the inside. Frost opened his ledger, riffling the pages until he came to the account for 930 Mendoza Street. He raised his hand to rap on the door, thought of something, checked himself. He quickly unbuttoned two buttons of his shirt, draping his tie to hide the bare skin. He might need his pistol....

He rapped sharply on the door and the sound rolled across the porch, astonishingly loud. All the neighbors must have heard it. He listened for an answering noise within; there was none. Faintly, far in the distance, a train whistle sounded, a passenger train, because the tone of the whistle was soft and mellifluous. Frost irrelevantly wondered if that train went to New York, thinking if it did he'd like to be on it....

He rapped on the door again, harder than before. Now there were sounds within the house, somebody was moving slowly towards the door. His pulse quickened. The sounds were distinct now, and he could make them out: the firm tread of a man. Frost heard him pause at the door, and in a moment the man spoke in a muffled tone.

"Yes?"

"Light man," Frost said, trying to imitate the regular reader's voice, as he remembered it.

"Whaddya want?"

"I want to read the meter. Open up," Frost said, his confidence returning with every syllable.

There was a moment's hesitation, and then something, a bar, thumped against the wood as the man dragged it back. The door swung open slowly, like a door in a mystery play, the man remaining concealed behind it. Frost stepped across the threshold into the kitchen, and for the first time saw his host. He was a smallish man, stout and squat and somewhat Mexican in appearance.

He closed the door and barred it again, with a four-by-four slipped through two iron supports. Frost acted as if he did not see this, his eyes rapidly covering the wall in search of the meter. He discovered it, strangely enough, exactly where they had said he would; to the right of the door.

He walked across the floor and picked up a chair to stand on while he made the reading.

"Who's that?" a hoarse voice called from somewhere towards the front of the house.

"Shut up!" the small, squat man said, glancing at Frost and hurrying out of the room.

Frost paused, breathless, and in a second heard them talking in stage whispers:

"It's only the light man!"

"Hell! Why'd you let him in?"

"Yeah—that would have fixed it!"

Frost was trying to place the voices. He hadn't time to investigate, he heard footsteps and he placed the chair against the wall and climbed up, looking carefully at the meter with a flash-lamp.

"Where's Mrs. Amato?" Frost asked. Mrs. Amato lived here. The light bill was in her name.

"She's gone away," the short man replied uncivilly.

Frost darted a swift glance at him.

"You must be the cousin she was always talking about."

"Yeah," the short man said, wetting his lips, "I'm the cousin, all right."

The telephone exploded suddenly from a room in the front; and the short man glided away, making not a sound now, walking on the balls of his feet.

"That's a good break," Frost thought, getting down off the chair and tiptoeing across the floor to the door the short man had gone through. Ahead there was a narrow, dark hallway.

Frost pressed himself against the wall, remembering that the acoustic qualities of walls sometimes are astonishing.

He heard the receiver click and recognized the short man's voice saying: "Yeah…" but then the voice dropped a full octave and Frost could hear only a hum of words, none of them distinguishable.

HE TIPTOED BACK across the floor to the meter, in a hurry to finish and get out of the house so he could summon help. Whether or not Giles was here, the plant seemed a phoney. These guys weren't natural.

He climbed on the chair as he heard the short man coming back, not so noiseless now, and then, when he was sure the short man had seen him on the chair, he got down and stood, making a few entries in his ledger.

When he turned to go, he saw the short, squat man was leaning inside the kitchen, against the door, his legs crossed. His attitude was very careless and indifferent. He held in his right hand a short-barreled pistol, which was pointed directly at Frost's chest.

"What's this all about?" asked Frost.

"Sit down," the short, squat man said softly.

"Say—"

"Sit down," he repeated; "and clasp your hands together over the top of that table!"

Frost sat down.

Another man came in then, a little bigger, a little older, better dressed, talking as he entered: "Who was that on the phone—" He saw Frost and stopped. "What's going on?" he demanded.

The short, squat man leered.

"This guy's a phoney—" the bigger man's face darkened immediately "—Eddie phoned that he tailed this bird. He saw him get out of a cab two blocks away. What we gonna do 'bout him?"

"Yeah?" the bigger man said. "A copper, huh?" He slanted his head from side to side, looking at Frost. "You got a lot of guts to bust in here," he said in an unpleasant tone.

"I don't know what you're talking about," Frost said.

"Yeah?"

The bigger man started forward; and Frost realized it was now or never. These men were desperate.

He whirled the table over quickly, sliding behind it, fumbling with his right hand for his gun. The short, squat man's pistol went off and Frost heard the bullet pass through the table an inch above his head, with a snap like the breaking of a stick of chalk.

He yanked his gun loose and poked it out before him, squeezing the trigger at the big man, who had been too astounded by what had happened to stop coming forward.

It spit fire like a flame-thrower. So close was the big man that the flame seemed actually to touch him. The big man grabbed his stomach and sank to the floor, looking like a broken, discarded Christmas toy.

With him down, Frost realized the line of fire was open again; and as he twisted he got a glimpse of the short, squat man, who had moved a few feet closer to the hall, patiently biding his time until he had a target. Now he had a good one and he cracked down. A perfect hail of lead broke through the table, spraying Frost with splinters.

Frost peeped around the table; saw a sudden jet of fire and tried to duck.

He had no luck. A bullet drilled through his shoulder muscles and almost knocked him down.

"Ugh!" he grunted, raising up and firing.

But the short, squat man had had enough of that. He had jumped through the door into the hall.

Frost shoved himself up from the floor with the muzzle of his gun. The room was suddenly deathly quiet; and then, just as suddenly, there were noises.

The big man was flat on his back now, his life fading swiftly. He was clawing desperately at the stings in his stomach, and he was making deep animal noises in his throat.

Frost stepped across him and proceeded to the hall door. As he started to turn in, he heard footsteps nearby, running up wooden steps. In a moment a door opened in the hall as a third man came up from the basement. Frost eased his arm into the clear.

"Put your hands up!" he yelled.

The third man whipped up a gun and fired; and Frost flicked his head without changing his base and let him have it. The man pitched backwards, his body rolling down the steps.

Frost pulled his head back to safety and was aware that his shoulder was hurting him terrifically. How many men the house contained, he didn't know: but he did know he would have to fight his way out.

He dared not step into the hall; ahead it was black and dim and somewhere was the short, squat man waiting for him to show himself. He reached out with his foot and hooked it under the rung of a kitchen chair, dragging it to him. He managed to lift it and toss it into the hall. It fell with a clatter.

Immediately there was a shot. The short, squat man had fired at the sound. That was what Frost had expected; so he leaned forward, himself presenting a superb target, in an effort to pick out the figure in the gloom of the hall. He shot at something… and felt that he had missed.

"Come out of there!" he yelled.

The short, squat man shouted an obscene answer to that.

Frost started to step forward when a strong acrid odor reached his nostrils, different from the smell of gunpowder. It rooted him to the spot, terrified him before he knew what it was; his animal instinct had responded to the menace of something yet undetermined.

It was a fire.

Frost sniffed. From the hall. He eased his head around now. He could see the ruddy glow through the door that was open to the cellar, could see the flames in the corner of the steps. His heart thumped heavily. The house was afire from below.

Boom! Boom! Boom!

Frost listened.

It wasn't a loud sound, but it was hollow.

Boom! Boom! Boom!

Something was happening down there in the cellar. Pain stabbed him in the shoulder all over again. He stepped into the hall, to the open door.

The cellar was an inferno. The man he had shot and knocked down the steps was not dead. Mortally wounded, he had dragged himself to a pile of papers and boards that evidently had been prepared for this very emergency, and lighted it. Or perhaps he had lighted it when he heard the shooting. Mixed with the smoke was the smell of kerosene.

Boom! Boom! Boom!

That noise again. Frost looked left and fell back, gasping with horror. Eddie Giles, bound hand and foot and gagged, had inched himself into a corner and was making those noises by beating the back of his head against a thick wooden bin. It was the only way he could attract attention.

Frost smothered a cry and bounded down the steps into that furnace. He shoved his pistol into his pocket and ducked his head to keep from striking the beams.

With his right hand he caught the ropes around Giles' feet and dragged him away from the flames; and then knocked the gag from his mouth in a single motion. Giles was making faces, trying to talk.

Frost fumbled with the ropes that bound his wrists, but they were too secure.

"Shoot 'em off!" Giles managed to say.

Frost yanked out his pistol and blasted the ropes. Giles rolled his arms in front of him. "I'm okey! Beat it!" he said in a ragged voice.

He reached out for the ropes that bound his ankles, but his fingers, cramped from a long, unnatural position, were useless. He could only move them feebly....

He turned over on his stomach, dragging himself across the floor like a legless man. It was becoming terrifically hot. Frost smelled human hair burning. He quickly bent over the ropes around Giles' ankles and tried to untie them. Despairing of ever doing this, he took Giles by the arm and dragged him to the temporary safety of the steps. Then he smelled that human hair burning again; and looked around.

It was the third man, the mortally wounded one, near the flames. A tongue of fire reached out every second or so and touched his hair, almost playfully. The man was dying; he couldn't move his arms or legs; but his brain was clear and alert and he knew what was happening. His mouth kept opening and closing like a fish's, saying nothing; but his eyes were eloquent, pleading that he be permitted to die in a manner befitting a human being.

Frost staggered back to get him. Above the roar of the flames and the pounding inside his skull, he could dimly hear pistol shots and shouts and footsteps banging on the kitchen floor. That would mean the finish of the short, squat man. Frost had wondered about him; but he had been too busy to do more than wonder.

Then a mighty voice bellowed: "Where the hell are you, Frost?" Frost reached for the wounded man's foot, to get him back a little for a better hold.

Suddenly a figure popped into the doorway at the head of the steps, a giant figure in a blue uniform and a grizzled gray mustache. It was Thomas Ryan, the bulldog, the hardboiled, and he came down the steps three at a time, bellowing profanity at the top of his lungs.

Frost heard and saw all this dimly. He reached over to pick up the wounded man; but swayed dizzily on his feet and slowly started to crumple.

The big arms of Thomas Ryan encircled him.

IT WAS LATE afternoon. Blue dusk lay on the window-sill of Thomas Ryan's office like a sifting of ash. A swift twilight of dust and fire: gray on earth and flame in the sky.

Jerry Frost, bathed, bandaged and interviewed, and not much the worse for any of these, turned in his chair, wincing slightly from the pain in his shoulder.

"Tell the Chief about the helmet, Eddie," he said.

"There isn't much to tell," Eddie Giles said. "The second day I was in the cellar I shoved my helmet into a box of garbage, praying it would be dumped out and somebody would find it."

Ryan nodded.

"How the hell did they get you in the first place?" he asked.

"Well," Giles answered, with a slow, apologetic smile, "I'd been in the habit of flying straight into the sun for an hour or so, and when I got hungry I'd drop down at a place I'd found for a Mex breakfast. On this side the river, of course. That morning there was company. They brought me up here in a car, at night. I didn't know where I was."

"Yeah," said Ryan. " 'Bout what you'd expect from those señoritas. On this side they're apt to be tied up with some gang or other."

Giles grinned. He didn't say anything.

"I hope this cures you of flying around at sunrise," Frost said.

"It does," said Giles, "until tomorrow morning. And then I think I'll head west."

Ryan laughed. The door opened and his uniformed secretary entered with a newspaper which he handed him.

"That's the final," he said.

Ryan picked it up. Frost and Giles saw the front page over his shoulder: *Kidnaped Ranger Rescued from Burning House by Local Police,* and beneath that there were sub-headings which said that Captain Jerry Frost, wounded in the gun-battle which claimed two lives, declared to reporters that Chief Thomas Ryan was solely responsible for the rescue of the kidnaped Ranger....

From somewhere in the dimness outside came the clang of a heavily loaded street car, carrying peaceful people to their homes....

Hardboiled Thomas Ryan looked at Frost, visibly moved by what he had read. He opened his mouth to say something.

"Forget it," Frost interposed. "You have to live here…."

The secretary entered again.

"You're wanted on the wire, Captain," he announced.

"Take it here," Ryan said, shoving a telephone across the desk.

"I don't want to talk to anybody. Did they say who it was?"

"I think it's the governor," the secretary said.

"Oh—" Frost exclaimed, reaching for the phone.

Somebody Must Die

Jerry Frost, flying Ranger, turns
stunt man to trap a crime leader

FORMALLY BOWING, ORTEGA, the Federal agent, handed his credentials to Frost, commander of the Border Patrol, standing stiffly, waiting for them to be inspected. But Frost merely glanced at the papers before handing them back; Jesus Ortega, the celebrated man-catcher, needed no identification anywhere in the Rio Grande country.

"The Adjutant-General phoned you were coming," Frost said, "but we expected you yesterday. Sit down."

Jesus Ortega bowed again and sat down. He was a slight figure of a man, thirty-odd years old, a little waxen in appearance.

"I wanted to get here yesterday," he said in precise, brittle English, "but I could not resist the temptation of San Antonio."

He lighted a slender black cigarro and inhaled deeply, holding the potent smoke in his lungs a long time, thinking of San Antonio, where the colors of the earth are rich and vivid, the air warm, the foliage lush, and life is slow and delightful, hoping he went there when he died.... Then he rolled the smoke from his lungs, turning his sharp, black eyes on Frost.

"I suppose the Adjutant-General told you why I am here?"

"Not exactly," said Frost. "He only ordered me to take a leave of absence, saying that you would explain when you got here. From that I presumed it was something important."

"Important, yes," said Jesus Ortega, sighing and looking a little pained, hating to stop thinking about San Antonio. "Very important. A vicious smuggling ring."

Jerry Frost frowned, remembering in his career with the Border Patrol there had been only one instance of organized smuggling, the Black Ship gang, which had been shattered after a long and bitter fight.

"The government is helpless," Ortega said, leaning forward in the chair. "*Capitan,*" he went on gravely, "you are the only man down here who can handle this, who can get on the inside of things with the opportunity presented us to reach the men we suspect. Our men can go no further."

Frost did not say anything. He did not feel flattered. He only felt weary.

"A perfect flood of narcotics is reaching the Middle West and East," Ortega said. "The source is in Mexico, somewhere in Chihuahua. I think we have located the distributing point in Texas at Salada."

Frost looked puzzled. "Then why can't you arrest these men yourself?" he asked.

"We don't know exactly who they are," Ortega replied, "and we want the leader. We can't risk scaring him off by using one of our own men and we must have a flyer."

Frost spread his hand, looking at the palm. Then he turned it over, looking at the fingers. The fingers were long and slender and very strong. "Why a flyer?" he finally asked.

"I'll tell you. The day after tomorrow Salada is opening a new municipal flying field with a big celebration. They are expecting a stunt flyer from the East by the name of Frank Curtis. Only Frank Curtis will not be there; we have secretly put him in jail in Pittsburgh. You will take his place." Ortega smiled genially. "Isn't that fine?"

"Yes, that's fine," Frost said slowly. "But have you thought of

what would happen to your plan if somebody at Salada knew I was not this Frank Curtis?"

"As nearly as we can determine nobody there knows him," Ortega said. "The Chamber of Commerce hired him by telegraph. Of course," he went on, divining Frost's thoughts, "even here, sitting like this—"

"I've heard that speech before, Mr. Ortega," Frost cut in. "Even here, sitting like this, one of us might die. But that's not a very cheerful thought, is it?"

He turned away to the window. Jesus Ortega watched him for a moment, then fumbled in his pocket, saying, "We have here Curtis' license and some clippings—" He took out a wallet and laid on the table a Department of Commerce pilot's license and a dozen newspaper clippings. Frost turned, picking up the license. It was made out to Frank Curtis, but with the corner bare of an identifying picture. All it needed to make it official was a passport snap of Frost.

"Study these," Ortega said, tapping the clippings, "and you will know Curtis as well as he knows himself. Tomorrow morning a regular transport plane will be delivered, an exact duplicate of his, including the same international number."

"You've thought of everything but the disguise," Frost said, half to himself.

"I beg your pardon?" Ortega said politely.

"Nothing," said Frost. "Nothing."

"You had better take another man, a mechanic," Ortega continued. "You may need him."

"From the looks of this set-up," Frost said, putting the clippings in his pocket, "I'll need the army and the navy."

Jesus Ortega shrugged, lighting another black cigarro from the butt of the first. His mission concluded, he seemed almost jovial. After all, it is distressing to ask a man to live with death, if only for a little while....

"Mr. Perry and I will leave for Salada tomorrow," Frost said.

For just an instant legitimate fear for the man he had maneuvered into this, flickered in Jesus Ortega's dark, aquiline face, then he thumped the wooden table in the customary petition for good luck.

Frost said nothing, thumping the table too.

NIGHT ON THE Rio Grande. Supper was over and Hell's Stepsons, guardians of a thousand miles of Border, sat on the sleeping porch in the darkness. Swift clouds flowed over the moon, sinking the country into changing moods of gloom. The twin radio towers, tall and grotesque, with red warning lights on top, looked like something out of a surgeon's nightmare. The hangar lay in the field, a humpbacked island of black.

Hans Traub, the ex-Bavarian ace, second in command, shifted in his seat, the chair groaning beneath his bulk. "I think he's got a—dam' nerve," he said, referring to Jesus Ortega.

"If he's as good as he thinks he is, why doesn't he go to Salada himself?" Eddie Giles asked loudly.

Skipper Hinsdell threw away his cigarette and walked into the circle of the conversation. "You guys have been arguing about that for an hour," he said. "Why don't you shut up?"

"You're—dam' right they can't risk sending one of their own men," Traub went on, paying no attention to Hinsdell. "But they sure as hell don't mind asking us to commit suicide!"

"Yeah," said Giles. "Why don't they do their own dirty work?"

"Don't you think if there's any complaining to be done Perry and I ought to do it?..." Frost asked mildly.

"All right, it's your funeral," Traub muttered. "It's a—dam' good thing he didn't ask me to go."

Frost knew that was exactly why they were grumbling, because they themselves hadn't been asked to go. In time of stress each man's concern was for the other....

Perry walked over to the radio, turned it on. "We ought to pitch in and get a new radio," he said. "It takes this one too long to get hot."

"You won't need a radio where you're going," Hinsdell called out. "Leave the money with me and I'll buy one."

Music began to come through the radio. It was Guy Lombardo's orchestra from the Ambassador in Los Angeles. Carmen

Lombardo was singing in a plaintive voice: "...*to the far-away ranch of the boss in the sky-i-i-i-i....*"

Frost got up, scuffling his boots on the floor, walking off the porch into the night.

THE NEXT AFTERNOON they reached Salada.

"Opening an airport is no joke to these people," Frost said as they rode from the field to town in a cab. The main street was gaily decorated.

"It looks like November the eleventh," Perry said.

The cab stopped. "This is the Chamber of Commerce," the driver said, coming around to open the door. As Frost got out the driver looked at him curiously. "Aren't you Frank Curtis?" he asked.

"Yes," said Frost. "I'm Curtis."

"I figured you were," the driver said, fumbling for change for the dollar bill. Frost motioned for him to keep it. "Thanks," the driver said, grinning. "I'll be out to the field today to see you do your stuff."

Frost and Perry started inside the building.

"That's a bad omen," Perry said.

"What's a bad omen?"

"That driver knowing you—"

They were inside. It was a long, narrow room filled with men and smoke and conversation.

"Did you want to see somebody?" a voice piped. Frost looked down. *Information,* said the sign on the desk. A young girl sat behind it.

"Is this the Chamber of Commerce?" Frost asked, thinking he had come through the wrong door. The inside of this place looked like a broker's office.

"Yes, this is the Chamber of Commerce," said the girl with the piping voice. Then she saw they were in flying clothes and said, "You're Frank Curtis, the stunt flyer," and looked at Perry.

"He is," Perry said, frowning at another bad omen.

The young lady with the piping voice was awed. "Just—just a minute," she said, fluttering from behind the desk, walking down the aisle with short, nervous steps to a group of men inside a railing.

"I don't feel so good about all this," Perry said in a low tone.

Frost did not reply, watching the girl. She had reached the group of men and they had turned, looking at him and Perry. One of them, tall and skinny, wearing thin gold spectacles on his nose, detached himself from the group, walked towards them with his hands held in front of him like a bumper, followed by the girl.

"Well, well, hello, hello," he said. "Mr. Curtis?" He paused, rubbing his hands.

"I'm Curtis," Frost said.

"I'm Presnell, secretary of the Chamber," the skinny man said, shaking hands with both hands. Pinned on his lapel were four enamel buttons, forming a large rosette: the Rotary Club, the Kiwanis Club, the Lion's Club and another Frost did not recognize.

"This is Fred Vinson, my mechanic," Frost said.

"Hello, hello," Presnell said, pouncing on Perry, giving him the same two-handed welcome.

"We came as soon as we got your telegram," Frost said. "We'd have been here earlier but we ran into a storm over Indiana."

"That's quite all right, quite all right," Presnell said. "Better late than never. Ha-ha-ha-ha."

Another man had left the group in the rear, walking towards them. He was big and heavy-jowled, wore a double-breasted blue suit and carried a derby in his hand.

"Well, well, Ray," Presnell said, turning to him, "here's your stunt flyer. This is Mr. Curtis and Mr. Vinson. Mr. Raymond Gulick. Mr. Gulick," he explained, "donated the ground for our new airport."

"It was nothing," Gulick said, shaking hands with Frost and nodding to Perry. "Nothing at all. Been reading a lot about you, Curtis. Glad you're here."

"We're glad to be here," said Frost.

"Come on back and meet the boys," Presnell said.

"Not now," Frost said. "We'd better get some rest. I just wanted to let you know we were here."

"You have lunch with me," Gulick said, taking Frost by the elbow.

"Really, we can't," Frost said. "We've got a tough afternoon ahead of us."

Raymond Gulick moved closer. "Well, then," he said, dropping his voice, "how about a little snort." He looked down at his coat pocket, which bulged. "Fine stuff," he said.

"Very, very good stuff," Presnell said solemnly, behind his skinny hand.

"Thanks," Frost said, "but we'd better get to the hotel. We'll have only a couple of hours' rest as it is."

"Tonight, then," Gulick said. "There's a party at my place—"

"Couple of hours' rest?" said Presnell, lifting his thick sandy eyebrows. "The parade starts in an hour. You're in the second car, right behind the mayor and Mr. Gulick."

"I'm sorry," Frost said. "We're too tired." There was another obvious reason, too, for not wanting to ride in a parade.

"Well—" Presnell said, disappointed.

"But you will come to the party at my place tonight?" Gulick said.

"If nothing happens."

"That sounds almost like you expected something to happen," Gulick said, rubbing his nose vigorously.

"In this business you never know," Frost said.

"It's going to be an elegant party," Gulick said, still rubbing his nose.

EVENING CAME, AND Frost, for one—Perry, for another—was glad that his afternoon's stunts were safely over. The crate was a good one, but Frost would have liked to know it better before pulling the hair-raising tricks in the sky he was supposed to do—and did.

They thought of no good excuse to refuse Gulick's invitation, so after a wash-up and change they started out.

Gulick's place, the Plantation Inn, was five miles from town on the El Paso highway, directly opposite the new airport. Everybody who knew what a roadhouse was, knew the Plantation Inn. It was the class. The floor show, the cuisine and the refreshments were excellent.

Frost and Perry sat at a table in a corner, where they were discovered by Gulick.

"What's all this?" he said. "What's the big idea? You're supposed to sit at the mayor's table."

"We didn't bring dinner clothes—" Frost began.

"The hell with that," Gulick said. "Come on with me."

They followed him to a table near the orchestra shell, heaped high with flowers. An elderly man in a tuxedo and a good-looking girl sat behind the flowers. Gulick took the flyers around to them.

"Mr. Mayor," he said, "Curtis and Vinson. This is Mayor Grant and his daughter, Jane. Isn't she a darb?" he said, in the same tone, admiring her.

Jane Grant was obviously embarrassed, blushing. She was very pretty, very sunburned. The mayor bit his lip, looking annoyed.

"Sit down, sit down, they won't bite you," Gulick said, shoving Frost and Perry into the chairs. "You folks ought to know each other. I'll be back in a minute."

"Great fellow, Gulick," the mayor said. "Do you fly too?" he asked Perry.

"Isn't he?" Perry said. "Yes, I fly a little."

"I thought your stunts this afternoon were exciting," the girl said to Frost. "Don't you ever get frightened?"

"Often," Frost said.

"Are you a stunt flyer too?" the mayor asked Perry.

"I leave the acrobatics to him," Perry said.

"He's very good," the mayor said. "I was just saying," the mayor looked at Frost, "how much I enjoyed your performance this afternoon."

"Thanks," Frost said....

There was a commotion behind them in the orchestra shell. Gulick was standing beside the orchestra leader, his arms lifted for silence. The noise gradually died down, like a waterfall being turned off.

Gulick raised his hands, as if bestowing a benediction. "Lissen, everybody! I've got an announcement to make.

Tonight the Plantation Inn passes into history." There was a loud chorus of "ohs" and "ahs" and a few scattered "no's." Gulick held up his hands grinning. The guests quieted. "In honor of the opening of the new flying field, the Plantation Inn will be known from now on as the Club Airport." Applause. Gulick waited patiently for it to die. "You all know the mayor has honored us with his presence," he went on, "—well, so has Frank Curtis, the famous stunt flyer. Here he is, right down here at the mayor's table."

More applause. Shouts. Frost's face grew hot, his neck reddened. He was forced to take three or four bows. The orchestra leader came to his rescue, swinging into the "Carioca."

Jane Grant looked invitingly at Frost.

"Dance?" he said, finally.

"I'd love it," she murmured.

As they got up from the table, Gulick returned. Frost nodded, following the girl to the dance-floor where a mob was struggling.

"You're very modest," she said after a while.

"It's nothing," he said.

"Doesn't all this bore you?"

"All what?"

"People staring at you. This fame. This hero-worship."

"Sometimes," he said, smiling into her hair, smelling perfume. "Not right now though."

They danced on, bump, bump, bump, excuse me, excuse me, excuse me....

"How long will you stay here?"

"That depends. With Salada air-minded, a flying school ought to do well."

"Really?"

"Really."

"I'd like to learn to fly."

"I'd like to teach you."

"Will you?"

"Well," Frost said slowly, "you have to have a special permit. There's always a lot of red-tape, a lot of politics—"

"You'd be surprised at the things you can use a mayor for," she said.

AN HOUR LATER Gulick drifted back to the mayor's table and sat down beside Frost.

"There's an old friend of yours here," he said. Perry stopped talking to the mayor, listening. They were all listening. "One of your old girls from back East," Gulick went on. "I told her it was all right to come over."

"Why, certainly," Frost said. "Er—who is she?"

"You wait, you'll see," Gulick replied, wetting his lips.

Sweat popped out on Frost's forehead. He looked at Perry. Perry's hands were clasped together on top of the table, but as Frost looked at him, he unlaced his fingers and moved them automatically, unconsciously, towards the gun, under his armpit.

"Here she comes," Gulick announced.

It was Tanya, the dancer featured in Gulick's floor show, but instead of her exotic costume she wore a conventional evening gown. She approached them in a languorous, well-rehearsed glide.

Fear suddenly clutched Frost's throat. He had never seen the woman before in his life.

Perry shoved his chair back slightly, ready for anything.

Tanya nodded to Jane and to the mayor. She was a stunning woman, black-haired, black-eyed, voluptuous.

"Hello…" Frost said, getting up and extending his hand. "It's been a long time—"

"Hasn't it?" Tanya said.

"You remember Fred Vinson," Frost said, nodding at Perry. There was a tight pause.

"Of course. How are you?" Tanya said, sitting down.

"The last time I saw you was in Detroit," Frost said in a voice he did not quite recognize, "at the *Black Bat*."

"Three years ago, wasn't it?" Tanya asked levelly.

"Mayor," Gulick put in, "these lovebirds haven't seen each other in three years. Shall we get some air?"

"Why—yes—yes," the mayor said, getting up. "Excuse me—" He and Gulick walked away.

Jane Grant gave Frost a venomous look, turning to Perry. "Shall we dance?"

Perry frowned, looking at Frost, not wanting to leave him alone. It's all right, Frost said with his eyes. "Certainly," Perry said to the girl.

Tanya lighted a cigarette, still in character; but when Perry and the Grant girl had moved away, she turned her black eyes on Frost.

"Just what in hell is the big idea?" she asked coldly.

"What big idea?" asked Frost innocently.

"Nix, nix," Tanya said, out of character. "You're no more Frank Curtis than I am. Who are you?"

It was in this crisis that the true nature of Jerry Frost was revealed. A lesser man might have been inclined to panic, but to Frost the emergency presented a challenge to his energy and resourcefulness; and if he had anything it was a thorough knowledge of human nature and a vast confidence in himself. If there was any way in the world to get along with this woman, he knew, it was to tell the truth.

"I'm not Frank Curtis," he admitted quietly. "I needed some money badly and I took his name just to get the job. That's all there is to it. And I didn't gyp 'em. I gave 'em plenty of stunts. I hope," he said, getting a wistful note into his voice, "you won't give me away to Gulick."

"Oh, that's all right," Tanya said, a little touched by the plea, "forget it. I wouldn't give away a dog to that—"

Frost, feeling relieved, pretended not to have heard what she called him. "I saw your dance," he said, "and I think it's swell. You ought to be in Hollywood or New York or some place. Why waste it on these yokels?"

"I know it," she said. "I'm only hanging around here until my boy friend, Kelly, gets back. Then we're going away." She took a drag of her cigarette, looking very wise. "This is a lousy town," she said, facing towards the orchestra, and then looked at Frost warmly, sympathetically. "Lissen, mister, take a tip from an old lady and don't get mixed up with Gulick."

"I'm not," Frost said. "But why? What's the matter with him?"

"Never mind," she said, "you take my word for it."

"You must be wrong," Frost said mildly. "The way people cheered him at the flying field this afternoon—"

"A lot of damn' farmers," she said. "They see him on his good behavior. I work for him. You know why he brought me over to this table tonight?" she asked suddenly.

"At first I thought he knew I wasn't Curtis and brought you

over to unmask me."

"That's not the reason," she said. "He heard that I used to know Curtis and he was sore because you danced with the Grant girl. He's jealous as hell of her."

"Then he's a great actor," Frost said, "because he smiled friendly enough."

"That's the way a lot of people kill, too," Tanya said, finishing with the subject of Gulick.

And nothing Frost could say would lead her into further conversation about him. Once one of his questions was so pointed, so significant, that it brought a flicker into her eyes, an ominous flicker that caused his stomach to do a full Immelmann. He realized in that moment he was being too curious, too anxious, like a badly trained bird dog in the brush… and he hurriedly changed the subject, studying her. When she smiled his stomach quieted down, and through the darkness of his assignment came the gleam of Tanya for a consolation. She knew things….

WHEN FROST ENTERED the hangar, several days later, Perry got down from the cock-pit and went over to him.

"If you don't stick around here everybody's going to know this flying school is phoney," he said. "This is the fifth day we've been open and we haven't taken a pupil up yet. When one does come, you're missing."

"Who's been here?"

"Who do you suppose?" said Perry, grimacing. "That Grant girl. Already she's started asking me questions about you. Every day you promise to take her up and don't do it. After a while she'll get tired of that."

"It can't be helped," Frost said. "Something important always happens."

"And another thing," Perry said. "I hope you realize that with all the publicity we've been getting we're laying ourselves wide open. One of these days somebody'll come along who knows the real Frank Curtis—"

"We've got to risk it," Frost said doggedly. "You can't take a blind assignment like this and pull results out of a hat. But at last I think I've got something from Tanya."

"You've spent enough time with her," Perry said. "You ought to get something."

"I had to take it easy. I damn' near upset the apple cart the first night I was with her by trying to rush things."

"Go on," said Perry.

Frost led the way to their plane in the middle of the hangar.

"Tanya hates Gulick's guts," he said. "From what I gather, they were pretty thick until Jane Grant came along about six months ago, just out of college, and Gulick gave Tanya the air. Tanya is not the sort to take a thing like that without being vindictive. She hung around, waiting to get even. Then she met this lad, Kelly, and fell for him hard. Real love, she says."

"What does Kelly do?"

"I don't know exactly. He works for Gulick in some capacity or other. Right now he's away on a business trip. He was due back a week ago. Tanya says Gulick won't tell her where he went or when he will return. She's worried. She thinks something has happened to him."

"What?" Perry asked.

Frost shrugged. "She's pretty morbid about it. Doesn't think he will ever come back."

"More and more," Perry said, "it begins to look like Gulick is the man we're after."

"Sometimes it does and sometimes it doesn't," Frost said. "This is one case where the slightest mistake would be fatal. He's a pal of the mayor, he's got the Chamber of Commerce in his pocket, and since the donation of the flying field he's practically king of the community. But if he is the man we're after, Ortega was right. He's the cleverest egg we've ever run up against."

"I'm beginning to understand why Ortega couldn't handle this case himself," Perry said reflectively.

Frost looked at the plane. "This buggy ready to fly?"

"It's been ready. Why? Where're you going?"

"Mexico."

"Mexico?" Perry repeated, astonished.

"To Chivatito in Chihuahua," Frost told him. "To the Santa Rosa Inn to talk to a fellow named Nick Harmon."

"For ——'s sake, why?"

"I told you I wasn't wasting time with Tanya," he said. "I'm going to take a look at the Santa Rosa Inn."

"You don't mean you're going to take seriously anything that dipsomaniac said?" Perry's tone was incredulous.

"We're working against time," Frost said, "and nothing is too insignificant to follow up. Besides," he added seriously, "she isn't always tight. She has her lucid moments."

"By ——" Perry said, wagging his head, "I give up. I think you're just plain nuts."

"Maybe," said Frost, "but I'm going."

He started to climb up.

"Wait a minute," Perry said. "Give me the dope and I'll go down. Then you can stay here with Tanya—"

"Nope," Frost said, "I'm going."

"Well, then," Perry argued, "we'll both go."

"Nope," Frost said, "I'm going alone."

Perry shut up, knowing further talk was useless.

"And while I'm gone," Frost said, "you stay away from the second floor of the Club Airport."

The second floor was given over to gambling games and devices.

"I'm making money," Perry retorted. "I'm about fifty bucks ahead of the wheel...."

Frost, leaning forward to reach the ignition switch, paused and frowned down at him.

"Keep it and stay away," he said.

FROST LAID THE nose of his ship SW by W and drove laterally across the Rio Grande into Chihuahua. The country beneath was flat, barren, hot and uninteresting. Some thirty minutes later, in the vicinity of Los Medanos, he picked up the gleaming steel ribbons that were the National Mexican railroad, and swung left, directly above them, his course now almost due south. This is the country's finest railroad, traversing the length of the republic, being halted only by the Chiapas jungles on the Isthmus of Tehuantepec.

His landmark located, Frost settled comfortably in the cockpit. He was at 2000 feet, flying 110 miles an hour, boring steadily into the country, which, say the legends, still is haunted by the burly, mustachioed ghost of the immortal Villa. This, Chihuahua, was his homeland, from this provincial theater did he spring to the stage of the world.

Past Lucero the land lost its flatness; hillocks and mounds

rose from the earth, covered with sage and cactus, slowly broadening, slowly ascending, slowly rolling southward. It is the beginning of the Tarahumare Mountains, which in turn are graduated into the terrible Sierra Madre range, whose height seems fabulous.

Frost took off his helmet, his black hair tangling in the breeze, his blood singing in his veins. In that fantastic moment he suddenly knew why he was what he was, an adventurer. I am true to my dreams, he thought exultantly. Elsewhere there are thousands and thousands of little creatures, trapped in the little cañons of life, chained to their little desks, thinking their little thoughts... But I, I have wings! Wings to carry me even to the uttermost isles....

He looked back from the diaphanous mountains to the cockpit, to the instrument panel, stupidly, through half-lidded eyes, as a man waking in a strange room stares perplexedly at the wall.

Then, instantly, his mind was acutely clear. He studied his instruments, making rapid calculations. He must be nearly there. He looked out. The gleaming tracks curved away from the mountains, and he eased off on his rudder bar, still keeping the shadow of his wings spanning the roadbed....

Presently he saw just ahead a goodly-sized town, spread out in a wide, irregular square, the whiteness of its buildings accentuated by the dead brown of its background.

He pushed his stick forward, nosing over, thinking this ought to be it, Chivatito. He was down to five hundred feet now, passing the edge of the town, his eyes seeking the railway station for its identifying signboard. The wind whined past his face, and he could see excited citizens, looking up at his plane and gesticulating. Others scattered like peasants in a war-time movie, expecting a bombing raid. A brood of children ran panic-stricken across the road, one *muchacho* falling flat on his belly in the dirt. From somewhere a bare-legged woman darted, like a hawk, dragging the child to safety....

Frost smiled, raising his eyes. Opposite the plaza was a red roofed, official looking building. He swung wide, dropping to two hundred feet and slowing his speed. He saw it was the rail-way station, skidding in closer. Chivatito, the sign said. Elated, he put his nose up in a wide climbing turn. Now to locate the Santa Rosa Inn. His description was meager. Tanya had said it was a big hacienda on the edge of town with a flying field adjoining. A flying field meant airplanes. Airplanes meant a hangar.

He looked over from a thousand feet, trying to pick out a hangar. There was none. A layer of intense heat lay along the earth, boiling up mirages, shimmering his vision, but when he had adjusted his eyes he made out a windsock. That would do. This must be the Santa Rosa Inn, he thought.

He circled and came down, bumping to a stop. The field, none too big, was home made. Climbing out, he checked his immediate reactions as methodically as he checked his instrument panel. He was first impressed by the fact that this field, although in a remote community far off the conventional air lanes, was being regularly used. Then he saw why there was no hangar. Instead, a portion of the hacienda's patio had been roofed over, with space for two planes, although he saw none.

He started gingerly towards the building, his legs slightly cramped from the long trip. Two men came out of the house, walking a few feet to the knee high rock wall that surrounded the patio, where they slouched into waiting positions. They were Mexicans, of medium age, one slightly taller and heavier than the other, both dressed somewhat foppishly in store bought clothes. Frost had a feeling they had been watching him some time.

"Buenos dias," he said, pausing at the gate.

"Hello," said the smaller one sulkily, in English, moving towards his comrade a little, blocking the entrance to the patio. In spite of himself Frost was amused. He wanted to tell them they had no finesse.

"I'm looking for Nick Harmon," he said calmly. "This is the Santa Rosa Inn, isn't it?"

The Mexicans looked at each other a moment. "Yes," the spokesman admitted reluctantly. "Who are you?"

"I'm an old pal of Nick's from the States," Frost replied. "A very old pal. Is he here?"

"He's inside," the little Mexican said, jerking his head towards the hacienda, but keeping his eyes fixed on Frost, making no move to admit him to the patio.

"Okey," Frost said, starting in. He brushed on past them and they fell in behind. Out of the corners of his eyes he could see their feet in step with his, one pace behind.

He looked up to see the outline of a man in the doorway. That startled him momentarily; only a second ago there was nobody there. The man was broad and compact, with long arms. The bulk of him almost filled the doorway. A brown paper cigarette drooped from his mouth. His eyes were hazel. His face was expressionless. He was an American.

"Are you Nick Harmon?"

"Yeah," the man replied, like a ventriloquist, not moving a

muscle of his face. Not even an ash flake on his cigarette was disturbed.

"I'm Frank Curtis," Frost said, sticking out his hand. "Some of the boys around Detroit said I'd find you here."

Harmon shook hands perfunctorily.

"Yeah?" he said, taking the cigarette out of his mouth, dropping it to the ground without looking at it. "So you're Frank Curtis," he said.

"Yes," said Frost, watching him closely. "And you're Nick Harmon, the guy I did a six-months' stretch for! Well, well, well. It's a pleasure finally to meet you."

"Yeah?" Harmon said, the suggestion of a smile on his flaccid face.

"Hell! I hated to see the government grab that swell load I was carrying for you that night. It must have been worth five grand."

"Ten," Harmon corrected.

"What ever happened to that old bunch? Bring any of them with you?"

"They broke up," Harmon said. He jerked his head at the Mexicans, dismissing them. Frost could hear them moving away. He felt considerably relieved.

"That your bodyguard?"

"You might call 'em that."

"They don't look very hot," Frost said.

"The big one," Harmon said quietly, "escaped from Devil's Island. The little one was a knife thrower in vaudeville until he got drunk one night and made a slight miscalculation." He moved out of the doorway. "Come on inside," he said.

A WAITER IN a dirty white jacket brought them their third round of beers. They were sitting in Harmon's wide bedroom, one corner of which had been made into an office, containing a desk, a telephone, a swivel-chair and an old fashioned floor safe.

Nick Harmon took a final look at the pilot's license and handed it back to Frost.

"I guess you were glad to be reinstated," he said, sliding down in his chair, hitching the knees of his pants. He was almost affable now....

"Yes. You know, Nick," Frost said, "it's damn' funny that with all the business we've done together we never met before."

"It's not so funny," Harmon said. "In those days I wasn't seeing many people."

He looked casually beyond Frost at the window opening into the patio. Just as casually Frost's eyes followed. The shadow of a man fell across the window sill. Frost pretended not to notice.

"And now you're running a flying school in Salada," Harmon mused.

"And starving to death," Frost said.

"I know some people in Salada..."

"Oh, the town's all right," Frost said; "only it's a little tough on a pioneer." He picked up a sheet of paper on the table and turned it over. Sketched on it in pencil was an architect's drawing of the front elevation of a pretentious home. *Design of a Villa in Provence, for Mr. Nicholas Harmon,* read the printed legend at the bottom. In a corner were the words, *Architect, Mr. Nicholas Harmon.*

Frost looked at him, surprised.

"You do this?"

"I'm an M.A. from M.I.T.," Harmon said.

"Provence, eh?"

"Sometime, maybe," Harmon said.

"It's very fine," Frost said, putting the paper on the table.

Harmon smiled warmly. He reached into his coat pocket. "Look at this," he said, holding up a Phi Beta Kappa key. "Know what that is?"

"Phi Beta Kappa—"

"Yes. You a college man?"

"Vanderbilt—"

Harmon's eyes brightened. "I know. In Tennessee. Great football teams."

Frost nodded. Harmon gazed wistfully at the Phi Beta Kappa key, dropping it in his pocket. He took the handle of his beer mug, twisting it, making circles on the table. He made six or seven, then stopped, picking up the design of the proposed villa in Provence, looking at it with transfixed, impersonal eyes, as a man in a dream might gaze upon his own dead image.

Frost was thoughtful enough to make a noise with his chair before speaking. "I was wondering what the chances were to pick up a little dough in this neck of the woods. I'm pretty flat."

"How do you mean?" asked Harmon, folding the paper in his hand.

"Well," Frost said, "I'm not particular when or what I fly. You know that. I was thinking maybe some of these Mexicans might like to make a trip across the Border...."

"Some of 'em might," Harmon said, "but that stuff down here is dynamite. The Border Patrol—"

Frost waved his hand disparagingly. "There was one in Canada too," he reminded him, "but that didn't stop me from smuggling in booze and Chinese—"

"Maybe so," said Harmon, "but that was kindergarten stuff compared with this. It's peonage down here and it's dynamite."

"Just the same," Frost said, "it's a good way to get rich in a hurry."

"Too much risk," Harmon said, shaking his head.

"Not for a guy with guts," Frost said with conviction. "Don't you think the idea has possibilities?"

"I'm not saying it hasn't got possibilities," Harmon said. "But you'd have to trust the flyer a hell of a lot. He might drink too much and shoot off his mouth, or lose his nerve in a tight place, or get caught and tell all he knew—"

"That's exactly what I'm saying: he'd have to have guts. Naturally, you'd pick a guy you could trust…."

Harmon regarded Frost studiously. "When do you have to go back to Salada?" he asked.

"Tonight or next week—it's all the same."

"Pepe, Pepe!" Harmon called, turning his head. In a moment Pepe came in. He was the little one, the one who used to be a knife-thrower. "Pepe," Harmon said, "Mr. Curtis is going to spend the night. Fix the upstairs bedroom for him." He drained his beer mug and stood up. Frost had a feeling Harmon was trying to make a signal to Pepe. "I guess you'd like to get in a tub, wouldn't you?" he asked.

"I'll say I would," Frost said, wishing he had eyes in the back of his head.

"Go along with Pepe then. He'll take good care of you." He looked directly at Pepe. "Take good care of Mr. Curtis, Pepe," he commanded.

"Oh, sure," Pepe said, not smiling.

"See you later," Harmon said, moving across the room towards the desk.

"This way," said Pepe.

"After you," said Frost, excessively polite.

Pepe shrugged, leading the way to the door. His patent leather shoes made no sound on the floor. Frost suddenly was aware of the noise his own boots were making; subconsciously he picked up his heels, walking on the balls of his feet. He had the impulse to turn and see what Harmon was doing at the desk, why he was so quiet. Then he realized that in situations like these it was generally the trivial thing, like a look or a movement at the wrong time, that brought disaster.

He went out the door without looking back, following Pepe along the patio to the outside steps, expecting anything—and ready for anything.

TWO DAYS LATER, Frost landed at Salada before dawn. He made his way to the quarters which he shared with Perry, and spent some time trying to arouse the sleeping flyer. Inside the room, Perry, hearing sound, came finally awake, fumbling for the chain on the night lamp with fingers that did not seem to be his own. *Bang, Bang. Bang.* It was the door. Someone was at the door. His clawing fingers pulled on the light and he swung out of bed. Taking his automatic off the night table, he crossed the room and opened the door.

Frost entered, his face haggard, his flying suit splotched with oil.

"Boy," he said, "how you do sleep! I've worn out my fist on that door!"

Perry nodded dumbly, closing the door, conscious that Frost

was staring at him, that he must have looked stupid, standing there, half awake, the automatic in his hand.

"Where the hell have you been for two days?" he demanded, unexpectedly belligerent. He pitched his automatic on the bed, slipping into a faded flannel wrapper, his face sour.

Frost smiled, lighting a cigarette, explaining what had happened, overlooking none of the panicky moments in the Santa Rosa Inn.

"You're a crazy fool!" said Perry bluntly.

"Since Harmon saw it my way," Frost went on unruffled, "I've been busy. I've brought over two loads of Chinese and tomorrow night I think I'm running some dope across."

"Where are you taking them?"

"To Montebello—east of here. I've already wired for Ortega to handle that end."

"When do you think we'll be able to wash this thing up?" was Perry's next question.

"I don't know. I'm almost certain Gulick is the big boss, that maybe the mayor is in with him."

"Grant?"

"That's only my own idea," Frost said. "Harmon hasn't peeped about that, but maybe he will when we're acquainted."

"What a chance you took!" Perry said. "It chills me even to think about it."

"As a matter of fact," Frost said, "it wasn't much of a chance. Harmon needed a flyer—needed one badly. His last one had an accident. His name was Kelly."

"Kelly? Tanya's friend? You think that—"

"It looks like it," Frost said seriously, sighing and rubbing out his cigarette. "That's another thing I've got to find out."

"Look here," said Perry, "you're not going back there alone. You're still in a spot."

"I'd be in a worse one if you went with me," Frost said. "What's happened here?"

"Nothing. Jane's been out every day and Tanya's been asking for you. I told them you went north to put on another show."

"So you've been to Gulick's place?"

"Hell!" Perry exploded. "Must I sit here and go screwy? I been having bad dreams as it is."

Frost was undressing, moving towards the bathroom. He paused at the bureau. On top of it be noticed the contents of Perry's pockets: some keys, an identification card made out to Fred Vinson, and a couple of dimes. Frost moved the wallet, looking for currency. There was none.

"I'll say you've been to Gulick's," Frost said. "He's cleaned you. You've lost all your dough at that roulette wheel."

"It wasn't the roulette wheel at all," Perry said. "It was the slot machine. I've worked my way up to the five-cent slot machine." Frost continued undressing. "If it isn't asking too much," Perry said, "will you please tell me where the hell we go from here?"

"I wish I knew," Frost replied, going into the bathroom.

AT THAT PRECISE minute, three-fifteen o'clock in the morning, Raymond Gulick sat in his office at the Club Airport, formerly the Plantation Inn, checking the night's receipts. Across the desk from him sat Alec, his manager. Both were in tuxedos.

Between them were several stacks of paper currency and four small columns of money: Halves, quarters, dimes and nickels, which Alec was stacking, taking them from the little silver lake in front of him. The only noise in the room was the clink of coins.

The clinking suddenly stopped. Alec was carefully inspecting something he had taken from the table, holding it up to the light. He dropped it back on the table. The sound was dull, leaden. He picked it up, dropping it again. The sound was still dull, leaden.

"Somebody's using slugs on us," he said, but thought no more about it, fishing around in the pile, separating the coins. He picked up two more slugs. "Here's a couple more," he said. Gulick nodded, saying nothing, not wanting to lose count of the currency he was fingering. Alec looked at the slugs again. "Hello," he said, "this is something new—"

Gulick finished counting the money, wrapping a printed paper band around it.

"Look, boss," Alec said.

Gulick took them casually, looking at them. He rolled one between his thumb and forefinger, reading the printing on it. The effect was startling. He sat upright in his chair, like a puppet jerked by a string. The muscles in his face were twitching.

"Where'd these come from?" he asked hoarsely.

"From the nickel slot machine," said Alec, wondering why the boss was so agitated.

"Bring Edwards in here..." Gulick commanded. Edwards was the bartender. The nickel slot machines were on either end of the bar.

When Alec returned with Edwards, a youngish man with a weak face, Gulick was on his feet chewing nervously on an unlighted cigar. Edwards took one look at him and mentally kissed his job good-by.

"Ever see these before?" Gulick bellowed, showing him the slugs.

"Why—no, sir, no, sir," Edwards stammered.

"See any strangers playing the nickel slot machines tonight?"

"I didn't pay any attention.... Is there something wrong? I'll make the slugs goods, Mr. Gulick—"

"Go on, get out, get out!" Gulick roared.

Edwards backed away, closing the door softly. Gulick went back to his desk, chewing viciously on the cigar. Alec sat down again.

"Why get upset, boss?" he said. "That's only fifteen cents."

Gulick looked at the slugs again, wrinkling his forehead. They were merchandise checks. On one side was printed: *Good for 5¢ in trade*. On the other side was printed: *Border Patrol Canteen*.

THE FOLLOWING EVENING, in response to a throaty, "Come in," Alec opened the door of Gulick's office in the Club Airport, and stepped inside. Between the opening and closing of the door the strains of "Little Grass Shack" floated through from the dance-floor amid sounds of revelry. Gulick was sitting at his desk, chewing on an unlighted cigar.

Alec advanced and stood awkwardly at attention. The routine of the Club Airport had changed a lot since last night. Before then he had fraternized freely with his employer, never bothering to knock on doors before he entered. But in the past twenty-four hours Gulick had changed. His manner was gruff, vicious; his deportment that of a wounded bear.

"Well, boss," said Alec lightly, "Tanya's finally stopped talking about her boy friend, Kelly. She's asleep in her dressing-room and she'll sleep for hours."

"You're sure you didn't give her too much?" Gulick growled.

"I gave her just enough, just enough," Alec said, highly pleased with himself. "But, boss, it seems silly to go to so much trouble just to shut up a dame. I can do it; I can shut her up so she'll stay shut…."

"Use your head," Gulick said angrily. "Is Curtis out there?"

"With the Grant girl," Alec said, nodding.

"Bring him in here," Gulick said.

Frost was neatly dressed in a gray sack suit with a dark blue tie, a white, soft shirt and black oxfords. As he stepped in, Alec backed out, closing the door. Frost took in the office in a single glance. Gulick kept his eyes on him, like a man hypnotized.

"You want to see me?"

"Yeah, sure," Gulick said. "Sit down, sit down. You're quite a stranger around here. How was the show up north?"

"It was all right," Frost said evenly, shifting the chair so the back of it was facing the wall. "They're all pretty much alike. People are always disappointed if you don't break your neck."

"I guess there's not much danger of that happening to you," Gulick said. "You're no rookie."

"No," Frost said. "What'd you have on your mind?"

"Oh, nothing," Gulick said lazily, licking the wrapper on his cigar.

"In that case," Frost said, pushing himself up from the chair, "I'd better see you some other time. I'm with a lady. I wouldn't want her to think I was impolite."

"Take it easy," Gulick said, smiling paternally. "If she gets sore I'll help you square it." He dropped his soggy cigar into a brass gobboon beside the desk and took a fresh one from his inside pocket, holding it like it was a sword. "I got a little job that ought to appeal to you," he said.

"Job?"

"Yeah. Something I want delivered tonight. A woman."

"Woman?"

"Yeah. She wants to go to the Santa Rosa Inn."

Frost never blinked an eye.

"Where's that?"

"Don't tell me you don't know where the Santa Rosa Inn is?" Gulick said, leaning back, rolling the cigar between his palms.

"I never heard of it," Frost said, looking blank.

Gulick seemed to think this was very funny. He laughed loudly.

"Nick Harmon said you were good, but you're better than that," he declared. "Why, you've almost got me believing in you."

"I don't know what the hell you're talking about," Frost said, pretending to be offended.

"Wait a minute, wait a minute," Gulick said, bouncing to his feet. "You can can all that crap and get down to cases with me. Nick Harmon's an old friend of mine. He told me all about you."

"When?"

"Day before yesterday. The day you went to work for him," Gulick said. "So you see, I find out things too." He rocked gently on the balls of his feet. "There's no danger in this. We take her out the back way and deliver her to your plane—"

"Take who out the back way?"

"Tanya."

Frost shook his head. "I don't want to get mixed up in anything like this, Gulick," he said. "She might yell or fall out—"

"She's asleep," Gulick said, grinning. "She took a powder that'll make her sleep till morning."

"I don't know—" Frost mused.

"There's two hundred bucks in it for you," Gulick said.

"Well, that's different. You should have said that before. But it's worth more. It's no cinch to land a plane on that field at night."

"I'll phone Nick to give you some lights," Gulick said. "Yes," he went on, looking sad, "Tanya needs some of that swell Mexican air to fix her up..." He started Frost to the door.

"I understand it's good for what ails you," Frost said.

"That's what they say," Gulick said, reaching for the doorknob.

BRIGHT MEXICAN SUNSHINE poured into Tanya's face, hot as a blow-torch, and she stirred uncomfortably, moving her head away from the cone of heat.

For almost an hour Frost had been trying quietly to rouse her out of her stupor, and now he was beside her bed, shaking her roughly, calling, "Tanya, Tanya," in a low voice against her ear.

Her eyelids finally fluttered, opening, but closing again as the glare of the sun struck her. She moved over, shivered and sat up, fully dressed, a wild look in her eyes. From somewhere in her throat a squeal of terror rose, to die suddenly as Frost clapped his hand over her mouth.

"Quiet!" he whispered, feeling her lips quivering against his palm. "Are you all right?"

She nodded.

"Quiet!" he whispered again, taking his hand away, dropping on one knee beside her.

"Where am I?" she asked. "What happened?"

"At the *Santa Rosa Inn,*" he said, speaking in a low voice. "Do you understand what I'm saying?"

She nodded dumbly, desperately trying to remember.

"They put something in your drink," Frost said. "They've brought you here to kill you. You know too much about Gulick. You've been talking too much. He's going to kill you."

For a moment this seemed incomprehensible to her, then terror and rage mingled in her face. She raised herself on one elbow, clutching Frost's arm.

"No!" she whimpered. "No! Gulick wouldn't—"

"Listen, Tanya," Frost went on, sweating a little. "Gulick killed Kelly and now he's going to kill you. He's going to kill you today. Your only chance is to get back across the Border."

Tanya was beginning to recollect.

"You brought me here," she said, pressing her fingers into his arm. "You—"

"Listen—it was the only way to save you. Now I've got to get you back across the Border. But you've got to help me—"

"All right—I'll do it. I'll do anything—"

"You know Gulick," Frost said, "and you know he's a dope smuggler. If you'll get on the witness stand and tell what you know about him, I'll see you get back to the States. Otherwise, he's going to rub you out just as he did Kelly—"

Tanya's eyes glittered. "Suppose," she said, "I tell them you're not who you're supposed to be?"

"In that case," Frost told her calmly, "I'd kill you myself—"

Tanya bit her lip. "Gulick's a dirty ——" she muttered through her teeth. "A dirty ——" She sat upright in bed. "But I'd never live to testify against him. He'd blow up the court-house to get me."

"We'll protect you," Frost said. "And think about Kelly. You're not going to let Gulick get away with that?"

"The dirty ——" she said again. "I'll tell what I know," she said fiercely, "yo're damn' right I'll tell. Say," she said looking at Frost curiously, "who are you anyway? How do I know you're on the level with me?"

"This," said Frost, turning back his glove and showing her a gold badge pinned inside.

"Texas—Ranger," she said dumfounded.

Frost nodded. "You lay there and pretend to be asleep. Nothing is going to happen for a while. And don't worry. I'll handle things."

He got up tip-toeing out of the room.

MEANWHILE, IN SALADA, Rowdy Perry heard a rush of noise outside the hangar as an automobile came rapidly down the tarmac, its vacuum-cup tires squealing on the asphalt. He started for the door to see who was abroad so early after breakfast.

A long green roadster slid to a stop in front of the open door and Jane Grant got out, hurrying inside, her hair tousled, her eyes flashing.

"Where's that impostor?" she cried.

"Who?" said Perry, mystified.

"You know who. Frank Curtis. Where is he?"

"Oh," said Perry, understanding now. "He went out early

this morning for a ride. He'll be back any minute now. Is there anything wrong?"

"I'll say there is," she said sarcastically. "He's insulted me for the last time. He won't walk off and leave me sitting at a table any more. The very idea, being introduced to my friends… what will they think?" She was moving around from nervous excitement. "I should forget the whole thing, but I can't. He can't impose on me that way. I'm going to show him up for what he really is."

"What brought this on?" Perry asked.

"This morning," she said coldly, "I got a clipping from a Pittsburgh newspaper announcing the engagement of a friend of mine. Right next to her picture was a story about some convicts breaking jail. One of them was Frank Curtis, a stunt flyer."

Rowdy Perry was paralyzed.

"I'm going to tell my father," she said, "and he'll show this man up for the impostor he is…."

"Now, now," said Perry, stalling for time, cudgeling his brain, "you're getting all worked up about nothing. Give him a chance to explain. Come on in the office and wait for him."

"No—" she fired at him.

"He'll only be a minute. Come on—"

He took her arm persuasively, but she jerked away, running towards the door.

"Wait a minute," Perry called, running after her.

If she ever got to her father, the mayor, with this story….

He caught her near the door, holding her arm. She was tugging, making throaty, frightened noises, her face shot with blood.

"Listen—" Perry said.

"Help!" she screamed.

Perry twisted her around, caught her with one arm about her shoulders and clapped his hand over her mouth.

Quickly he carried her into the office, found some rope handy and lashed her arms loosely at her sides so that he could gag her without their interference. That finished, he completed his task of tying arms and ankles securely, brought over a blanket and laid her as comfortably as possible behind the desk. Then he ran out to her long green roadster, driving it into the hangar and covering it with a plane tarpaulin.

He returned to the office. The Grant girl glared at him with eyes that tried to tell all the things she thought about him, which her mouth could not utter. Perry shook his head at her.

"It's your own fault, being so darned stubborn," he told her. "He isn't the bad guy you think he is. You wouldn't wait for him to explain and here you are—and here you'll stay till he does come."

He shrugged, coming outside, feeling somewhat like a blind-folded man reaching for the curbing. Then he made a show of having something important to do which kept him in a position where he could watch through the open door of the hangar.

Directly opposite, across the road but a little distance away, was the Club Airport. Perry could see the white letters on the slanting roof just over the shrubbery that surrounded it.

For some reason, Perry's eyes returned again and again to the white lettered sign, as if, almost, he suspected what was at that moment going on inside the club, in Gulick's private office where Mayor Grant, in great excitement, had just arrived with news for his fellow conspirator.

Breathing heavily, Mayor Grant leaned over the desk, looking down as Gulick read the newspaper clipping. *Noted, stunt flyer in jail break. Frank Curtis, charged with smuggling, one of six who escape,* the headings read.

"I found that wadded up by Jane's plate when I came down to breakfast," Grant said. "What does it mean?"

Gulick placed the clipping on his desk, and opened the middle drawer. Silently, he took out the three slugs he had found in one of his slot machines, the Border Patrol canteen checks, and one by one he dropped them on the clipping.

"What does it mean?" Grant asked again, fearing the worst.

"It means," Gulick said, reaching for the telephone, "that this guy who's working for us is somebody else, that's all." Into the telephone he said: "I want long distance."

"Then who is he?" Grant asked, moving around in front of the desk.

"Long distance," Gulick said, "this is Mr. Gulick at the Club Airport. I want the Santa Rosa Inn at Chivatito in Mexico.... No, I'll hold on—" He put his hand over the mouthpiece, waiting. "Somebody," he explained to the white-faced mayor, "got drunk and dropped these things in the slot machine, thinking they were nickels. When I found them I did some investigating. Two men were missing from the Border Patrol. I think this guy is Frost."

"Jerry Frost!" exclaimed the mayor, shaking as if he had the palsy.

"Yeah," Gulick said almost placidly.

"What are we going to do?"

"Keep your pants on," Gulick said. "Hello," he said into the mouthpiece, motioning for Grant to keep quiet. "Nick

Harmon? Nick?… This is Gulick. Did Curtis get there with that party?… Well, wake 'em up and send 'em right back… and listen, put one of them things in his wing, just like you did Kelly.… Who is he? He's nobody but Jerry Frost of the Border Patrol.… Don't apologize, the damage is done. Just see there ain't no mistake.… Yeah, I'll stick right by the phone…" He hung up, beaming expansively at Grant. "Everything is gonna be all right," he said. "We'll just stick here for a while."

Mayor Grant licked his dry lips. "I must go to my office," he managed to say, not looking at Gulick. "I've some appointments…"

"You'll stay right here," Gulick rasped, moving to the door and locking it. "You're not getting out of my sight."

"Why—why—" Grant made a pitiful effort to bluster.

"Sit down," Gulick barked.

The mayor sat down, wiping his forehead with his coat sleeve.

JERRY FROST JUMPED from the trellis to the window-sill, clutching it, pulling himself into Tanya's room. She threw back the sheet.

"Somebody just telephoned Harmon," he said. "I've got a hunch we'd better beat it right now. We'll make a break for the plane—"

He stopped talking. Footsteps sounded in the corridor, becoming louder as they drew near—two or three men.

"Back into bed quick," he said. "And don't lose your nerve!"

Tanya jumped back into bed, pulling the sheet up to her chin. Frost glided to an overstuffed chair in the corner near the bed, dropping behind it. He took out his automatic.

The door opened, Pepe and the other Mexican came in. They moved to the bed, looking at Tanya.

Pepe bent over the bed, shaking her. Tanya finally opened her eyes, sitting up.

"Come on," said Pepe in English.

"Who are you?"

"Come on," said Pepe again, doggedly.

Tanya forced sounds of fear through her tight throat, yanking the sheet over her head as she fell back. The bigger Mexican grunted, moving around to the opposite side of the bed. This brought him within a few feet of the overstuffed chair. Frost got up noiselessly, starting forward. The bigger Mexican heard the slight sound, and whirled. Frost crashed him with the barrel of the heavy automatic, laying it against his temple. Blood spurted, the bigger Mexican dropping like a log.

Pepe's arm went back like lightning, metal in his hand. Quick as a thought, his hand came over his head, the arc marked by the gleaming steel. It was a knife. Twisting his body out of the line of flight, Frost dived across the bed, dropping his gun at Tanya's knees. Behind him there was a click as the knife struck the wall. Frost fell at Pepe's feet, clutching them in a low tackle. The impact carried Pepe backward and they rolled over the floor, Pepe underneath.

The little Mexican had one thumb hooked in Frost's mouth, with the other hand he was gouging at his eyes. Frost finally worked his teeth over that loose thumb, grinding down hard. Pepe squealed, jerking back his torn thumb. Frost quickly clambered up, dragging Pepe with him, holding his lapel with the left hand, beating him in the face with his free fist. Pepe put up both hands to save his face and Frost swung back and turned loose a terrific right. Pepe staggered his own length, then crashed to the floor.

"Come on," Frost said to Tanya.

He retrieved his automatic from the bed, leading her to the door. Cautiously, they went outside, making no sound in the corridor. Half-way down the steps to the patio they saw Nick Harmon and the waiter emerge from the door below. They saw Frost and the girl at the same time.

"Put your hands up and stand still!" Frost yelled.

Harmon slowly complied, but the waiter leaped for the door through which he had just come. It was a tragic mistake. Frost squeezed the trigger, the automatic rearing in his hand. The waiter clutched for air, falling flat, rolling over on his face.

Frost pulled Tanya down the steps behind him.

"Go ahead to the plane and keep your hands up," he said to Harmon.

Without a word Harmon turned, marching to the plane.

"Climb in that one," Frost said to Tanya, indicating the rear cockpit.

Tanya obeyed.

"All right, Harmon, you in front."

"Aw, now, wait a minute," Harmon said, turning around, his hands clasped together over his head.

"Get in!" Frost barked.

"Take it easy. Let's talk this over," Harmon said, easing a step closer to him. Quickly he brought his arms down, sledge-like, but Frost had expected something like this. He stepped back, bashing him in the head with the flat side of his gun, a murderous blow. Harmon bared his teeth, shaking his head like a groggy prize-fighter, still coming in. Frost measured him, striking again. This time Harmon stood still, a leer on his fat face, then his muscles flexed and he melted to the ground.

Frost shoved his automatic in his belt, bending over him, tugging, sweating, lifting. It was no easy job. Blood streamed from the two gashes in Harmon's head. Frost slowly worked the unconscious man on to the wing, rolling him on his back, hooking his limp legs over the side of the front cockpit. With a tremendous effort he shoved, Harmon falling into the pit like a sack of sugar, one arm dangling out.

His shirt and hands covered with blood, Frost climbed in beside Tanya, pressing the starter.

The motor caught, sputtering and the plane moved forward. It rocked unevenly, quivering, the motor spitting, still cold. Frost realized this was a violation of the first rule of flying, but there was no time now to nurse the temperature of his motor. He pushed the throttle. The motor spit furiously, increasing its speed in jerks. Frost looked ahead. He didn't have much of the field left, directly ahead was stubby, shoulder-high vegetation. Across his mind flashed a news-reel picture he had seen of de Pinedo burning to death.

He slapped his throttle forward, easing back on the stick, his left hand on the switch to cut it if he crashed. The motor gasped under the impetus of the gas flow. For an awful split-second it hung over oblivion. Then it caught in a roar, purring rhythmically, like a great symphony.

Tanya wondered why his face was so white....

"Watch your feet," he yelled in her ear. "Don't get 'em caught in those cables!"

He looked out. Harmon's arm was swinging in the slip-stream like a pendulum. Frost leaned forward, pulling the arm back inside. A piece of paper, wind drawn from a pocket, fluttered back. It was the design for a proposed villa in Provence....

TEN MINUTES LATER Harmon's head eased up above the fuselage, turning around. Little stalactites of dried blood hung from his hair and forehead. There was a frightened expression on his face. He was yelling something Frost could not hear, pointing frantically at the right wing.

Frost paid no attention, but when Harmon kept on yelling and pointing, he wriggled up and leaned over the cowling, the prop wash tugging at his hair.

"Bomb!" Harmon was screaming. "Bomb!"

Frost looked at the right wing. A small square of linen on the underside was flapping in the wind.

"Bomb!" Harmon was screaming. "Bomb!"

Frost looked at the flapping linen again. It had been cleanly cut. He slid back into the cockpit, quickly lashing the controls. Putting his face close to Tanya's ear, he yelled, "Sit tight and don't touch a thing!"

He climbed over the fuselage, past the front cockpit, the wind tearing at him with millions of fingers. He restrained the impulse to slam his heel into Harmon's face. Carefully, he worked his way out on the wing. It was a perilous job. It is not child's play even when your ship is specially built to stand it, even when you have somebody at the controls to keep her keel even as you gradually shift the center of gravity. There still are many things which can happen. If the ship hits a pocket, suddenly lurching....

Frost braced himself against the wind, slowly reaching into the square hole in the upper wing. His fingers groped in the blackness, then closed over something solid, something hot. Searing pain stung his fingers, but he held on, pulling it out. It was a small object, no bigger than the palm of his hand, round and very heavy for its size. He stuck his arm over the side, dropping it. When it struck the ground there was a puff of gray smoke and a geyser of dirt showered upward....

RAYMOND GULICK, PACING up and down the floor of his office, threw his cigar against the wall irritably. He had been waiting a long while for reassuring news from across the Border and his companion had stood for the suspense less stoically than he.

He whirled on Mayor Grant, who cowered in his chair.

"For ——'s sake, shut up!" he roared. "You're in this thing too—right up to there!" He slashed his finger across Grant's Adam's apple.

The telephone rang, Gulick grabbing it in a single move.

"Hello, hello," he shouted, no longer calm. "Yes, yes, this is Gulick. Who is this?... Pepe!" he exclaimed, astonished., "Where's Harmon?... Gone *where?* Why didn't you phone me before?" he demanded, his voice rising. Mayor Grant was on his feet. "Huh—you were knocked out?..."

Gulick slammed down the telephone, starting for a wall closet. "Frost escaped with the girl," he said, talking as he went. "He's kidnaped Harmon too—and that yellow ——'ll spill his guts—" Gulick grabbed a small kit bag, moving swiftly to the safe. "That's why I put Harmon in Mexico—to keep him away from the cops—" He threw open the safe. He began to pile currency into the kit bag.

"Where are you going?" Grant asked, falling to pieces.

"I'm getting out," Gulick said over his shoulder. "I'm no dummy. I been waiting for this blow-off for days—" He closed the bag. It bulged.

"You're not leaving," Grant muttered. He had drawn a pistol from his pocket and held it leveled at Gulick. "You're not going to run away and leave me to face a charge for murdering that Kelly."

"Put that gun away," Gulick said calmly, as if he thought it was a joke.

"I'll take the rap for what's coming to me," Grant said, "but murder's another thing—"

"Put that gun away," Gulick said, surprised at the other's courage.

The inside of the office exploded, the walls rocking with the sound. For a stunned moment Gulick thought he himself had been shot. Then he saw Grant pitch forward, not uttering a sound. Gulick looked around. Alec was half inside the window, a gun in his hand.

"I thought I'd see why you didn't open the door," he said.

"You got here just in time," Gulick said, stepping across the body of Grant, moving to the window. He handed the bag to Alec, climbed out.

NOT MANY MINUTES later, Frost put his plane down, pulling it in beside the hangar. Rowdy Perry ran to meet him.

"Watch these prisoners," Frost yelled, jumping to the ground.

"That Grant girl—" Perry said.

"See how badly that man is hurt," Frost said, running inside to the office. He grabbed the telephone, calling police head-quarters.

"This is Captain Frost, Texas Rangers," he said. "Send a squad to the *Airport Club*... whaddya mean, they're all there now?... Who's been shot?... Oh! When?... Huh.... You say Gulick went towards the Border in a black roadster?..."

He rushed outside. Perry had Tanya and Harmon on the ground, covered with his gun.

"Where're you going?" Perry shouted.

Frost didn't answer. He wound his starter, then clambered inside the pit. He turned his switch, his motor roared and he jerked away, swinging back to the south whence he had come.

At five hundred feet he leveled off, directly above the highway that led to the Mexican Border in an unbroken white line. Ahead he saw two cars, one behind the other, both traveling rapidly. He dropped down for a better look.

As he passed the first one he overhauled he could see uniforms. Police. He opened his throttle. The threnody of his motor increased. He reached into a black bag hanging from the panel, taking out three extra clips of ammunition, laying them in his lap. He wished he had his own plane, mounted with machine-guns. Well....

A mile ahead he saw the black automobile. He nosed over to two hundred feet, gaining on the car. He looked down, trying to identify the occupants. It was a roadster with the top laid back. A white face looked up at him, then he saw a puff of smoke and flame from a pistol. A bullet pinged through the fabric of a wing.

He swept his plane in a long skid, that came close to the speeding car. Pushing the nose of his automatic over the side, he took deliberate aim, firing fast. He could see the men in the roadster crouching low. The man who was not driving stuck his arm up, firing again. Frost kept his plane in the skid, emptying his gun.

The black roadster suddenly went crazy, wobbling, then shooting off the road down a small embankment, turning over and over and over.

Frost came out of the skid, going straight down to the highway, almost cracking up on the hard road. He jumped out of his plane, running to the wreck, slipping in a new clip of cartridges as he went. Somewhere behind rose the thin wail of police sirens.

The roadster had rolled into a cotton field that long since had been picked of its product. Gulick was pinned under the wheel and broken windshield of the car, a terrible gash in the back of his head. The other man had been thrown clear and now lay face down, jerking his arms, unable to get the rest of his body to respond. Frost turned him over. It was Alec. He was breathing in wheezes.

Between him and the battered roadster was a small kit bag, burst open, loose currency scattered on the ground among the bare cotton-stalks like dead leaves.

The wail of the sirens came closer....

NIGHT ROLLED OVER the steaming city and rain streamed down from low-hanging clouds, crashing against the hotel window like water thrown out of a bucket. Noises from the street below seeped into the room; the hollow rattling of street cars, the strident screeching of automobile horns, the hum of traffic, the hum of people hurrying home, rushing to get out of the rain.

Perry and Jesus Ortega, the thin little Federal agent, stood beside a table, looking at the headlines in the final edition. *Mayor Grant Murdered; Dies Martyr's Death. Killed as He Tries to Arrest Criminals. Crime Crusader Pays for Ideals with His Own Life.*

Jesus Ortega looked at Perry with quizzical eyes. Perry jerked his thumb at Frost, who was standing by the window, looking out.

"He gave out that story," Perry whispered, "on account of the girl—Grant's daughter."

"But—" Jesus Ortega started to protest.

"Have you a daughter?"

Jesus Ortega shook his head.

"Then you wouldn't understand," Perry said.

A crash of thunder rocked the world. Frost pushed up the window, thinking what an ugly thing physical violence was. The rain beat against his face, wetting his shirt.